Gothic Fog

A DCI Finnegan Yorkshire Crime Thriller

Ely North

Red Handed Print

To contact ely@elynorthcrimefiction.com

Author Website: https://elynorthcrimefiction.com

https://www.facebook.com/elynorthcrimefictionUK

Cover design by Cherie Chapman/Chapman & Wilder

Cover images © Adobe Stock / Stokkete (circus tent), jes2uphoto (fog), VFX GUY (Fog) and LittleART (tent opening)

Published by Red Handed Print

First Edition

Kindle e-book ISBN-13: 978-0-6459958-0-0

Paperback ISBN-13: 978-0-6459958-1-7

Also By Ely North - DCI Finnegan Series

Book 1: **Black Nab**

Book 2: **Jawbone Walk**

Book 3: **Vertigo Alley**

Book 4: **Whitby Toll**

Book 5: **House Arrest**

Book 6: **Gothic Fog**

Book 7: **Happy Camp**

Book 8: **Harbour Secrets**

Book 9: **Murder Mystery** – Pre-order (Dec 2024)

DCI Finnegan Series Boxset #1: **Books 1 – 3**

DCI Finnegan Series Boxset #2: **Books 4 – 6**

Prequel: **Aquaphobia** (Free ebook for newsletter subscribers)

*Note: All books are available from Amazon in ebook, paperback, and in **Kindle Unlimited** (excluding Aquaphobia). Paperbacks can be ordered from all good bookshops. **Boxset print editions are one book compiled from three books. They do not come in a box.** *** Pre-orders only apply to ebooks.

1

Thursday 29th October – 8:30 pm

The waning moon casts a watery glow across the ebony canvas of the frigid autumn night. It hangs aloof, alienated, like a pariah at a funeral—resented, uninvited. Far below, life persists in its dutiful rhythm. A sequence of habitual evening events unfold—shared family meals, the hypnotic lull of televisions, the digital escape into computer games. Mundane chores fulfilled, warm baths relax, intimate revelations whispered, trivial chats conducted, profound topics discussed, and, for some, perhaps many, an enveloping silence.

Loneliness.

To this backdrop, the elements of mortality flare—petty frictions gradually escalating into thunderous disputes, tantrums rupturing the calm, affection transmuting to spite, hasty goodnight stories, gentle maternal kisses, firm paternal embraces. Conflict and harmony blend uneasily, producing scenes of deceit, torrid words of passion, veiled affairs, ringing laughter, short-lived transgressions, a tender touch.

Hidden secrets, once discovered, bear down like a ponderous weight—seldom forgiven, merely acknowledged, tucked away in the recesses of the mind. Acts of aggression seen and unseen, a harsh word, a forceful shove, a raised fist—violence in its myriad forms. Amidst all this, love stoically strives, forever swept up into the whirlpool of human conflict; pummelled, battered, accosted, but never defeated.

Humanity in the raw.

His breath comes in ragged gasps, reflecting an intensity that's mirrored by the unmistakable form rising beneath the fabric of his trousers.

He peers through a knot in the wood.

Recently daubed with a fresh coat of protective sealant, the lap-fence radiates a heady brew of aromatic chemicals. The tingling sensation in the pit of his stomach grows stronger with each passing minute. She flits across the room, but he can barely see her as the curtains are almost fully drawn.

Almost.

With arms raised, her silhouette is more discernible. Her hands disappear around her back as she unfastens her bra. The shadow disappears. Scanning the garden, he spots a wooden framed compost box close to the fence. He covertly studies the surrounding houses. All emit light from various rooms, but blinds and curtains prevent anyone from seeing out... or peering in.

All bar one.

Dropping from the fence, he lands silently on the springy lawn and pauses. Half crouched, he scurries like a sewer rat towards the washing line and pulls at a pair of scanty knickers. He stuffs them into his coat pocket, creeps stealthily to the house and presses up against the wall. Fear and excitement emulsify, creating an irresistible cocktail of sexual craving. He dips below the windowsill, then gradually rises, inch by inch, and peers through the crack in the curtains. A bedside lamp casts a creamy orange glow in the bedroom. As he waits in quivering anticipation, his pulse quickens, mouth dries, heart throbs. Unexpectedly she materialises with a towel wrapped around her. For a moment he cannot breathe as he experiences a dizzy rush so powerful, he is in danger of passing out.

The click of a latch and an obstinate back door being yanked open sends a volley of panic his way.

'Come on Bruno, last pee of the night.' A gruff male voice, long marinated in nicotine, encourages the dog.

The nighttime prowler freezes and closes his eyes as if it will help him become invisible.

Hears the animal sniffing up against the adjoining fence.

Cigarette smoke drifts through the air.

A soft patter of liquid as the canine relieves itself.

A guttural growl erupts into frenzied barking. The hound has one eye resolutely fixed against another knot hole in the timber.

'Bruno, what's the matter?' the man scolds, alarmed at the dog's manic behaviour.

Thwarted, the prowler rushes back across the lawn and attempts to traverse the fence, the same way he arrived. The next-door neighbour is on tiptoes, scanning the adjacent garden.

'Oi, you! What the bloody hell's your game?' he bellows.

The intruder's first attempt snaps a panel. With his second endeavour, he gains purchase and, with effortless dexterity, fuelled by adrenalin, he straddles the top rail, drops to the other side and slithers into the dark shadows that swallow him up.

2

Frank flops onto the settee, kicks off his shoes, and slides effortlessly into his slippers. Meera throws him a disapproving glare, which goes unnoticed. She bends, picks up his shoes, and deposits them in the hallway behind the front door. Frank grabs the newspaper from the coffee table, fumbles his spectacles on, and focuses on the unfinished crossword as Meera returns.

'That was the best meat and tatty pie you've ever made, love,' he says absentmindedly as his wife nudges the dial for the central heating up a notch.

'If I served up a tin of dog food, you'd say it was the best meal you've ever had,' she replies, seating herself in a comfortable armchair opposite him.

'Nowt wrong with dog food. Is there Foxtrot?' Frank says with a chuckle as the dog stops its nightly ablutions and peers at his master.

'Now, Frank, you haven't forgotten that Emily is arriving tomorrow night for the weekend. I'll be picking her up from the train station at six, so you need to be home at least fifteen minutes earlier.'

'Forgotten?' he replies, mildly astonished. 'I'm hardly likely to forget my favourite niece visiting for a couple of nights, am I? I've been looking forward to this for weeks and have everything mapped out like a military exercise.'

Meera's eyes narrow. 'What do you mean?' she asks suspiciously.

Frank puts his newspaper down and grabs his carefully planned itinerary from the table.

'Tomorrow night, after dinner, I thought we'd take a walk along the promenade and spend an hour or so in the amusement arcades. Then I'll buy us a hot chocolate and some freshly minted donuts. Then back home to watch a good kid's film. Maybe Harry Potter, or what about Willy Wonka? And guess what's kicking off on Saturday afternoon?'

'What?'

'Henderson's Magical, Mysterious, Carnival of Wonderment.'

Meera groans. 'Oh, not that old ramshackle, retro circus again. I was hoping they'd have gone out of business by now.'

Mortally wounded, Frank removes his glasses in astonishment. 'Meera! That circus is living history. It's a cultural heritage.'

'It's a cultural antiquity which should have been closed down years ago.'

'What is the matter with you?' he bristles. 'It's how circuses used to be in the Victorian era. Clowns, stilt-walkers, fire-eaters, acrobats, sword swallowers, trapeze artists, contortionists, fortune-tellers, magicians. The sound of Wurlitzers. The smell of blood and sawdust and greasepaint. The roar of the crowd. It's a spectacle.'

'It's a debacle. I'm surprised they don't have a freak show and bearded ladies.'

'If they did, your mate Sandra would be able to earn a few quid on the side.'

'That's not funny, Frank,' she scolds.

'Anyway, the last time I took Emily, she absolutely loved it,' he retorts in his defence.

Meera sighs. 'Frank, that was over two years ago.'

'So?'

'She was eleven then. She's now thirteen and a half. I think she'll be more interested in the Goth weekend than in the blasted circus. She's not a little girl anymore, Frank. She's a young woman.'

'Nonsense! Not my Emily. She'll always be a little girl in my eyes. I remember how she loved Ginger Jack in his stage show—The Strawman Cometh. Had the kiddies eating out of his hand. Jack and I go back many a year. He's a grand old lad. The consummate children's entertainer,' he adds with a warm, reflective smile.

'He's a grubby, dishevelled, smelly old man. He must be eighty if he's a day. And half the kids are terrified of him. Hobbling about on a wooden leg, smelling of whisky. The man's a walking biohazard.'

Frank stands up and reaches for his coat off the back of the settee. 'Okay! We'll see what Emily has to say about it, shall we?' he snaps, clearly offended by his wife's cutting remarks. 'If she wants to go to the circus, then *I* will take her to the circus. With or without your blessing. Come along Foxtrot. Time for your nightly walk.' He hurriedly slips his coat on and departs the house, accompanied by the dog. The door slams shut behind them.

Meera chuckles. 'Daft, old man,' she mutters as she reaches for the TV remote control.

3

Friday 30th October – 11:15 am

PC Kylie Pembroke parks the patrol car outside the address in a cul-de-sac of nineteen-sixties bungalows. It's a pleasant residential area on the outskirts of Whitby. The homeowners have maintained the houses studiously, which has helped them weather well despite being over sixty years old.

Exiting the vehicle, she walks up a narrow garden path bridged between two strips of lawn. A blackbird hops over the grass, cocks its head, then tugs at a worm. With its prey in beak, it skims over the grass into a neat privet hedge. Kylie presses the doorbell, which chimes her arrival. She's usually partnered with another officer, but he's off sick and there are staff shortages, so she's solo today. She doesn't enjoy working alone. It makes her vulnerable. All it takes is one weirdo, one crack addict having a meltdown, or a violent alcoholic on a bender, and she could be in trouble. At least with a partner, there's someone to come to your aid or call for back-up. Safety in numbers, even if it numbers only two.

The door cracks open a fraction, its movement impeded by a chain.

'Yes?' a woman's voice asks hesitantly, with a distinct Australian twang.

Kylie flashes her card, although the police uniform should have introduced her.

'PC Kylie Pembroke, Whitby Police. Are you Miss Hannah Turnbull?'

The chain rattles and the door fully opens. 'Yes. Please come in,' she says, nervously scanning outside. Kylie strides into the hallway as the woman swiftly shuts, locks, and chains the door. She leads Kylie into the living room, where both young women take seats opposite each other.

'You called the station early this morning to report a prowler,' Kylie begins as she takes her cap off and pulls out her notebook.

Hannah appears sheepish. 'Yes. Sorry. I hope I'm not wasting your time. It could be nothing.'

'Don't apologise. Just tell me what happened. In your own time.'

'Last night, about eight-thirty, I went into the bedroom and undressed to get a shower. I heard Bruno barking, then

Harry's voice call out. I thought little of it until a moment later he was banging on my front door.'

'Who is Harry and who was banging on your front door?'

'Sorry. My next-door neighbour. Harry Brewer. He's a retired widower. Bruno is his dog.'

'I see,' Kylie says, taking notes. 'And what did Harry want?'

'He said he'd seen someone in my back garden. He shouted at them, and they ran. Jumped over the back fence into another neighbour's garden.' She clasps her hands together and rocks forward. 'I didn't worry about it. I thought it would be kids. It's that time of year with Halloween and Mischievous Night coming up. Then this morning I went to bring in a few items of washing I'd hung out on the line yesterday afternoon.' Hannah pulls a red bra from the back of her chair. 'The matching knickers to this were missing,' she adds holding the skimpy bra in the air.

'Ah, I see. Anything else taken?'

'No.'

'And you're certain you hung the knickers out yesterday? Could they still be in the washing machine? Small items sometimes stick to the drum.'

'No. I've checked, and I clearly remember hanging them out. I only bloody bought them last week.'

'No signs of a break-in?'

Hannah is horrified. 'No... I mean, well, I haven't checked. You don't think...'

Kylie smiles reassuringly. 'Sorry. I didn't mean to alarm you. How about I take a wander around the house and check your security? Not that I'm suggesting for one minute anyone intended to break-in. It's simply for your own peace of mind.'

Hannah relaxes somewhat. 'Feel free.'

Kylie performs a quick reconnaissance of the bungalow, accompanied by Hannah.

'Hmm... your windows all have lever locks on them. Sixty years ago, the standard locks on your windows might have been considered secure, but not today. Anyone could break the glass and release the lever. You any good at DIY?' she enquires as they enter the kitchen.

Hannah shakes her head. 'No. Useless.'

'Do you have a partner or a man around the house?'

'No. We split up last year.'

'Any family members or friends who are handy with a drill?'

'My brother's okay with that stuff, but he lives in Leeds.'

As Kylie turns to head back to the front room, she spots the small doggie flap installed at the bottom of the external kitchen door.

'Do you have a dog?'

Hannah follows Kylie's gaze. 'No. It was here when I moved in. That's too small for anyone to get through, though.'

Kylie inspects the door and dog flap. 'The lock on the flap is broken,' she says, dropping to her haunches. 'It has been known for burglars to put their arm through and, with the aid of a stiff wire, dislodge the key if it's been left in the lock.' She rises. 'But I see you have a top bolt and chain. Do you bolt it every night?'

'I sometimes forget. But I won't from now on.'

'Good. I can recommend a good locksmith. I had him put locks on all my windows last year. Wasn't too pricey.'

'Thanks, that would be great.'

'Five Star Locksmith's. They're based in Whitby. And I'll also pass your details on to our Crime Prevention Officer. He can call around to offer some other tips.'

Hannah escorts Kylie to the front door and slides the bolt and chain back.

'Thanks for your visit,' she says meekly, with arms folded firmly across her chest. 'God, there's some weirdo's out there.'

Kylie notes her apprehension. 'I understand incidents like this can be unsettling, but you must remember, it's extremely rare. And you may have been right... possibly it was kids messing around,' she adds with a reassuring smile.

'Hmm...' Hannah murmurs, less than convinced.

'I tell you what; I'll ask the boys on nightshift to send a patrol car out for the next couple of nights, to do a drive past. Would that make you feel any better?'

Hannah smiles. 'Yes, it would. Thanks again for your help.'

'I love your accent. Whereabouts in Australia are you originally from?'

'Brisbane. My parents are English but me and my brother were brought up in Oz.'

'How long have you been here?'

'Three years.'

Kylie glances at the adjacent bungalow. 'Your next-door neighbour, Mr Brewer, do you know if he's home?'

'I think so. I heard his TV earlier, and he doesn't get out much.'

'I'll have a word with him to get his account of last night, and also take a quick walk around your garden, if you don't mind.'

'Go for it.'

'Try not to worry, Hannah. And call the locksmith as soon as.'

Kylie saunters up the path and knocks on the front door. A net curtain is swished aside and an elderly gentleman gazes out at her.

'Go t'back door,' he gesticulates in a gruff Yorkshire accent. Kylie ambles around to the rear of the house and waits while the kitchen door is unlocked.

'Now then, lass. Is this about last night?' Battered by age and failing health, the dishevelled old man is rough shaven, his skin flaky and as weathered as an old barn.

'Yes, it is, Mr Brewer. If you could spare me a few minutes,' she replies as an old Labrador pushes past the man and sticks its snout into Kylie's groin.

'Get outta there, Bruno! You nosey little bugger,' he says, grabbing the dog by the collar and dragging it back into the house. With the aid of a walking stick, he steps outside and closes the door. 'Sorry about that,' he says, mildly embarrassed.

Kylie grins. 'Dogs, eh? They're like men... no foreplay, is there?' The old man laughs as she pulls out her notebook and pen. 'Can you recount what happened last night, Mr Brewer?'

'Aye, lass. It was about half-eight,' he explains, sparking up a rollie, 'and I came out for my last fag of the night, and to let Bruno take a leak. I was standing in this very spot. I'd just lit up when Bruno went off like a pork chop. He was up against the fence,' he explains, nodding to where the dog was standing.

Kylie inches forward and crouches. 'There's a hole in the wood. He obviously saw something through it.' She rises to her feet. 'Which way was Bruno facing?'

'Gun barrel straight towards the back of Hannah's house.'

'I see,' she replies, taking notes. 'Then what?'

'Whoever it was must have been spooked by Bruno because he scarpered back down the garden.'

Kylie frowns as she does a double-take at the fence, then back to Mr Brewer. 'How do you know he ran down the garden? You can't see over the fence from where you're standing.'

'Because Bruno took off like a bloody whippet along the fence line, heading that-a-way.' He points towards the back of the garden.

'You said the intruder was male?'

Mr Brewer scratches at his mottled jowls. 'Aye, well, I didn't know it was a he at that point. It wasn't until I went up on my tippy-toes and stuck my noggin over the fence that I realised it was a man.'

'Can you describe him?'

'Not really. I only caught a fleeting glance, and it was dark. He was dressed all in black. Tall. He had two goes at getting over the back fence into the other neighbour's garden.'

Kylie notes Mr Brewer's diminutive height and wonders what he means by tall.

'Was he slow, fast, old, young?'

'He wasn't old, not by the way he leaped that fence. He was nimble, like Spring-heeled Jack. The bugger.'

'But not a boy, or a youth?'

'Now you're putting me on the spot,' he says, stroking the grey stubble on his chin thoughtfully as he spits out a loose strand of tobacco. 'Definitely not a young lad. But he could have been a tall teenager.'

'You still haven't explained why you think the intruder was male?'

He cackles and rocks back on his heels. 'And how many lasses do you know who would go peeping through a woman's bedroom window? It was obvious what the bugger was up to. I've heard of Peeping Tom but never of Peeping Tess.'

'Hmm... fair point.'

4

Prisha drops to a gentle jog, then a walk, allowing her pulse to slow. She rounds the corner into the police car park and spots PC Pembroke alighting from a patrol car.

'Hi, Kylie!' she shouts, offering a little wave.

Kylie advances towards her, smiling. 'It's like a drug for you, isn't it?'

'What is?'

'Running.'

'Got to keep those natural endorphins flowing,' she replies with a grin as they meander toward the station entrance. 'Are you going to the Goth Festival this weekend?' Prisha asks.

'Yes. I'm bloody working it. For once, it would be nice to attend as a member of the public, *not* in uniform. And apparently, there's a weather front moving in from the north. Let's hope it hits after the weekend festivities have finished.'

'What's your shift?'

Kylie grimaces. 'The shite shift... 3 pm to 1 am. And I'm on call, so I can't even go out and have a drink afterwards. What about you? Are you going?'

'Yes. I'm on call tonight, but I have the weekend off. Me and Adam are going tomorrow night.'

'Ooh! The big romance is still on then, is it?' Kylie teases as they enter the station reception.

Prisha pouts at her. 'It's not a big romance. We're getting to know each other. It's not serious.'

'At the moment. What's he like in the sack?'

Prisha hits her playfully on the arm. 'Shush, keep your voice down,' she whispers peering at the other officers in reception coming and going. 'For your information, we haven't done it yet.'

Kylie chuckles. 'Christ, who are you, Mother Teresa? How long's it been now?'

'Five weeks. What with his work on the farm and my shift pattern, it's hard to find the time.'

'I wouldn't hang about, girl. A guy who's as drop-dead gorgeous as Adam won't want to be kept waiting. If I was dating him, I'd have...'

'Yes, well, I'm not you, am I? Anything happening out on the streets?' she asks, quickly changing the subject.

Kylie frowns. 'A prowler nicking women's knickers from a line and peering through a bedroom window. Mind you, it could have been kids messing about, but I don't think it is. I've just returned from the woman's place. Her security leaves a lot to be desired. I've told her to get a locksmith in. I said I'd send the Crime Prevention Officer around to give her some advice, but they'll have to come from HQ, so I'm not sure when that will be.'

'Hey, I can pay a visit if you'd like? I did a stint as CPO when I was in the Midlands.'

'Okay, that would be good. Thanks!'

'I'll put it in my calendar for Monday morning,' Prisha says, heading towards the back security door.

'And what's happening in the CID engine room?' Kylie asks, with a cheeky grin.

'Oh, it's abuzz with excitement,' she replies drily. 'We had an interactive whiteboard delivered yesterday. Dinkel is like a kid on Christmas morning, whereas Frank eyes it suspiciously, as though it's going to stab him.'

'Frank would be a blackboard and chalk man, wouldn't he?'

Prisha laughs. 'Yes. We confiscated his chisel and stone tablets last year. Right, I better take a quick shower and finish my bloody paperwork for the week. Can you let me know when you've written up your report on the prowler and I'll read through your notes?'

'Sure thing. And Prisha, remember what I said about Adam? Get a wriggle on, girl, otherwise he may slip from the hook.'

5

Frank scrapes the tinned dog food into Foxtrot's bowl and watches contentedly as the little Yorkshire Terrier performs his nighttime ritual. He approaches cautiously, as if he's been offered month-old roadkill. Sniffing the food, he recoils as though it's the first time he's encountered Royal Canin wet food, the doggy equivalent of beluga caviar. Foxtrot throws Frank a disgusted glance, then advances towards the bowl for a second time, tentatively jerking a morsel into his mouth. As if chewing on a brussel sprout, he gives his master another disapproving stare before accepting he may as well take what's on offer because there'll be nothing else on the menu tonight.

'Daft bugger,' Frank chortles, staring down at the fur ball. 'You act as if I'm trying to poison you, Foxtrot. I'm tempted to eat that food myself; it looks that good.' The front door slams shut as animated voices flood the house. Frank rubs his hands together and dashes from the kitchen.

'Where is she?' he bellows. 'Where's my little girl?'

The hallway door bursts open as Frank's cherished niece rushes forth.

'UNCLE FRANK!'

She launches herself onto Frank's stout frame, and clings to him in what could only be described as a reverse piggyback, her head snuggled into the folds of his neck.

'Oh, sweetheart, how I've missed you!' he yells, spinning her around and around as Meera enters the living room carrying a schoolbag and a small holdall. She grins at the scene.

'Look at you two!' she cries. 'Like two peas in a pod. Emily, don't be too rough with your Uncle Frank. He's got a dicky knee. We don't want him keeling over.'

'Nonsense,' Frank roars as Emily drops to the ground. They both stare at each other as Frank rests his palms on her shoulders. 'My God! Those eyes! They could melt the hardest of hearts. Bugger me, you've shot up. How tall are you now?'

'Five-six, last time mam measured me,' she replies, grinning and performing a twirl. 'But I think I might have grown another inch since then.'

He grabs her head and pulls her into his chest.

'Let go of her, Frank. You're smothering the poor girl,' Meera admonishes.

He releases her, chuckling away to himself. 'I've got a right weekend lined up for me and thee, lass,' he states proudly.

Emily throws Meera a concerned look. 'Great. Aunty Meera, can I get a quick shower, please?'

Frank glances at the clock. 'Shower? It's not even six-thirty. Don't tell me you're ready for your jim-jams this early? I was planning on us taking a walk along the promenade after dinner and visiting the amusement arcades, then maybe some sugared donuts and a cup of hot chocolate on the way back.'

Emily whispers in her aunt's ear. 'I see,' Meera says. 'You run along and get your shower and take as long as you need. Take your bags up. The spare bedroom is all set up for you.'

Emily excitedly grabs her luggage, hastens from the room, and clatters up the stairs. Meera eyes Frank disapprovingly.

'What?' he asks, patently perplexed. 'And why a shower at this time of night?'

'I told you yesterday, she's not a little girl anymore. She's on her period, hence the shower.'

'Oh,' is Frank's crestfallen reply. 'That didn't take long. Is that normal for a girl of her age?'

'Yes, Frank. Perfectly normal. To say you're a copper, there are plenty of things you're still in the dark about. Now, did you put the casserole in the oven?'

'Yes,' he says, nodding thoughtfully.

'Good. I'll put the dumplings in shortly,' she replies, bustling into the kitchen.

The trio are huddled around the dining table, eagerly tucking into their evening feast. All the while, Emily is delivering a frenzied update of her life, filled largely with minor school disagreements, her current favourite bands and music, and the latest trends in fashion. Most of it flies way above Frank's head, but he listens patiently, invigorated by her youthful exuberance. There's a break in the chatter as Emily attacks her last dumpling.

'So,' Frank begins, 'tomorrow after breakfast I thought we'd have a walk along the beach to the harbour and watch the trawlers come back to port. Then we'll pay a visit to that little knick-knack shop you like so much on Church Street. I dare say I can treat my favourite niece to whatever takes her fancy. Followed by a walk up to the Abbey, work up an appetite, then fish and chips at the

Jackdaw; take away or sit-down, your choice. And guess what? The circus is back in town. You remember the last time you came, and we went to see Ginger Jack in his show, The Scarecrow Cometh? Well, he's back. We can spend Saturday afternoon at the circus and catch the matinee show. And you won't believe what I've got lined up for Sunday.'

'Frank,' Meera interrupts, pursing her lips.

'What?'

An almost imperceptible shake of her head, followed by guilty glances between Emily and Meera.

Emily finishes chewing. 'Ahem, Uncle Frank, me and Aunty Meera plan on clothes shopping tomorrow,' she says, blushing as she averts her gaze.

'Clothes shopping?' he states clearly confounded by the concept. 'Okay, well, that won't take longer than thirty minutes. I'm sure we can fit it into the schedule.'

Meera cocks her head to the side. 'Frank, clothes shopping will take up most of the day. We plan on driving to Middlesbrough.'

'Middlesbrough!' he exclaims, as if it were Timbuktu.

'Yes... Middlesbrough. There's a sports shop that sell... what are they called?' she questions, turning to Emily, as Frank scrapes at his empty dish, in danger of removing the enamel.

'The Loewe, Cloudventure Running Shoe. They're in a sale. Two hundred and ninety-nine pounds,' Emily explains.

Frank drops his spoon into the dish, coughing violently.

'Frank!' Meera shouts.

He pulls a handkerchief from his pocket and dabs at his mouth. It takes him a few seconds to compose himself before issuing forth the Yorkshire battle cry.

'How bloody much!'

'Two hundred and ninety-nine pounds,' Emily replies, grinning. 'They're normally three hundred and forty-nine pounds.'

'Sweet merciful shit-on-a-stick!'

'Frank! Language!'

'Some folk have more brass than sense. Three hundred and forty-nine quid for a pair of bloody pumps!'

It's Emily's turn to be confused as she shoots Meera a glance. 'Pumps?'

Meera pouts. 'It's what your Uncle Frank calls trainers. Back in the dark ages, that's what sports shoes were called.'

After his near-death experience, Frank contemplates the news more serenely. 'It looks like you and your aunty have the daytime sorted out tomorrow, then?' he says, trying to sound cheery.

Emily offers him an apologetic wisp of a smile. 'Yes. Sorry, Uncle Frank, but I've been wanting to get these trainers for ages. I've saved up two hundred pounds and Aunty Meera said she'd pay the difference.'

'Did she now?' Frank replies, eyeballing his wife suspiciously. 'Okay, well, how about tomorrow night at the circus?' he suggests hopefully.

More nervous exchanges. Emily taps the edge of the bowl with her spoon, staring into the abyss of a beef and vegetable casserole with dumplings. 'It's the Goth Weekend,' she murmurs, almost ashamed.

'Aye. So?'

'I wanted to get dressed up and walk around and take in the sights. There'll be street buskers and nighttime market stalls and all sorts.'

'Oh... I see.'

'You can come if you want?' she states excitedly, beaming at him.

Frank dabs at his lips with a serviette. 'Ahem, no, I don't think so. That's not my sort of thing. Anyway, an old fuddy duddy like me would only cramp your style. It would be better if you went with Meera. A girl's night out. Actually, there's an excellent series starting on TV tomorrow night I wanted to catch. And it's Newcastle against Liverpool later on.'

'Oh. Okay,' Emily mutters.

'That's Saturday ruled out. How about we do the circus on Sunday?'

Meera clasps her hands together and gazes at her husband with a mixture of impatience and tenderness.

'I think Emily feels she's a bit old for the circus.'

'Nonsense! You're never too old for the circus. I'm old enough to be your grandfather and I still enjoy it,' he says, offering Emily an impish grin.

'You're not listening, Frank.'

Emily says nothing, simply prods at her last remaining dumpling.

'Ahh... I see,' he says rising from his chair. 'I best get my coat and take Foxtrot for his nightly constitutional. Come along, Foxtrot!'

'Yes. Good idea,' Meera agrees.

The dog plods in from his bed in the hallway and stares without enthusiasm at Frank.

'Have you ever known a dog that doesn't enjoy its food, and also hates going for a walk?' he grumbles as he slips into his overcoat. 'He's not right in the bloody head.'

The front door shuts quietly. Meera reaches out and places her hand on top of Emily's.

'I feel so bad, Aunty Meera,' she whispers, almost weeping.

Meera expels a gasp of air. 'That's life, sweetheart. He doesn't want you to grow up. Wants things to always remain the same, and they can't.'

'I know, but he looked so hurt. It breaks my heart,' she says, bursting into tears.

Meera walks around the table and embraces her niece. 'There, there. Don't go getting all upset. I tell you what, after we've done the dishes, why don't we put our heads together and see if we can come up with something you'd both enjoy doing on Sunday? Remember, life is about compromise sometimes. How does that sound?'

Emily wipes her tears on Meera's jumper, letting out a gasp that's half chuckle, half sob. Composing herself, she nods at Meera and says, 'Yes, yes. Let's do that. Thank you, Aunty Meera.'

6

Hannah Turnbull yawns and holds her thumb down on the remote control. The TV screen clicks and fades to black. She rises and tightens the belt on her dressing gown. Exiting the living room, she turns the lights off.

Gargles, spits, and stares at her reflection in the bathroom mirror.

Sighs.

She paws at a few unwelcome wrinkles on her face, then applies nighttime moisturiser. Room to room, she double checks all the windows are shut and secured with their antiquated levers. Front door: locked, bolted, chained. Back door: locked, bolted, chained.

No way in.

As she exits the kitchen and flicks the light off, she gives the back door one more suspicious glance. Satisfied, she retires to her bedroom, slips from her dressing gown, and climbs into bed.

It's been an exhausting week.

The soft orange glow from the bedroom lamp casts dubious shadows on the ceiling as her heavy eyelids droop. She could turn the light off, but it offers her comfort.

Another yawn, then, like a powerful sedative before a major operation, melatonin chugs through her blood vessels.

Sleep.

The nightmare is intense.

So real.

Engaged in an internal battle, her subconscious grapples with reality. The struggle to untangle fact from outlandish, surreal fiction is fierce. Instinctively, her right hand claws at an obstruction over her mouth, meeting with formidable resistance.

A smell.

Has something fallen on me? Has there been an earthquake and the roof's collapsed? What is gripping my mouth?

Finally, after winning the battle against slumber, her eyelids reluctantly open.

Blink. Flicker.

Unfocused vision recalibrates.

Rapid heartbeat as the realisation slaps her awake.

This can't happen to me! Please God, no! I'm dreaming. I remember the police officer and Harry from next-door. How did he get in? Impossible!

He speaks in a low, measured whisper. 'Make a sound and I'll cut your fucking head off.'

The words make no sense... at first.

Not until he raises his hand, and she witnesses the vicious, serrated grooves in the hunting knife, which hovers inches above her neck.

Hannah is now wide awake. Fight and flight have well and truly dragged melatonin from the dancefloor and ejected it from the venue, with a brutal kick to the head.

Her screams are muffled by his other hand.

The smell creeps further up her nostrils.

He speaks. 'I'm going to take my hand away from your mouth now. If you scream or utter a *single* word, then you're dead. Blink your eyes twice if you understand?'

Blink. Blink.

'Good. I won't hurt you unless I need to. Be a good girl and you'll come out of this alive. I'm not a bad man. I'm not a killer... yet,' he adds. The final, calculated word hangs like a bad smell in the air, unwilling or unable to disperse.

The pressure from her mouth is released as he slowly relinquishes his grip. He passes the knife into his other hand. It's no longer above her throat, yet still lingers menacingly above her eyes.

Why me? Should I believe him? I've seen true life crime TV where rapists kill their victims afterwards to cover their tracks. Without a witness, it increases their chance of not being identified. That's why they do it. Who is this monster?

Deep breaths.

You can do it, Hannah. Keep quiet. Accept he's going to rape you. Don't resist. Don't scream. Let it be quick and pray he leaves afterwards. That's all you have. You must stay alive.

Sober comfort.

With her eyes bulging, some semblance of reasoning resurfaces. She takes in his height, the ski mask pulled down over his face, the eyeholes. And... something odd.

His eyes.

They're not right, not normal.

A faint scent, not from the leather glove that clamped her mouth, but something else. A perfume, a musk she can't define.

Terrifying fear returns.

I'm going to die!

No, no you're not, Hannah. You'll survive this.

Calms.

You must believe!

Bedsheets are ripped violently back. His free hand pulls roughly at the band around her pyjama bottoms. He tugs them down to expose her knickers.

Pauses.

Leers.

His excitement swells.

Gasping, the sound of spittle is involuntarily sucked back and forth in perverse pleasure.

The taboo, the forbidden, awaits the human monster.

His for the taking.

Another victim. No name... not yet.

Glances at her face with his peculiar eyes.

Fingers slide under knicker elastic.

Hannah presses her buttocks firmly into the mattress to make it harder for him, then relents, thinking he may see it as resistance.

Be passive. Don't anger him.

The insatiable urge for control, power, and a warped, fucked-up mind is all it takes to produce a killer.

He yanks her knickers down in two, three, four, clumsy movements.

Stops.

Stares.

Bends.

Lowers his head.

Weird eyes squint.

Confusion.

Realisation!

He recoils backward as if bitten by a snake, as the knife is jerked high above Hannah's head.

This is it! He's going to kill me.

Decides not to scream because he has all the power.

Seething and disgusted, the would-be rapist glowers at her with hatred and loathing.

This time, he doesn't whisper. An aggravated yell. 'You dirty fecking bitch!'

She dare not believe as the shadowy figure rushes from the room, whimpering like a spanked puppy.

Lying completely still, silent, traumatised, she's confused what to do.

Will he come back? Has he left the house? I heard a rattling noise from the kitchen. He could still be here. Where the fuck is my phone? Wardrobe... I can hide in the wardrobe!

Paralysed by fear, she does nothing.

Far from the coast, lurking above the North Sea, a thick fog silently drifts towards shore.

7

Prisha pulls up behind two patrol cars outside the bungalow, exits, and zips up her puffer jacket. As she trots up the garden path to the front door, PC Kylie Pembroke advances towards her.

'A sexual assault?' Prisha questions, forcing her hands into a pair of latex gloves.

'Yes.'

'But not raped, or otherwise harmed?'

'No. Not physically, anyway.'

'Give me the details before I go inside,' she says, slipping into shoe covers.

'Hannah Turnbull is the Australian woman I told you about this morning, the one who had a prowler last night. Stole a pair of knickers. She had the morning off. Went into work at midday and arrived home at five-thirty. Had her dinner, got a shower. Watched some TV. Went to bed around ten-thirty. Fell asleep, then woke up with some guy holding his hand over her mouth, and wielding a bloody great big hunting knife. Told her to be quiet, or he'd cut her head off.'

Prisha rolls her eyes. 'A real charmer, then.'

'He pulled down her pyjama bottoms, then her knickers, and stopped. Called her a dirty fucking bitch and left.'

Creases run across Prisha's forehead. 'Is she on her period?'

'Yes. Wears a pad on a nighttime. There was menstrual blood on it.'

'Fuck. Who'd have ever thought a period could come in handy? How is she?'

'Scared to death.'

'To be expected. Husband, boyfriend, partner, relatives?'

'No. Lives alone. Split from her boyfriend last year. Has a brother in Leeds, who is on his way now to collect her and take her back.'

'And how did the attacker get in?'

Kylie shrugs. 'Good question. No signs of forced entry. The back door was unlocked but Hannah was adamant she locked, bolted, and chained it before she went to bed.'

'So, it's likely the attacker left via the back door?'

'It appears so. If it was actually locked, as Hannah said.'

'Why the doubt?'

'She admitted to having a very hard week and was unusually groggy and tired. Maybe she thought she locked the door, but there's always the possibility she didn't. How else could he have got inside?'

'Hmm... Okay, lead the way.'

PC Pembroke turns on her heels and leads Prisha into the hallway.

'We've searched the back garden and the gardens of the houses in the vicinity,' Kylie explains. 'The house opposite has a security camera, but the owners are away for the weekend.'

'And what about the next-door neighbour immediately adjacent?'

'Single elderly male. Lives alone apart from his dog.'

'Potential suspect?'

Kylie frowns. 'Nah, definitely not. Harry Brewer uses a walking stick and is not the most agile, and he doesn't fit the description of the attacker. And he's the guy who alerted Hannah to the prowler in her back garden last night.'

'And what is the attacker's description?'

'Tall male, dressed in black, ski mask, gloves. Matches the prowler from last night.'

'Great. That narrows it down a bit,' Prisha huffs with a hefty dose of sarcasm. 'A male dressed in black wandering around Whitby on the opening night of the Goth Weekend.'

'I know. Like looking for a piece of hay in a haystack.'

'Have you informed forensics?'

'Yeah. Still forty minutes away. A Family Liaison Officer should be here soon, though. She's coming from Scarborough.' Kylie leads the way into the living room where Hannah is sitting wrapped in a blanket in an armchair, nursing a cup of hot chocolate. 'Hannah, this is Detective Inspector Kumar from CID. I know you've already given me a statement, but DI Kumar would like to go over it again with you. Is that okay?'

Hannah puffs out her cheeks. 'I guess,' she replies dolefully.

Prisha makes herself comfortable and offers her a warm, sympathetic smile. 'PC Pembroke tells me you went to bed around ten-thirty?'

'Yes, that's right. I'd just finished watching a re-run of Call the Midwife.'

'Then what?'

'I checked every window latch and both doors, then brushed my teeth and got into bed.'

'Had you anything alcoholic to drink or are you taking any medication?'

'No alcohol, but I am on a very mild dose of Xanax.'

Prisha nods. 'Is that for anxiety or have you trouble sleeping?'

'Bit of both.'

'And when did you take your dose?'

'About ten.'

'Let's jump forward to when you realised someone was in your bedroom. Take your time and step me through it second by second. If at any time you feel distressed, then let me know and we can do this another time.'

Hannah nods meekly and takes a sip from her cup. 'I thought it was a bad dream. Something was pressing against my mouth. I eventually opened my eyes and saw him. I leave my bedroom lamp on. He had his hand over my mouth and a big knife above my throat. He said he'd cut my head off if I made a noise. And then...' she hesitates, unsure of her recollection. 'He said something like, I'm going to remove my hand now. If you make a noise, I'll kill you. Blink twice if you understand. So, I blinked twice, and he removed his hand. Then he said if I was a good girl, he wouldn't hurt me and that he wasn't a bad man, and he didn't kill people—yet.'

Both officers exchange glances. Prisha inches forward. 'Let's go over that in a bit more depth. When you awoke he had his hand over your mouth?'

'Yes.'

'Which hand?'

Her eyes swivel from side to side. 'His right hand. The knife was in his left.'

'Now this is very important; did you detect his skin colour?'

'Yes. He was white.'

'How do you know?'

'Because when he lifted his hand from my mouth, I saw a small part of his inner wrist.'

'And what about accent?'

'I couldn't say. It was a forced whisper.'

'You couldn't tell if he was British or foreign?'

'He didn't sound foreign.'

'Scottish, Irish, Welsh, English?'

'I'm... I'm not sure. I struggle with the different accents. When I think someone's Scottish it turns out they're Irish. When I think they're Welsh, they're from Cornwall. We don't really have strong regional accents in Australia.'

'I understand. You're doing well. You've told me what you saw, but what about your other senses? Hearing, smell, touch?'

Hannah pouts and scrunches up her eyes. 'Oh, yes, that's right. There was a smell, I'm trying to think... leather! Yes, definitely leather. He was wearing gloves; I remember the smooth feeling on my mouth.'

‘Excellent. Okay, continue.’

‘Erm...he pulled the bedsheets back... no wait, he swapped hands. He changed the knife from his left to his right hand, then he pulled the bedsheets back. He pulled my knickers down, then stopped and sort of stooped closer. Then the prick called me a dirty bitch and left.’

‘As we did with the previous exercise, let’s go through it again and see if you can pick out any other details using different senses.’

‘Okay.’ She stares at the carpet, shaking her head. ‘I’m sorry, but I can’t...wait, his eyes.’

‘What about his eyes?’

‘They were odd.’

‘In what way?’

‘The skin under the eyes was peculiar, white, creased. And he had a smell about him, but I can’t place it.’

‘Alcohol fumes, cigarette odour, aftershave, sweat?’ Prisha prompts.

Hannah shakes her head ‘No. Nothing like that. I’m sorry. It was faint, but not unpleasant. Sort of oily.’

‘Oily. Like motor oil?’

‘No. The smell is hard to pin down; it was faint, kind of like the smell you get when you walk into a church or an antiques shop. Oily waxy, but I can’t... I’m sorry. I’m not being much use.’

'That's okay. When he left the room, did he run, walk, limp?'

She shrugs. 'He sort of darted.'

'Did you hear him leave?'

She ponders for a moment. 'Yes... well, sort of. There was a noise. A metallic sort of clank. It could have been the bolt or the chain.'

'Unlocking the back door in the kitchen?'

Shrugs. 'Yes. I guess so.'

Prisha reaches out and touches the back of her hand. 'Okay, nearly done, Hannah. You've been super helpful. The more information we get on this man, the better chance we have of catching him. Just a few more questions. Over the last few weeks, months, have you noticed anyone following you, or staring at you? Any unwanted advances or suggestive comments?'

Her head wiggles. 'No.'

'Nothing at work?'

She nearly laughs. 'No. I work as a secretary for Dixon Accountants in town. It's a partnership, and both brothers are past retirement age, and neither of them are in the best of health. There's been no funny business with either of them since I started working there.'

'What about clients? Anyone who gave you the creeps or made you feel uncomfortable?'

'No.'

'PC Pembroke tells me you split up from your boyfriend last year. Can you tell me why?'

Hannah's eyes flicker, bemused at the question. 'I found out he—Ben—had been cheating on me, so I ended it.'

'Was it acrimonious?'

'Too fucking right, it was acrimonious! Well… on my part, at least.'

'Did he leave quietly?'

'Yes. Packed his bags and left. Last I heard, he was living in Spain. Bought a bar apparently, with his bit-on-the-side.'

'I see. This is a little personal and please don't feel obliged to answer if it makes you feel uncomfortable. Did Ben ever suggest any sort of role-playing games which you found distasteful?'

Her face contorts. 'No. I mean, we mixed things up occasionally, but if you're suggesting fantasy rape, then absolutely not. Anyway, this guy was a good five inches taller than Ben and a lot skinnier. So, unless Ben has had a growth spurt and lost three stone, then it wasn't him.'

'Was Ben ever violent or abusive to you in any way?'

'No. He was as soft as.'

'What about finances? Who owns the house or is it rented?'

'I own it. Or at least the bank does until I pay the mortgage off in thirty years.'

'No money disputes when Ben left?'

'No. None. I'm sorry, inspector, but I think I've had enough now.'

Prisha smiles. 'I understand. That was my last question, anyway. Thanks, Hannah. You've been very brave.'

The slamming of a car door has Kylie peering out of the window.

'Ah, that's the Family Liaison Officer. She'll take care of you from here on in, Hannah,' Kylie explains. 'She's not here to question you. She's here to offer you emotional and practical support.'

Prisha nods at Kylie and makes her way into the hallway, followed by the young PC.

'You said her brother is coming from Leeds to collect her. How long will that take?'

Kylie performs a mental calculation. 'If he takes the fastest route along the A64, it will be about an hour and a half, maybe two, depending on the fog.'

Prisha ponders for a moment. 'Right, I don't want Hannah here when forensics arrive. She's been through enough. Organise for her to be driven by patrol to a designated halfway point and meet the brother there.'

Kylie winces. 'We're stretched to the limit, Prisha. What with the Goth Weekend, and staffing shortages, we...'

'Make it happen,' she says sternly. 'And have you taken DNA swabs and fingerprints?'

'Yes, all done.'

'Good. I'm going to have a wander around. Where's the bedroom?'

'Down there on the left,' she replies with a tilt of the head.

Prisha steps into the bedroom and assesses the scene. Double bed pushed up against a wall. Headboard towards the window into the back garden. Bedside lamp with a weak orange glow. Neat, tidy, clean. Bedsheets crumpled. A photograph on the wall of an older couple on the steps of the Sydney Opera House, presumably Hannah's parents. Another photo on her dresser is of a handsome man in his early thirties, holding a surfboard, beaming. He bears an uncanny resemblance to Hannah—probably her brother. She spots another frame, face down next to it, and delicately picks it up. The image has been ripped in half. All that remains is a man with chubby cheeks, bearing an innocent smile... but unfortunately his eyes have been gouged out.

'Hell hath no fury,' Prisha murmurs, replacing the frame in its original position. Carefully, she investigates each room of the bungalow before ending in the kitchen. She inspects the back door. Notices the tiny pet hatch, pulls out her phone and takes a photo of it.

Kylie saunters in behind her. 'Spot anything I missed?'

'Not really. The pet hatch is too small for a grown man to get through, and if she bolted and chained the door, then the old wire through the flap trick would have been nigh on impossible to achieve.'

'I agree. That's why I'm dubious if she locked it. With the medication she's taking, she may have forgotten.'

'Hmm... I don't buy that, though.'

'Why?'

'Last night she had a prowler, a Peeping Tom. I reckon she'd have shut up shop early tonight and double, treble checked all the doors and windows. Wouldn't you?'

'Well... yes. But as I said, the drugs could have confused her recollection.'

'She didn't take her dosage until ten o'clock. She would have locked up immediately after arriving home from work.'

Kylie raises her shoulders and holds her palms out. 'I don't know then. I'm baffled.'

'You said when you arrived, you did a thorough inspection of every room?'

'Yep. All the rooms, wardrobes, under beds. Hang on... you don't suspect he's still in the house, do you?' she questions, her tone carrying a hint of apprehension.

Prisha takes a step closer and lowers her voice to a murmur. 'What about...' She lifts a finger in the air and points at the ceiling hatch above them—the entry to the loft.

8

Saturday 31st October – 1:30 am

The FLO accompanies Hannah outside to an awaiting patrol car to take her to the rendezvous point with her brother. Once she's safely in the car, and it departs, Prisha and PC Pembroke reconvene in the hallway.

Both officers tilt their heads and stare at the ceiling.

Kylie is mightily concerned and whispers in Prisha's ear. 'I don't think you should do this. I think we need armed response. What if he's waiting with the knife?'

'Don't worry. I'm not doing it. You are,' Prisha murmurs. Kylie takes a step back, eyes as wide as saucers. Prisha stifles a snigger. 'Calm the farm. I'm taking the piss. Right, here goes nothing.' They tread carefully into the kitchen. Prisha picks up the ladder pole and snares the handle on the loft hatch, then tugs at it. The ladders noisily rattle downward. With torch in hand, she swiftly climbs the rungs. She sticks her head into the gloom of the loft and flashes the light around. It's still, empty, nothing but dust, cobwebs, and an icy silence. The torchlight flickers, fades, then dies.

'Damn it!' she hisses.

'What's the matter?' Kylie asks, her stomach in a knot.

'Bloody battery has gone on my torch. Here, hand me yours,' she says, lowering her flashlight. A draft of air on the side of her face takes her by surprise and she lets out a yelp.

'Prisha!'

Her left foot drops from a rung and she almost falls. She snatches Kylie's torch and takes another two steps up the ladder, her upper body now in the loft. Scanning the tiny space, she sees it hurtling towards her. Unceremoniously, her feet lose purchase, and she clatters down the ladder, grazing her shins in the process. She lands in a heap on the floor.

Kylie screams, as she fumbles with her Taser. 'Fuck! Is it him?'

Prisha looks up at her, half grinning, half grimacing as she rubs at her legs. 'No. It was a bloody bat. My God, there's not much that creeps me out, but those things give me the heebie-jeebies. Flying rodents.'

As a small team of bunny suited forensics analyse the house, Prisha, and Kylie talk outside.

'We know a lot more after your questioning than from my initial attempt,' Kylie says, with an element of disappointment in herself.

Prisha offers her a sisterly smile. 'Hey, buck up. I have ten years on you. You'll get there. We all go through the learning process. Anyway, it's all good experience. Put some of what you witnessed in your memory bank.'

Kylie sniggers. 'Don't you worry. I have a journal at home called Inspector Kumar. I jot down all the little things I learn from you.'

Prisha's nose creases. 'Not sure I like the sound of that. It makes you sound like a stalker,' she replies with a grin. 'Right, so what do we have?'

'Tall IC1 male, maybe six-foot two. British. Unsure of accent. Has weird, wrinkly bags under his eyes. He emits a peculiar smell that hasn't been identified yet, but it's not offensive. And…' she pauses as her eyes roll from side to side. 'Probably left-handed,' she adds, reticently.

'Excellent! And what makes you think he's left-handed?'

'He had his right hand over Hannah's mouth and held the hunting knife in his left hand. Typically, you'd hold a weapon in your favoured hand.'

'Go on.'

'As he went to pull Hannah's pyjamas down, he switched the knife from left to right.'

'Indicating?'

'Once again, he used his favoured hand to undertake the task. It's involuntary. He's not unique. We all do it unless we're born ambidextrous.'

'Which is about one per cent of the population. Anything else?'

Kylie considers the question. 'Possibly has a phobia?'

'Why?'

'His reaction to period blood.'

'Explain?'

'He's a rapist, or at least a potential rapist. He somehow got into the house with one intention. But... he stops when he sees blood on Hannah's pad.'

'We assume that's his reason. Only he would know.'

'True. But what else could have stopped him? Anyway, he could have either hemophobia, or menophobia, or both. A fear of blood, or periods. But I suspect the latter due to him calling Hannah dirty. Some men are plain weird when it comes to women's menstruation.'

'Very good deduction. Anything else?'

Kylie grimaces and lowers her voice. 'I'd say he's extremely dangerous.'

'I agree. He issued Hannah with a veiled threat... he hadn't killed... yet. He's a nasty piece of work who could turn from prowler to rapist to murderer. Always remember about escalation, Kylie. Your average Joe Blow, with an unblemished record, doesn't wake up one day and decide they're going to kill. Escalation, stepping stones. The thrill must always increase.'

'A bit like taking drugs?'

'Exactly. We need him off the streets ASAP. Anything you'd like to add?'

'Yes. The prick is a Houdini. He can enter a house that is locked,' Kylie adds, deep in thought. 'Hey, here's an idea. What if he broke into the house while Kylie was at work? She only has Yale locks on the doors. One door wouldn't have been chained and bolted, and Yale locks are notoriously easy to pick.'

'It's a possibility. But why wait until Hannah went to bed to carry out the attack? That means he would have needed to hide for at least four to five hours.' She checks her wristwatch. 'Shit! It's one-thirty already. Right, I'm away to bed. I'll nip into the station later today to write up my report. Sleep tight.'

9

With a spring in her step, Prisha bounds up the stairs that lead to the second floor and the incident room. Although she's rostered off for the weekend, she wants to write up the sex assault from the previous night as soon as possible, while the details are still fresh in her mind. Stopping at the antiquated coffee machine, she jabs at a button and awaits impatiently as the black liquid splatters into a cardboard cup.

Taking a sip of the predictably acrid coffee, she enters the room and immediately spots Dinkel messing around with the new interactive whiteboard.

'Morning ma'am!' he declares, as happy as a pig in shit, holding the instruction manual in his left hand.

'Morning, Dinkel. Up to speed with your new toy?' she replies, taking a seat at her desk.

'Just about. Nearly finished the manual,' he says with a cheeky grin. 'It's amazing. Once it's set up correctly, we'll be able to pull up ongoing investigations, and every detail associated with them; mug shots, street maps, witness statements, forensic reports. You can even colour code them in order of importance. Of course, it's connected to the internet, and the PNC and Holmes, so we'll have everything at our fingertips in one place. Once I've mastered it, I can show you the ropes, if you like?'

Prisha jabs at her keyboard, hoping to get out of the office as soon as. 'Won't be necessary, but thanks,' she says, distracted. 'We had interactive whiteboards in the West Midlands Police ten years ago.'

The smile falls from Dinkel's face. 'Oh, I see.'

She pauses from bashing the bejeezus out of the keys and glances at his crestfallen face.

'But, as you're on duty this weekend and I'm not, I have a little job for you. It can be the first case you enter onto the whiteboard.'

His idiotic grin returns. 'Excellent! What is it?'

'Hannah Turnbull was sexually assaulted last night in her home. All the details will be in my report. I want you to trawl through the HOLMES database and compile a list of all unsolved rapes and or attempted rapes from the last ten years. Group together any cases where the attacker matches the profile of our suspect, not that we have much to go on at the moment. The man we're after is white, British, tall, thin, and agile. Aged anywhere from mid-teens to mid-thirties. Possibly also steals underwear from the victim's washing line a night or so before his attack, maybe as a trophy, or a marker for his next victim. Can you handle that?'

Dinkel warms his palms with a rub. 'Certainly, ma'am! There's no better teacher than experience itself.'

'You walk on the wild side, don't you, Dinkel?' she teases under her breath.

'Should I notify you once I've processed all the data?' he asks.

Prisha fixes him with a disapproving glare, the glint of warning unmistakable. 'No, absolutely, bloody not. I'm taking the rest of the weekend off. It can wait until Monday.'

'Roger Moore, that!'

The pen misses Dinkel's head by mere millimetres.

10

Frank glances at his wristwatch, releasing a gusty sigh. With Meera and Emily embarking on their early-morning Middlesbrough shopping spree, he finds himself in a peculiar situation—at a loose end. From a ruthlessly critical point of view, one could even describe his current state as boredom. Foxtrot is sprawled out on his bed in front of the gas fire, contented, drifting in and out of consciousness. Frank stares at him.

'Come on, Foxtrot, let's go for a walk?'

The dog lazily lifts his head and gazes back. He may not be fully fluent in Yorkshire English, but he understands his name and the meaning of the word—walk. And yet, he's confused. He's already had his morning walk, and his evening stroll doesn't occur until after his dinner. There must be some mistake.

'Come on, lad! What's the matter with you? It's time for walkies,' Frank shouts, grabbing the dog lead.

Foxtrot rises and does an all over body shake. He was quite happy where he was, thank you very much. Alas, he learnt a long time ago he has no say in these matters. He reluctantly sits and throws his master a disgruntled glance as his lead is attached.

Frank shuts the garden gate as a blast of cold air swirls in from the sea. He buttons up his long overcoat and pulls on a stylish herringbone flat cap. Hanging left, he hastens towards the Cleveland Way walking track, stopping briefly to watch a bunch of golfers teeing off.

'Never seen the attraction,' he mutters to no one apart from his befuddled dog. Heading along the track, he turns back on himself and follows the path along the coast towards the harbour. In the distance, he sees the big top and occasionally catches a slurry of incomprehensible shouts and commands carried on a stiff breeze. As he nears the circus, he slows to a shuffle and absorbs the action.

The sun pierces the chill of morning, as the briny zest of the North Sea blends with an intoxicatingly sweet aroma wafting from nearby candy floss stalls. The air is electric with anticipation; a testament to the jovial grandeur of an old-fashioned circus pulling into town.

Performers hurry about, a ballet of organised chaos. Stilt-walkers, towering above the rest, drape swathes of crimson and blue ribbons across the entrance to the main marquee. Five-foot-high letters announce, "Henderson's Magical, Mysterious, Carnival of Wonderment".

Fire-eaters test their skills with an occasional blast of flame from their mouths. Sword swallowers sit calmly on the sidelines, their gleaming blades glinting menacingly, a silent promise of the daring spectacle to come. A deep neighing punctuates spirited chatter, echoing from the makeshift animal farm, replete with majestic horses. The rustic scent of hay, mingles with the warm, comforting fragrance of buttery popcorn, creating a striking contrast against the clean, crisp smack of ozone.

Untamed merriment saturates the site as clowns flirt with laughter, tripping over enormous shoes and honking oversized horns tucked under the ruffles of their outfits. Their infectious laughter breaks the rhythmic cadence of mallets hitting giant pegs, as guy ropes are secured. Nearby, acrobats, compact and agile, weave in and out, their lithe forms twisting with an effortless grace as they sporadically break out into a spectacular display of aerial flips.

The initial melodies of a joyful waltz resonate from a Wurlitzer, evoking the splendour of a bygone Victorian era. Food stalls prepare, as smaller marquees are erected with speed and dexterity. The air thrums with the charm of yesteryear. Already, a steady stream of visitors are sampling the delights on offer from the food stalls, which have opened early.

Frank grins, soaking it up as if he were a wide-eyed, eight-year-old boy again. He spots a familiar figure in the distance hobbling towards a huddle of caravans.

'Jack! Hang on a mo!' he bellows, attracting the old man's attention. 'Come along, Foxtrot. You remember old Ginger Jack, don't you?' he says as they set off at a brisk pace.

The dog emits a wary growl, more concerned with keeping a close eye on the freakish giants and human, fire-breathing dragons.

11

Jack flings open the door of an antiquated, shabby caravan and clumsily ascends the two metal steps, muttering a string of curses. Frank notes the name 'Matilda' on the caravan's nameplate as he and Foxtrot trail behind Jack into the dim, confined space, reeking of pork fat. He spots six sausages sizzling in a frying pan on a small stove. At one end of the caravan is a built-in bed with a rumple of old sheets and blankets tossed across it. In the centre of the room, opposite the gas hob, is a squat wood burner radiating heat. To his left, a cupboard, a small fridge, and a sink. Frank, with his detective mind, records the scene to memory. Although grubby, and smelly, the van is kind of cosy... that is, if you're a single male who long ago abandoned any semblance of order, or cleanliness.

Jack smiles and points at a bench seat behind Frank. 'Take a pew and tell me how you've been these last couple of years.'

Frank sits down and takes his cap off as Jack prods the sausages with a fork. 'Not much to tell, really. Same old, same old,' he says with a weary sigh.

'Still putting villains behind bars?'

'Oh, aye. There's never a shortage of those buggers.'

'Not thinking about retiring?'

'I'm always thinking about it. Meera brings it up every few months.'

'But?'

Frank grimaces. 'I don't know, Jack. I've still got something to offer. I can feel it inside me, like a fire. Once the fire is out, then I'll know it's time.'

'I'm the same. My granddaughter keeps telling me it's time to call it a day. Buy a small bungalow on the coast. But what would I do all bloody day? The circus life is all I've ever known. It's where I want to die.'

Jack sticks his grubby hand into a plastic bag and pulls out a slice of white bread. Picking up a sausage, he drops it into the middle and folds it over on itself then hands it to Frank.

'Cheers. It looks scrumptious,' Frank says, having second thoughts about accepting Jack's invitation for a bite to eat.

Jack rubs his nose on the back of his overcoat sleeve and coughs. 'They needed eating. Another day or two and they'd have grown legs and walked out of here,' he says, chortling. He pulls two tumblers from a cupboard and grabs a whisky bottle off the countertop. Tapping at the bottle, he holds it aloft. 'I take it you're off duty, Frank?'

'Yes, but it's a little early for...'

'Nonsense. Helps keep the chill out.' He deftly pours two generous glasses of scotch and passes one to Frank. 'Bottoms up,' he says as both men clink glasses.

Frank takes a wholesome sip, whereas Jack knocks his shot back in one before grabbing a sausage and slapping it into a slice of insipid, white bread. He wriggles backwards and flops onto the bed, placing his sandwich on the bedsheets. Huffing and puffing, he lifts his trouser leg, undoes the leather straps attached to his wooden prosthetic, then leans it up against the bed, emitting a pleasurable groan.

'I see you've still got the peg leg,' Frank comments.

Jack eyes him warily. 'Hardly likely to grow a new one, am I?'

'No, I meant why haven't you got a modern, lightweight prosthetic?'

'I've tried a few out over the years, but never take to them. I always return to Jake.'

'What happens when the ground's wet?' Frank enquires casually, staring at the small, wooden disc at the end of the leg as he munches on his food.

'I unscrew the bottom disc and replace it with a larger one,' he says, finally attacking his sausage sandwich with gusto. 'I take it you'll be coming to the show, Frank?'

'Wouldn't miss it for the world,' Frank lies, not wishing to hurt the old trouper's feelings.

'Matinee starts at three and the evening show begins at seven.'

'I'll attend the evening show with my niece. We won't have time to hang around afterwards, though. She wants to head into the old town and soak up the Goth Weekend atmosphere. I brought her two years ago, and she loved The Strawman Cometh. She was a little frightened at first, but she soon got into it.'

Jack chuckles. 'I've had to shorten the performance to thirty minutes. I get out of puff these days. I've also tweaked the finale, slightly.'

Frank cannot recall the ending. 'Remind me again?'

'You remember the fat kid who taunts and bullies the scarecrow, but by the end of the show, they're best friends?'

'Oh, aye. That's right. A nice feel-good ending.'

'Well, I've changed the final scene. Plus, the lad who played the bully is no longer with us. His father was one of the circus performers. Hazardous Harry, the axe juggler. Unfortunately, he left the circus.'

'What happened?'

'Misjudged an axe one day,' he explains soberly. 'There's not much demand for one-handed jugglers.'

'Poor bugger.'

'Indeed. Although, looking on the bright side, he picks up seasonal work at Christmas as a town crier,' he muses reflectively. 'I've replaced the chunky whippersnapper with a dwarf from the clown troupe.' He fishes out a couple of VIP tickets from his pocket. 'Here, on the house. They'll get you prime seats at the show.'

'No, I couldn't!' Frank exclaims.

'Nonsense. Us old-timers must look after one another.'

Frank reluctantly accepts the tickets, a little miffed Jack's lumped him into the same age bracket as himself. 'Okay, if you insist. That's very generous of you.'

'Grandad!' a female voice cries from outside.

Jack lifts himself upright and peers out of the grimy window. 'In here!' he bellows.

Frank courteously rises and steps aside as an appealing woman, early thirties, enters the caravan. Dressed in snug-fitting jodhpurs, sturdy boots, and a chic black jacket, she projects an aura of serene, confident control.

'Oh, sorry. I didn't realise you had company, granddad,' she states.

'Frank, this is my granddaughter, Abby Henderson. Abby, I'd like you to meet an old friend of mine, Frank Finnegan. Mind what you say now, he's a detective chief inspector,' he adds with a chuckle, followed immediately by a hacking cough. Pulling a handkerchief from his pocket, he spits into it, grizzles, then slides the offending article back inside his coat.

Frank and Abby purposefully ignore the display as they shake hands and exchange pleasantries.

'Has old Jack got you on the payroll as well?' Frank asks, attempting small talk.

Abby smiles discreetly. 'You could say that.'

'It's the other way around,' Jack says, cackling as he reattaches his wooden leg. 'If my granddaughter hadn't joined the show eighteen months back, then we'd have gone under. She's been a godsend.'

'Oh, nonsense, grandad. You'd have soldiered on. When you've got a moment, I want to give you an update. One of the acts isn't feeling too well and we may need to pull something together to utilise the marquee. We don't want it left empty. Anyway, I'll leave you two old blokes to it. Nice to have met you, Mr Finnegan.'

'Same here,' Frank says, trying to push aside the old bloke comment.

Jack wrestles himself up from the bed to snatch another sausage. 'Feel free, Frank.'

'Thanks. But one was plenty.' His focus is on Abby Henderson as she marches with determination across the grassy area, embraced by the circular arrangement of caravans and vehicles. She steps into a shiny luxury motorhome.

'Don't jump to conclusions,' Jack cautions perceptively.

'About?' Frank asks, turning to face him.

'The whole living situation; me in this rundown caravan and her in that fancy-dancy new-fangled thing. Truth is, she's always nagging me to upgrade to a new van, paid for by the business.'

'Then why don't you?'

'I bought Matilda when I was twenty-one. I've lived in her for the last sixty years. She caters for all my needs... which are few. I couldn't send her to the knacker's yard, not now. It would be a betrayal.'

'A few home comforts wouldn't go amiss.'

Jack snorts. 'I have a wood burner, a stove, a fridge, a bed, running water and a cupboard full of food. What else does a man need? I live a simple life, Frank. Always have. We'll go out together, me and Matilda. That's how it'll be.'

'Fair enough.'

'That girl, my granddaughter, would buy me the moon if I asked for it. I'm just thankful Henderson's Carnival has now passed into the family. She even has my last name. Never married. I keep telling her to find an eligible young man so she can have an heir. Doesn't bloody listen, though. That's modern women for you.'

'And older women,' Frank replies, reflecting on his own wife. 'Is it true what you said about the circus folding?'

'Yes, it is. Abby was a dancer with the Royal Ballet for years. Then about five years ago, she left to study business management at university. She came to see me one day with ideas on how to modernise and expand the circus. I mean modernise in a business sense, of course. She laid it all out for me; business plans, profit and loss, social media strategy, streamlined electronic payments. The whole kit and kaboodle. To be honest, Frank,' he says, refilling the whisky glasses, 'I didn't have a bloody clue what she was on about. That's when I decided to relinquish control and hand over the entire shooting match to her. I'm not sure how much longer I have left. None of us are getting any younger, are we?'

Frank has a thick skin, but three age related insults in as many minutes is irksome.

'Ahem, no. So legally, Abby now owns the circus?'

Jack chuckles. 'No. It's now a private limited company, and she's CEO, with fifty-one percent of the shares. The other forty-nine per cent are owned by investors. That's how we were able to expand and buy a lot of smaller marquees. The days of having one big top are long gone. By having many tents, we can put on more diverse shows throughout the day. And for each show, there's a cost of entry, instead of one price fits all. I tell you what, if I'd had my granddaughter onboard five years ago, I'd be a millionaire by now. Not that money's any good to me, these days. A bed to sleep in, a bit of grub, and a life on the road is all I need to keep me happy.'

'No more hoarding of cash under your mattress?' Frank says with a chuckle.

'No. It's nearly all card payments now. Which means we have to pay tax. But she even employs experts in that department to reduce our liabilities. She certainly didn't get her brains from me. And she's also general manager of day-to-day operations and MC for the main big top show—hence the riding clobber. Prances in on a beautiful white mare.'

Frank swills his whisky down and glances at his watch. 'It's been good catching up with you, Jack,' he says patting the old man on the shoulder.

'Aye, always a pleasure to see an old mate.' As Frank steps from the caravan, Jack calls him back. 'Hey, Frank... do you still like a wager on the nags?' he asks in a whisper, scanning the camping area surreptitiously.

Frank grins. 'Occasionally, in moderation. Have you some red-hot tips for me?'

'As it happens, I do. Let's call it inside information,' he replies with a wink, tapping his nose. 'You got any paper on you?'

Frank scrabbles about inside his coat but can only locate a pen. 'No, sorry.'

'Call yourself a copper? Never mind.' He grabs a circus flyer from the door of the fridge and hands it to Frank. 'Three-fifteen, Kempton, Black Meg. Three-forty, Aintree, Yosemite Sam.'

Frank repeats the tips as he jots them down on the back of the leaflet, then carefully folds the sheet and slips it into his coat pocket.

'Cheers, Jack. I may have a wander down to the bookies right now. Come along Foxtrot.' He turns on his heels and heads away.

Jack chuckles as he leans out of the caravan. 'Go big, Frank. These are guaranteed. Keep it to yourself, mind. Remember what I said... go big!'

'Will do!' Frank raises a hand as he continues walking.

Going big for Frank Finnegan means five pounds each way.

12

Saturday - 3:00 pm

With the crowd seated, there's a ripple of expectation in the marquee. Frank smiles as he looks around the tent. Hard plastic chairs mounted on terraced platforms accommodate at least two hundred children and parents. Frank pulls out a packet of jelly babies from his coat pocket and offers them to Emily.

'I got them earlier,' he says. 'Your favourites.'

Emly grins. 'Thanks, Uncle Frank.'

Frank relaxes back into the chair. 'Did your Aunty Meera put you up to this?'

'Up to what?' she asks, dropping a sweet into her mouth.

He chuckles. 'You know very well what. Last night, you were too old for the circus. You were going shopping all day. Now you're sitting here with me.'

'I told you. We bought the trainers, had a bite to eat, then headed back. I thought I'd like to spend some time with you, so why not visit the circus. I know you enjoy it.'

'And you don't mind seeing The Strawman Cometh again?'

'No. I'm looking forward to it. Even though I know the ending,' Emily says with a giggle.

'Ah, well, here's an exclusive for you; Ginger Jack has tweaked the finale a little.'

'Aw! I liked it the way it was.'

'I'm sure it won't be much different.'

The faint overhead lights fade as a voice booms from the speakers.

'Ladies and gentlemen, boys and girls, and non-binary...'

'So help me God,' Frank mutters, for which he receives a slap to the thigh from his niece.

'The Strawman Cometh!'

The crowd erupts into ecstatic applause as the curtain slides back, revealing a black stage, as a backing-track plays. A whistling, raging storm conjures up images of a cruel, bleak winter. After thirty seconds, the tempest subsides, followed by the gentle chirruping of birds and bleating lambs, representing spring. The agreeable sound of buzzing bees and crickets paints a picture of an idyllic summer day. Lastly, maudlin caws of crows, dry rustling leaves, and the hoot of an owl reverberates around the marquee—autumn. A spotlight abruptly focuses on centre stage, highlighting a scarecrow, standing alone to the backdrop of a barren ploughed field with desolate trees in the distance. Gnarled, bony branches reach out like skeletal fingers, denuded of foliage. The strawman's head droops, its arms in a crucifix position. One wooden pole juts into the earth.

Emily slides her hand into Frank's. 'This is always the sad part,' she whispers as Frank's heart soars.

The sound of children's voices, laughing, joking, grows louder. A little girl sings a wistful lullaby as she emerges on stage. She has the voice of an angel.

"As the leaves fall, whispering their last goodbyes,
Autumn hangs her head and sings a wistful lullaby.
Underneath the moon's soft light,
Ghosts of summer fade to night."

The girl stops and stares at the strawman. 'Hello, Mr Scarecrow. My name's Jemima. What's your name?' she asks as a dwarf dressed as a little boy enters the scene.

'Why are you talking to that dumb scarecrow?' he asks mockingly.

Emily shoots Frank a concerned look. 'That's not the same boy from last time. He's different,' she whispers.

Frank shifts uneasily in his seat. 'Aye, you could say that. He could have really done with a shave.'

The action on the stage continues.

'He's not dumb!' Jemima declares, clearly annoyed.

'Yes, he is! Big fat ugly scarecrow,' chants the boy as he dances around the strawman. He picks up a handful of stones and pelts the effigy.

'Stop it, Tom!' Jemima screams. 'Don't you think his life is hard enough, stuck in this field year in year out with no one to talk to? Why would you be so mean?'

'Because he's a big fat ugly scarecrow, that's why?' Tom states, no stranger to a Mars bar or two, himself.

'That's no reason to be cruel.'

'I hate him. He's not like us.'

The show continues for the next thirty minutes, exploring the complexities of built-in prejudice in simple terms that children can comprehend.

From what Frank remembers, the play is nearing the final scene.

Contrite and with head bowed, Tom is alone with the scarecrow in the field.

'Hello, Mr Strawman. I'm here to apologise. I've been horrible to you. Throwing stones, calling you names, simply because you're different from me. I was wrong. I can see that now. Can we be friends?' the little boy says, reaching out and touching the scarecrow's straw hand.

To the surprise of the audience, who had presumed it was merely a prop, the scarecrow abruptly raises its head to the sound of gasps.

'Yes, Tom. We can be friends.'

The boy takes a step back in disbelief and fright. 'You *can* talk!'

'Indeed, I can, Tom. I've always possessed the ability to speak. But only those whose hearts are full of love can hear my words. To those consumed by hatred, they are forever deaf.'

Tom steps forward and folds into the scarecrow's embrace. As straw arms encircle him, a tide of relief washes over the audience, and the stage plunges into darkness.

'Shouldn't that be the end?' Emily whispers to Frank.

'I thought so. Maybe there's another scene.'

The stage is suddenly bathed in light again. Tom emerges from the wings, and laboriously scales a wooden fence. In his left hand he carries a chainsaw. Approaching the scarecrow, his face contorts into a manic grin.

'You didn't really believe me, did you? Stupid, daft, hideous strawman!'

He yanks the ripcord, and the roar of the chainsaw reverberates around the marquee. The lights fade to black. The audience reaction is hard to judge but concerned murmuring and a few gasps possibly telegraph a slightly negative response.

'I'm not sure I like where this is going,' Emily cries, squeezing Frank's arm.

'No, nor me,' he says, feeling decidedly uncomfortable.

The saw's menacing hum slowly dwindles into an unsettling silence, until an echoing clomp, clomp, clomp upon the stage heightens the atmosphere of dread. A sliver of light pierces the darkness, illuminating the edge of the stage.

Clomp, clomp, clomp.

As the scarecrow lumbers into view, the audience is transfixed. The spotlight abruptly expands, illuminating the entire stage with glaring intensity. A momentary swell of confusion sweeps over the crowd as they grapple with the horrifying spectacle before them. The tentative peace shatters like a broken bottle as the marquee erupts into a cacophony of terrified screams, shrill screeches, indignant boos, and utter pandemonium.

'In the name of all that's shitting holy,' Frank whispers, his eyes widening in terror as they take in the grotesque sight.

Tom's twitching body lies on the ground in a gruesome pool of blood as the scarecrow stands above him brandishing the boy's severed head by the hair.

Ginger Jack smokes nervously outside at the rear of the marquee.

'I'm not entirely convinced the crowd enjoyed the new ending,' he says to Frank, pulling a rogue piece of straw from his collar.

'You don't say.'

'Do you think I misread their reaction?'

Frank massages the back of his neck. 'Crowds—they can be difficult to gauge. Although, I suspect the trauma wing at Scarborough Hospital will be filling up very shortly with mentally scarred youngsters. If I were you, Jack, I'd keep a low profile until the next show and revert to the original ending.'

'You think?'

'Yes. The new finale is closer in style to a Quentin Tarantino film than a children's pantomime. I mean, at its heart, it's a morality play about empathy and understanding. Leave the audience feeling good about life, not reaching for their vomit bags.'

'Yeah. Maybe you're right. How's your niece?'

'She's gone for a walk to get some fresh air. I'm sure she'll regain the power of speech soon enough.'

'Tell her I'm sorry. I thought it would spice things up a bit.'

'You got that right. But it's a show for youngsters, Jack. It even says so on the billboard outside—suitable for children five years and above. Put it down to one of life's little speed bumps.'

Frank strolls to the front of the tent and scans the crowd, searching for Emily. There are still a handful of parents remonstrating with the harassed ticket attendant for the show.

'I demand a refund,' an angry father shouts, red in the face.

'As I've explained, sir, it's not our policy to offer refunds.'

'I'll be reporting you to the authorities!' a woman shrieks as her petrified little cherub clings to her leg, crimson-eyed and sniffling.

'Can I be of assistance?' Abby Henderson arrives on the scene, the epitome of calm professionalism.

'Who the hell are you?' the angry father shouts.

'I'm the general manager.'

He and the other parents reiterate their request for a refund.

'Certainly. Not a problem. If you'd care to follow me to the ticketing stall, I'll reimburse your money. And I must apologise for the performance. Unbeknownst to me, it deviated from the usual script somewhat. If I had known about the alternative ending, I would have rectified it. I can assure you it won't be happening again. As a way of apology, I'd like to offer you complimentary tickets for tonight's main performance in the big top.' Her voice trails off as she leads the angry parents away.

'Hi, Frank!' a gruff Yorkshire voice bellows.

Frank spins around and squints at the approaching figure. 'Keith bloody Miller! How are you going?' he says, beaming widely as both men shake hands.

'Oh, you know me Frank, keeping out of trouble.'

'Good to hear it. Who are you here with?'

Keith throws a glance over his shoulder. 'That little scamp over there,' he says, jutting his thumb in the direction of a young girl who is trailing a jester on stilts, mesmerised. 'That's my granddaughter, Rosie.'

'I remember you telling me about her. She's your Scarlet's girl.'

'Aye, that's right.'

Frank frowns. 'You said her father was a bad 'un?'

'Yep. Doing time in Armley Jail.'

'Can't be easy on Scarlet, being a single mum.'

'Me and Jenny are always on hand to help out. Who are you here with?'

Frank spots Emily at the candy floss stall. 'My niece, Emily,' he says, nodding in her direction.

Keith peers over at her. 'She's a bonny-looking lass. Who's the lad she's talking to? Is it her boyfriend?'

Frank frowns. 'No, it bloody isn't. I don't know who that little toe-rag is.'

Keith chuckles. 'Did you watch the show—The Strawman Cometh?'

'Yes, we did. We caught it two years back. Had a more satisfying ending that time. How did Rosie react?'

'Oh, she thought it was a blast. She loves blood and gore. She's a right little terror, I can tell you. Anyway, they see far worse on the internet.'

'I'm not sure you can get much worse than a decapitation, but I take your point. And how's your lad, Riley, doing? Last time we spoke, you said he had some of the big rugby league clubs sniffing around?'

Keith's eyes nearly pop out of his head. 'Great news! He's playing his final game for Whitby today up at Darlington. On Thursday he signs with Leeds Rhinos,' he explains, barely able to contain his excitement.

'Well, I'll be!' Frank exclaims, patting Keith on the shoulder. 'Tell him congratulations from me. Although,' he pulls a grave expression, 'it's going to be a big step up from amateur to professional... and a different code. He does realise that?'

'Yeah, he's sick of me telling him the same. But you remember what it's like when you're twenty-one—you know it all. Hey, they're paying him a pretty penny for signing on. He'll be able to put a hefty deposit down on his first house. Of course, me and Jenny will be sad to see him move out, but Leeds isn't that far. A couple of hours by car. Watch out for him Frank, he's a future England captain!'

'I will. Let me know when he's playing his first game, and we'll watch the lad together.'

Keith is distracted as he searches for his precious granddaughter. 'Aye, I will... now where's that little madam gone to now? She's a right handful, Frank. Ah, there she is, sticking her tongue out at the clowns. I'll be in touch. Give my regards to Meera!'

Frank saunters over to his own treasured girl, who is still happily chatting to the mystery lad.

'Oh, hi, Uncle Frank. I got myself some candy floss.'

'So I see.'

'Sorry, I should have asked if you wanted some.'

'Aye, I think I will,' he says, reaching for his wallet.

'No, don't. I'll get it. You've paid for everything else.'

Frank relents as Emily turns away to join the queue. He fixes his eyes on the young lad.

'And what's your game?' he growls.

'What?' The boy shuffles back a step.

'You heard. What are you up to?'

The boy is confused and clearly intimidated. 'I'm up to nowt,' he states defensively.

'Well sling your hook, and get up to nowt somewhere else… understand?'

The lad slopes away, chuntering to himself and melts into the crowd. A moment later, Emily returns and hands Frank candy floss on a stick.

'Here you go,' she says, all smiles having recovered from the horror show in the marquee.

'Thanks, love.'

'Where's Danny gone?'

'Who?'

'The boy I was chatting with.'

'He said he had to meet his girlfriend,' he replies nonchalantly, taking a bite of his treat.

Emily appears crestfallen for a moment. 'Oh, he never said he had a girlfriend.'

'Aye, well, you need to watch out for his type. A bad egg through and through. His eyes were too close together. Always a dead giveaway. Right, what's next? The hall of mirrors? Oh, and one small matter; I wouldn't tell your Aunty Meera about the ending of The Strawman

Cometh; she doesn't think highly of Ginger Jack at the best of times.'

13

Prisha squeezes the nozzle on the bottle of Euphoria, releasing an intoxicating scent of pomegranate, orchid, and sandalwood—a seductive potion that conjures up a sense of mystery and depth. She places it on the counter and stares into the bathroom mirror. Rubbing her lips together to smooth the lipstick, she makes one last adjustment to her hair. A shard of excitement tickles her tummy. It's her fifth date with Adam Rushford and tonight's the night when she'll suggest he stay over at her flat. She briefly ponders if it's too soon, then considers if she's waited too long? All they've indulged in so far is some passionate kissing. And even that only happened on the third date. She has no idea what the required etiquette is these days. The harsh buzzer from the main entrance gives her a start.

Rushing to the hallway, she peers at the intercom screen. 'I'll be down in a jiffy,' she says, beaming at the grainy footage of Adam.

'Okay,' Adam replies. 'Make sure you've got a warm coat. It's brass monkeys tonight.'

She slips into a long overcoat and stashes a small purse into a pocket, then skips down the steps, excited and eager.

'Calm down, Prisha. You don't want to come across as too keen. Reel him in slowly,' she murmurs to herself.

As she yanks the door open, he automatically leans in and gives her a quick kiss to the lips.

'Wow! I like your hair. I've only ever seen it in a ponytail before. And I love your coat. Very... what's the word... Victorian chic.'

'Thanks,' she says closing the door.

'Did you get us booked in at a restaurant?' he asks as they hold hands and bounce down the front path.

She cringes. 'Sorry. I left it too late. I've been flat out at work and forgot about the Goth Weekend. Everywhere is chockers.'

'Never mind. I'm sure we can find something else to do. As long as I'm with you, I don't care.'

Her heart misses a beat. *Can this be really happening?* 'I thought we'd go to the circus. I don't mean the main show in the big top, but the sideshows and stalls. Then we can wander into town and find a cosy pub, although they'll all be packed out. There'll be plenty of street food to choose from.'

'Perfect,' he says, squeezing her hand. He pulls his collar up against the cold. 'I reckon we could be in for a sea fret.'

'A what?'

'You know, a thick fog which creeps in from the sea. It was a mild day for the end of October, which means there'll be moisture in the air. Once it hits the chill of the North Sea, it condenses and converts to fog. I hope I'm wrong. I don't fancy driving home through pea soup.'

Prisha seizes her chance. 'Actually, you don't have to drive home. You can stop at my place tonight. If you want,' she says, adding a touch of flippancy to her final words. She doesn't want to appear desperate.

He raises an eyebrow. 'On the couch?'

'That depends,' she replies, acting coy.

'On what?'

'I haven't decided yet.'

They chatter excitedly as they turn onto North Terrace, then hang a left and head towards the flashing lights and distant strains of carnival music. The main thoroughfares are already teeming with crowds of people dressed for Halloween. Prisha spots a tall man ahead. He sports a ridiculously long, grey coat with gold buttons. A black bow tie encircles a round collar. His face mask is alien in nature, white and gold, all sharp points, and angles. He holds an old book in his left hand. It resembles a diary or a ledger of some sort. Most disconcertingly, he's stood mute to the spot, staring at the spectacle.

'Christ!' Prisha hisses. 'Take a look at him. He gives me the creeps.'

Adam chuckles. 'I bet he's an accountant by day.'

'Yeah, and a weird creep by night. That's the only problem with things like this; the majority of people are ordinary folk who like to dress up and have a good time. But I'll bet you anything there are a small percentage of people who are deviants. Lurking in shadows. Hiding in plain view.'

'Do you ever switch off from being a copper?'

She winces. 'Sorry. It's ingrained in my nature.'

As they enter the circus area, Prisha spots a stall doing a roaring trade selling various ghoulish masks. 'Someone's onto a winner,' she comments. 'Five quid a pop. Nearly every kid under the age of twelve is wearing a mask.'

Adam sniggers. 'It's a talent, isn't it?'

'What is?'

'Having the foresight to spot a good business opportunity. That guy probably ordered five hundred masks a few weeks back for a couple of hundred quid. My mind doesn't work like that.'

'Some people are born hustlers.'

Sauntering through the stalls and sideshows overlooking West Beach, they stop to watch a troupe of jugglers, fire-eaters, and sword swallows who are entertaining a crowd mainly made up of parents with young children. People snack on toffee apples, donuts, and candy floss, and sip on hot chocolate, and coffees. The jugglers finish their act to rapturous applause as they pass a hat around. People throw in coins of various denominations as they disperse.

Adam takes in his surroundings and spots something of interest. Away from the main crowd is a solitary, small, black marquee, shabby in appearance compared to the other tents.

'Come on,' he encourages as he tugs at Prisha's arm.

'What?'

'The fortune teller. I'll pay for you to have a reading,' he says with a roguish grin.

'Oh no! I hate all that old tosh. You realise it's all bullshit?'

'Now, now,' he chastises. 'Don't be so judgemental. Go in there with an open mind.'

'Why don't you go in?'

'I saw her last year.'

'Really? And did she foretell the extraordinary changes that your life has recently undergone?'

'She said good fortune was coming my way if I could find empathy and understanding in my heart.'

'Hmm... bit vague and woolly.'

They hear voices from inside the tent.

'She must have someone in there already. We'll wait.'

Prisha stares incredulously at the sign outside the tent.

"Cassandra The Fortune Teller. Step inside and unveil your destiny. £20 per reading."

Two teenage girls, dressed in the ubiquitous black, wearing Goth make-up, emerge from the tent laughing and giggling.

'How did she know all that?' one of them squeals in amazement.

'OMG! She really is psychic.'

Prisha rolls her eyes and pouts at Adam. 'You're wasting your money.'

Adam grins. 'It's my money to waste.'

'You don't believe in this nonsense, do you?'

A frown supplants the grin. 'There are many things science cannot explain. Believe me, I've experienced some weird shit in my life. Especially up on the moors.'

'Next!' a disembodied voice calls out from inside the tent.

'You sure you want to blow twenty quid?' Prisha asks.

Adam nods. 'Leave your cynicism outside,' he replies, smiling.

'Very well.' She pulls at the flap of the marquee. 'And by the way, I'm a sceptic... not a cynic. Big difference.'

Inside, the tent is illuminated by eight candles in a single candelabra positioned towards the rear. A pair of rickety chairs rest in front of a small wooden table, covered in a purple tablecloth, behind which, a woman of indeterminate age is sitting. A domino mask covers her eyes, and a dark cloak is swathed around her skinny frame. Her long, black locks, speckled with shards of grey, hang limply over bony shoulders. On the table rests a crystal ball, chaperoned by two smaller candles in glass tumblers.

She welcomes them in without looking up. 'Greetings, seekers of truth. Cross the threshold and permit the shadows of tomorrow to unveil themselves.'

'Christ,' Prisha mutters under her breath, taking a seat as her inquisitive nature evaluates the woman.

Thin lips... collagen loss. Her fingers have deep wrinkles, indicating she's way past middle-aged or she's had a hard life. Hair is lank. A rough guess—I'd say she's diminutive—between five-two, five-four. There's no meat on her. A strong west country accent; Cornwall, Devon, Somerset? And most likely from a rural area, by the way she rolls some of the vowels and consonants at the end of words.

The woman holds out her palm. Adam pulls a twenty from his pocket and hands it over. Opening a small black purse, she carefully folds it around another clutch of notes.

'This reading, or whatever you call it, is for...' Prisha begins.

The fortune teller raises a hand. 'It is for you. The non-believer,' she states without emotion.

Prisha is unimpressed. A fifty-fifty chance. You either believe or you don't. Or possibly she has very good hearing and overheard the conversation outside, she thinks.

Adam smirks at her. 'See.'

Prisha pokes her tongue out as the crystal ball reflects the languidly dancing flames of the candles.

'What is your name?' the woman asks.

'You're the clairvoyant, you tell me?' Prisha replies with a hint of cockiness.

The woman lifts her head. Her dark eyes bore into Prisha's. 'I am a scryer foretelling the future, *not* a clairvoyant. I have learnt my craft. A clairvoyant is born with it. Now, your name, or would you prefer I return your money?' she questions sternly.

Adam gives Prisha a gentle tap on the shin with his boot. She huffs, raises her eyebrows, and plays the game for everyone's sake.

'My name is Prisha.'

'Ah, Prisha, meaning God's gift. It is a beautiful name. Your parents chose well.' She refocusses her attention on the shimmering glass sphere, her hands hovering over it, as if performing reiki. 'Your mother and father miss you dearly. They think of you often. Although you are a strong, independent woman, to them you are still their little girl.' She releases a half chuckle. 'Your brothers also think about you... but not as much. Nanni has a photograph of you on her bedside cabinet. She says goodnight to you and good morning every day. She misses you dearly. You should visit more often, Prisha.'

Internally, Prisha ho-hums. *Most people have a mother and father, and maybe a remaining grandparent. She knows by the colour of my skin and my name that I'm either Indian or Pakistani and it would be more than likely I'd have siblings. She's merely playing the percentages. As for Prisha, meaning God's gift, it would be wise in this game to find out the meanings behind a lot of names. Although, ten out of ten for her memory recall.*

'I sense a powerful force around you, a burden, a duty. It weighs heavy on your shoulders. You seek truths, secrets that others wish to keep buried. It is in your nature. I see a flame flickering brightly amidst shadowy gusts; you bear the torch of justice, carrying its weight willingly. You don't trust people. Forever on your guard. And yet...' she pauses, smiles and peers at Prisha, then at Adam. 'Your heart is on fire. You are in love.'

Prisha is grateful for the gloomy light as it hides her blushes.

It's obvious we're a newly dating couple. There are signs. We want to be close, but we are still treading carefully, not wanting to rush things. It's our body language. But fair credit, she's good at observing people. She should have been a copper.

The fortune teller returns her gaze to the crystal ball, her narrow lips spreading into a knowing smile. 'The Guardian—,' she begins, her voice a mere whisper, '—that's you. Always protecting, watching out for something... or someone. A rock-strewn path you have travelled, my dear. You do not suffer fools gladly. You're impatient, always in a rush. Slow down, Prisha. Life is long, the journey is far, and we all eventually arrive at the same destination.'

What a crock of shit.

The fortune teller falls silent as her genial demeanour gradually evaporates. The discordant tune from a haunting Wurlitzer seeps into the tent. The once merry oompah-pah rhythm is slower, twisting into a requiem. High tones scrape darkness, the lower timbres gurgle and growl, like an unseen beast. Each note strikes an ominous chord, spinning a chaotic symphony perfectly complimenting the macabre dance of the quivering candle lights. The foreboding melody conveys a hidden truth; beneath the carnival's colourful facade lies something rotten. Prisha shivers as the ghoulish music conjures up images of creepy clowns and animated marionettes dancing in her bedroom in the dead of night.

For the first time, she's slightly disconcerted. She throws Adam a nervous glance, then refocusses on the woman.

'Go on?' she prompts.

'I can see a solitary raven sitting on a fence in a barren field. Mist rolls in. You are alone. Abandoned. Something catches your eye, and you stoop to pick it up,' she whispers as the creases in her face deepen.

'What do I pick up?' Prisha urges unnerved yet intrigued.

As the distant strains of the carnival organ become more sinister to Prisha's ears, the woman holds her bony hand aloft.

'Shush!' she gasps. Her eyes narrow. She grimaces. 'A toy… a child's toy. A headless doll, also abandoned.'

Prisha swallows hard. 'And then what?'

The woman removes her face mask, revealing an old face, wizened, and deeply concerned.

Her voice rises in pitch and intensity. 'The picture is fading fast. There is a shadow that stalks you. An evil darkness above you... waiting, watching.'

'Waiting for what?'

'For the right time. You are in grave danger, Prisha.'

'What sort of danger?'

'Give me your hand,' the woman demands.

'What?'

'Your hand!' she yells, making her jump.

Prisha hesitantly stretches her arm out. The old woman seizes her palm and holds it near the crystal ball. Squinting, she traces the creases of skin with her finger. Gasping, she drops the hand as though it were molten iron.

'What is it?' Prisha barks.

Rocking back and forth, she speaks in an ancient tongue. 'Fios agam agat anois. Na faigheann tú riamh seachad an t-éan dubh, ná meas a bhfuil tú slán.'

'What the hell does that mean?' Adam murmurs, spooked by proceedings.

'It means listen to the knowledge I impart to you, Prisha. Beware the *raven!* Her eyes are on the earth *and* in the sky. She watches over you, planning your demise. You must slay the raven before she slays you.'

Prisha has heard enough and pushes back in her chair. 'You know what? People like you should be banned. This is subliminal messaging. You may be able to mesmerise pubescent teenage girls, and the hard-of-understanding, but to any rational human being you are nothing more than a cheap charlatan, a shyster, charging twenty quid a throw for five minutes of hammy bullshit! Come on, Adam, let's go,' she shouts, heading towards the flap of the tent.

'I speak from the heart, detective. The third eye does not deceive,' the woman states coldly.

Prisha stops dead in her tracks and turns at the speed of an ocean liner. 'How do you know I'm a detective?'

'I see it in the crystal.' She pulls open a table drawer and retrieves something. 'Take this,' she adds urgently, thrusting it towards Prisha.

Prisha gazes at the chain and tiny black object attached. 'What is it?'

'A talisman. A wolf's claw carved from Whitby jet. It has magical properties. Wear it around your neck always. It cannot *protect* you from evil... but it will warn you when evil nears.'

'And how much do you charge for it?' Prisha sneers.

The woman shakes her head. 'It is my gift. If the spirits are willing, they shall repay my generosity.'

'Take it,' Adam says, his face a conundrum of fear and bafflement.

Prisha grabs the necklace and studies it. A long silver chain, in the centre, a small but exquisitely carved black claw.

'You said it would give me a warning. How?' she demands, annoyed as hell she's been suckered into this morbid fairytale from a scam artist.

'You will know. When it warns you, Prisha, take heed and be on your guard for you will be in mortal danger. Wear it always. It is your only chance against the evil that pursues you.'

Prisha storms from the tent as a peculiar and unwelcome chill ripples down her spine.

14

They saunter silently through the crowds, an intriguing blend of Victorian aristocrats, steam punks, vampiric enthusiasts and cyber-goths, their eccentric outfits steeped in varying colours. The festivalgoers are a diverse collection, spanning different age groups and backgrounds, bound by their shared appreciation of the alternative world.

Adam tries to slide his hand into Prisha's, but she pulls away and jams her fists firmly into the warmth of her coat pockets.

'I'm sorry,' he mumbles. 'I thought it would be a laugh.'

Prisha had her doubts about their relationship. She wanted to believe, so buried her qualms, but now they've resurfaced.

She turns to him. 'Look, Adam, this isn't going to work.'

He's stunned. 'What?'

'Us,' she sighs. 'You're a farmer. I'm a police officer. You believe in all this spiritual stuff, and I don't. We're complete opposites. You're laid-back and easy-going and I'm... uptight and neurotic. It's a recipe for disaster. What's the point of continuing a relationship we both know won't last? We're setting ourselves up for pain.'

Adam grins nervously. 'She was right, the fortune teller. You are in a rush. Prisha, this is only our fourth date and...'

'Fifth,' she corrects, interrupting him.

'Sorry, fifth,' he states apologetically before frowning. 'Why are you getting so ahead of yourself? Let's enjoy the moment, right here and now. To hell with tomorrow.' He leans in and gently kisses her lips, then plants a lingering smooch on the side of her neck. It melts her resolve. He pulls her hands from her pockets, then tenderly rubs them. 'Cold hands, warm heart,' he whispers, bearing a cheeky smile as their eyes lock.

Embarrassed at her outburst, she relents. 'You're right. I can be such a fixated bitch sometimes. I think I've forgotten how to enjoy myself. Can we start the night again?'

He beams and takes her arm. 'Great idea. Do you like roasted chestnuts?'

'I've never had them.'

'You're in for a treat, then. There's a stall up here selling them. We'll grab a couple of bags, catch a few more circus sights, then head over to the old part of town and see if we can squeeze into a pub for a drink. How does that sound?'

She exhales deeply, her breath hanging in the frigid air. 'It sounds wonderful. I'm sorry for my little rant. Here, take this. I don't want it,' she adds, passing him the amulet. 'Give it to your sister for Christmas. She's into all that malarky.'

Reticent, he wavers before taking the necklace, wishing to avoid any further quarrels.

'Fine,' he says. 'Let's get those chestnuts.'

As Adam places his order at the front of the queue, Prisha hangs back and studies the crowd. She spots four teenage boys in a cluster near to a contortionist entertaining a small crowd. One of the boys pulls a twenty from his coat and hands it over. The other lad takes it and moves his clenched fist forward. They shake hands and pat each other on the shoulder, exchanging fake farewells.

'Good to see you, buddy. I'll see you around, yeah?'

'Yeah. Cheers.'

They disperse.

'Dealing drugs,' Prisha murmurs. Her eyes wander across to another clutch of youths, this time all girls. Their make-up and goth outfits age them, but she'd guess they're all in their early teens. One of them surreptitiously hands a water bottle around. As each girl takes a swig, they grimace before passing the bottle on.

'And those young ladies are necking neat gin or vodka, I suspect.'

Adam returns with the chestnuts. 'Here we go. Watch out. They're hot.'

She takes the bag as her eyes flit onto the contortionist, who is earning gasps from the crowd as he manipulates his whole body through a stringless tennis racket.

Adam notices her faraway look. 'What's the matter?'

She snaps from her day job back to reality. 'Nothing. Just soaking up the atmosphere,' she lies as something niggles at her.

Sauntering through the bustling throng, they absorb the spectacle and the palpable sense of excitement.

'Oh, that's a shame,' Adam states.

'What is?'

With a nod towards a marquee board outside a tent, Adam replies, 'I saw him last time, and he was amazing.'

Echoing the words inscribed on the board, Prisha reads aloud. 'Samson Durat the World's Greatest Illusionist. Show cancelled due to unforeseen circumstances. Refunds available from the ticket kiosk.' She chuckles. 'Samson

Durat is an anagram of Nostradamus. The irony is rich, don't you think?'

Adam's puzzled expression suggests he missed the inference. 'He has a black casket and secures his assistant inside, padlocking it firmly shut. Then, the box levitates off the ground. He parades around swirling his cane above and below. Absolutely no wires or hidden mechanisms in sight. A black curtain descends and...'

Intervening with the punchline, Prisha concludes, 'And in a miraculous turn of events, it's the assistant who unlocks the box to reveal the illusionist inside.'

Perplexed, Adam stares wide-eyed. 'You've seen it?'

'Variations of it,' she says, less than impressed. 'How old are you?'

'You know how old I am.'

'I meant your mental age.'

He grins. 'True. I'm still a child at heart.'

Prisha pokes her head inside the tent and spots a short, portly, older male with a long, grey goatee beard below a handlebar moustache. A younger, attractive woman is busy packing flight cases. The man spots Prisha as he straps a black casket to a trolley and pushes it towards the back entrance and a waiting van.

In a croaky voice, his face glistening with sweat, he explains, 'I'm sorry, my dear, but tonight's show is cancelled. I'm afraid I have the flu.' He pulls a handkerchief from his pocket and dabs his forehead. 'If you purchased a ticket, you can obtain a refund from the ticket kiosk.'

'Kevin, it's simply a head cold,' the woman says, rolling her eyes. She momentarily stops packing and glances knowingly at Prisha. 'If he were a woman, he'd have the sniffles. But being a man, he has the flu.'

'Ah, the dreaded man-flu,' Prisha says with a grin.

The illusionist ignores his assistant. 'If you wish to witness Samson Durat, the world's greatest illusionist, our next show will be at the Theatre Royal in Newcastle on Friday night. If I haven't expired by then,' he adds, as a miserable afterthought. Closing his eyes, he sneezes violently into his hanky. Prisha offers the assistant a commiserative shrug and retreats from inside the tent.

'Nosey bugger, aren't you?' Adam says.

'I prefer the term inquisitive,' she replies, picking a warm chestnut from the bag.

'Prisha!' a voice calls out.

Half-turning, she doesn't immediately identify the older woman and teenage girl approaching.

'Ah! Meera, I didn't recognise you.'

Meera chuckles, her hands wafting over her Victorian outfit. 'I'm not surprised. I look like a rather plump

Madame Bovary. You won't have met my niece. This is Emily, my youngest sister's daughter.'

Prisha smiles at the girl, who is in full-scale goth regalia. 'Pleased to meet you, Emily. Frank has mentioned you many times. Talking of Frank, is he around?'

'No. He's at home watching the telly. He and Emily visited the circus this afternoon. I think it's worn him out,' Meera explains as her eyes fall onto Adam.

Prisha clears her throat nervously. 'Oh, Meera, let me introduce you to my... ahem, my friend, Adam,' she says.

Adam nods. 'Pleased to meet you.'

'Likewise. Right, we better leave you two lovebirds alone. Me and Emily are going to catch the illusionist show then head towards Church Street where all the action is.'

Prisha grimaces and pulls an apologetic face. 'You're out of luck, Meera. It's been cancelled. Samson Durat has the sniffles.'

'Oh, no!' Emily cries. 'That was the only show I wanted to see tonight. Come on, Aunty Meera, let's head into the old part of town now.'

'Very well, dear. Although, I must grab a coffee to pep myself up first. I'm not used to these late nights.'

'It's not even eight-thirty,' Emily exclaims.

Prisha and Adam watch on in mild amusement as the pair saunter off, arm in arm.

'That's nice,' Adam notes.

'What is?'

He turns to her, puzzled. 'You know... aunty and niece, out together.'

Prisha considers it for a split second. 'Yeah. Suppose.'

Adam stares at her thoughtfully for a moment before his eyes light up as they fall on a tent in the distance.

'Hey, how about the hall of mirrors? That's always a giggle.'

Studying his expectant face, she replies, 'Okay, man-boy. The hall of mirrors it is. Then let's head down to the harbour. I'm just about over the circus.'

Hand in hand, they creep into the marquee, a row of mirrors stretching out before them. Their reflections cavort in the distorting glass, creating a symphony of silhouettes to accompany the shared laughter. It's a welcome respite, a step away from the strains of earlier. As they round a corner, the atmosphere shifts abruptly. They're unexpectedly confronted by a formation of towering clowns, each one an intimidating caricature, garbed in jarring, psychedelic chequered uniforms, their porcelain faces grinning maliciously.

'Christ, they're creepy,' Adam states.

Prisha scoffs. 'Big tough, Yorkshire farmer! Scared of a set of giant dolls.'

As they hesitantly edge past, the clowns spring to life. Their arms jerk into mechanical motion as their heads swivel to track the intruders in an eerily fluid dance. Several of the mannequins break into sudden bouts of low, hysterical laughter, which echoes off the mirrors. The chilling spectacle shoots a ripple of unease through the couple as their fingers interlock. They shoot a quick glance at each other, scream, laugh, and sprint from the tent.

15

With great difficulty, Adam squeezes past the hordes of people in the pub and makes his way outside onto a balcony overlooking the harbour. Clutching two pint glasses, he spots Prisha squashed up against a balustrade in the corner.

'Scuse, scuse, coming through,' he shouts as he turns sideways to slink through the merry crowd of revellers, a Duran Duran song blaring from a speaker. He hands her a pint of shandy.

'Cheers,' she says, beaming.

'Cheers. And thank you for a wonderful night.'

They clink glasses.

'And it's not over yet,' Prisha adds with an enigmatic smile. 'Sorry about earlier. You were right. I need to live in the moment. I've had such a laugh.'

Adam leans in and plants a tender kiss on her lips. 'Me too. The best times happen when you just go with the flow.'

'I didn't think I'd enjoy the circus, but it was a ball.' Her smile slips, replaced by a frown. 'Apart from the fortune teller and the clowns in the hall of mirrors.'

'God! Those clowns gave me the creeps. Whoever thought of that was clever.'

'Or sick.'

'No... clever. To take your emotions from one extreme to the other is hard to do. One minute laughing, the next moment screaming and running for our lives.'

Prisha turns and gazes out at the twinkling lights that festoon the West Pier, experiencing a sense of wonderment and a slight euphoric tingling she hasn't felt in a long time. Her elation is short-lived. As she takes a sip of shandy, her eyes focus on the yawning entrance to the harbour.

'Now *that* is spooky,' she murmurs, transfixed as an unexpected apparition materialises — sea fog. The loud babble of the patrons melts to silence.

Adam follows her gaze. 'Hell! I've never witnessed a sea fret roll in that fast before,' he says in astonishment.

Like a stalker, it tumbles and roils towards them, its foggy tendrils billowing wildly as they barrel into the harbour, swallowing both piers as it gathers pace. Its shadowy form is dense, unnaturally so, moving with an unsettling speed. The sight sends another uncanny shiver through Prisha, a postscript to the eeriness of a night she won't forget soon.

They stare at each other. A click breaks the impasse as the convection heater thermostat temporarily turns off the heat in the bedroom.

Prisha tries to hide her nervousness. It's nearly two years since she had sex with anyone. Adam does not appear nervous. On the contrary, he looks like a man who has recently finished a twelve-month stint in prison. And yet, he's restrained, considerate. He makes the first move and imparts a long sensual kiss, which Prisha gratefully accepts and fully reciprocates. His lips fall on to her neck as her heart thumps against her chest. She wants this to be long, slow, so she can savour every moment. He gently lifts her arms in the air and pulls her jumper up, the static from the wool causing strands of her hair to stand on end. He throws the sweater onto a chair.

'Wait,' Prisha whispers, eyes on fire. 'I want to undress you.'

Adam grins. 'Best offer I've had all day.'

Slowly, she unbuttons his shirt and disrobes him, then lifts his T-shirt over his head. Her hands stroke his muscular chest, slide across his taut abdomen and drop to his belt buckle. Deftly, she unhitches the clasp and slides the leather apart, pops the top button on his cargo pants, and pulls at the zipper.

Then stops.

Lascivious thoughts are abruptly interrupted as she strains to hear the sound again.

Nothing.

Her hands slip around to the back of his pants, her thumbs delve inside and grip the fabric.

Adam again kisses her neck, then nibbles on her ear.

This time Prisha's heart does not skip a beat.

'Can you give me a moment,' she declares, as if she were a librarian who'd just been asked to check if they had a certain book on the shelves.

Adam is confused. 'What's wrong?' He receives no reply as Prisha heads to the bedroom window, pulls the curtains back, and lifts the sash window. She peers out but cannot see anything because of the thick fog. She cocks her head to one side and waits.

Nothing.

'Hmm...' Shutting the window, she draws the curtains and turns back to Adam.

'Sorry about that. I thought I heard something. Now, where were we?'

'You were about to pull my trousers down.'

'That's right,' she says, smiling sweetly and leaning in to kiss him.

'You're odd,' he says as their lips touch.

'I know,' she mumbles, smiling.

She stops again, returns to the window, pulls the blinds, lifts the frame.

'For God's sake, Prisha! What's the matter?' Adam is not only baffled, but extremely sexually frustrated.

'Shush!' she replies. 'There, I heard it again.'

'What?' he grumbles.

'Voices, angry voices, and a lot of them. It's muffled by the fog, but there's something going on.'

'So what? It's just another Saturday night where dickheads who can't hold their drink decide to have a punch up.'

'A police siren in the distance... no wait, two or more sirens. It must be big.' She leans precariously outside the window, dangling three storeys above the ground. A repeating blue light intermittently stabs through the grey murkiness. The voices come to her again, this time more strident, angry, violent. She pulls herself back in and slams the window shut as she grabs her jumper and slips back into her boots.

'What are you doing?' Adam asks, alarmed at her peculiar behaviour.

'There's something kicking off, and it's big. I think it's coming from the circus. I better go check it out,' she explains, hurriedly fashioning her hair into a ponytail and collecting her phone.

'Isn't that uniform's job? Sorting out the drunks?'

'Like I said, this doesn't sound like a few drunken yobbos trying to kick the shit out of each other. It sounds like a crowd. And baying crowds don't suddenly materialise at this time of night, in the freezing cold, without good reason. Sorry, I'll be back as soon as I can.' She pecks him on the cheek and pats him on the groin. 'Keep it warm for when I return. And don't help yourself. Save it for me,' she says with a chuckle.

'Wait a minute.' He pulls the amulet, gifted from the fortune teller, from his pocket and releases the clasp. 'Wear this,' he says as he attaches it around her neck.

'Really?' she groans, staring at the claw on her jumper. 'You're scared of your own shadow. It's all bunkum. People believe what they want to believe, it doesn't mean it's true.'

'Please, for me.'

'Okay.' She relents, pulling at the neck of her sweater and dropping the chain inside.

'Thanks.' Adam watches despairingly as she strides across the room. 'You know I've got to be at the farm by six, which means leaving here by five?' he calls after her, glancing at the clock on the wall, the hour and minute hands precariously close to midnight.

'Yep. I'll be back long before then!' she yells as she clatters down the dormer stairs.

Adam slumps onto the bed, dispirited, as his ardour rapidly diminishes. 'Maybe she's right. Maybe we're not suited.'

16

Sunday 1st November – 12:01 am

Frank steps from the patrol car into the bitter, foggy night. The carnival atmosphere has long ago evaporated, now replaced by violent shouts, and a tangible crackle of violence in the air. He takes a moment to reconcile the happy, vibrant colours dancing in the circus lights with the scene of confusion playing out before him.

'This could turn ugly very quickly,' he mutters to himself, slamming the car door shut. He turns to PC Pembroke, who collected him from his house a few moments ago.

'Do you have a megaphone in the boot?' he asks.

'No, sir. But I could try one of the other patrol cars.'

'Aye. Do that and make it quick before this thing really gets going.' He strides towards the raucous crowd baying for blood as his name is called out.

'Frank!'

He stops and spins around as Prisha jogs up to him. 'What's happening?'

'Not entirely sure yet. All I know is an eight-year-old lass went missing a few hours ago. For some reason someone's formed the impression Ginger Jack is involved in her disappearance.'

'What's the girl's name?' she asks as they both hurry towards the scene.

He shoots her a worried sideways glance. 'Rosie Miller. Keith Miller's granddaughter. I was only speaking with him earlier today at the circus.'

'Shit! How long has she been missing?'

'Not sure.'

Frank surveys the landscape. A dozen uniformed officers, with arms entwined, are providing a wall of protection in front of the circus caravans, preventing the mob from advancing towards the motley crew of performers, who, in turn have formed into a tight circle around Ginger Jack. He shivers in the cold, wild staring eyes, fearing for his life. His granddaughter, Abby Henderson, has her arm around his shoulder, offering him comfort. Frank and Prisha bustle their way to the front of the throng, joining Zac, who is already in attendance, pleading with the crowd to calm down.

'That's the bastard!' A man shouts, pointing at Ginger Jack.

'Where is she, you sicko?'

'What have you done with her?' voices scream, jabbing fingers towards the petrified old man. A surge from the crowd engulfs Frank and Prisha, squeezing them back into the line of blue.

'What the hell is happening?' Frank bellows at Zac.

'God knows! For some reason they suspect the old man knows of the girl's whereabouts, but I cannae get any sense out of them. A lot are rugby lads and most of them are pissed out of their heads! Uniform have already completed a thorough search of all the tents and caravans.'

Frank suddenly has a megaphone thrust into his hand. He ducks under the police cordon and stands on the step of a motorhome. The loudspeaker goes into feedback mode as he turns it on.

'Right, listen up, you lot! I'm DCI Frank Finnegan. I understand feelings are running high, but this is not the way to find Rosie! You must disperse and let the police do their job!' His appeal is met with a barrage of insults and invective. He spots Keith Miller and his son, Riley, in the middle of the pack, and gestures towards them. 'Keith! Keith, step this way. Let's have a chat.'

Zac and Prisha escort Keith through the police line as reinforcements arrive to the sound of screeching tyres and wailing sirens.

Keith's jowls harden, his eyes ablaze with fury. 'You don't understand, Frank,' he spits as Frank drops from the step.

'No, you're right, I don't. Ten minutes ago, I was about to slip into a nice, warm bed. Now I'm standing here freezing my nuts off. Give me a quick summary of what's happened.'

'It's our Rosie, Frank. She went missing, and I believe that dirty old bastard over there,' he points towards Ginger Jack, 'knows something about it. If he's laid a single finger on her, I'll skin the bugger alive!'

Frank takes him by the elbow and leads him aside. 'Take a deep breath and calm down. I haven't got my head around the facts yet. Now start again.'

Anger is replaced with concern as Keith rubs at his face. 'Rosie said she'd been invited for a sleepover at her mate's house, India Anderson. They're best mates. India lives across the street and they're always having sleepovers. Anyway, the little buggers snuck out. India's mother was at the bingo and arrived back about eight. The older brother, Dylan, was supposed to be babysitting, but he was in his room playing video games so didn't notice them missing. As the girls neared the circus, India got cold feet and told Rosie she didn't want to go. They had a tiff and India ran back home. When her mother got home, India was pretending to be asleep in bed. Then about two hours ago India's conscience got the better of her and she spilled the beans to her mother.'

'Hang on... wasn't India's mother aware of the sleepover?'

'No.'

'Rosie made India promise not to tell anyone she'd gone to the circus. She wanted to see that bloody Strawman play again,' he adds throwing a vengeful glare at Ginger Jack, still closely guarded by his troupe.

'What time did the girls set off for the circus?'

'Not sure. But they were specifically going to see the Strawman play and that started at seven.'

'And it's about a fifteen, twenty-minute walk from your place to here.'

'Aye, about that.'

Frank shoots a glance at his watch—it's ticked past midnight. 'And why do you think the old man has anything to do with Rosie's disappearance?'

'Because today, not long after I'd spoken with you, she disappeared for a few minutes. Apparently, according to India, she bumped into Ginger Jack at the back of the marquee. He gave her two free tickets to tonight's show. He said that after the show, if she went to his caravan, he had something special for her. Sick old bastard!'

'Hell fire,' Frank mutters, a wave of dread washing over him. 'Does Rosie have a mobile phone?'

'No. We've been putting it off as long as we could. I'm regretting that decision now,' he reflects wistfully. 'I want this whole place searched, Frank. We're wasting bloody time!' he shouts as his ire returns with a vengeance.

'It's been searched once, but we'll conduct another one. Right, give me a minute,' he replies as he walks over to the ring of performers. 'Jack, we need to talk,' he states without emotion as Jack and Abby are released from the encirclement. 'The girl that went missing; they're saying you handed her two free tickets this afternoon for the evening show, and you asked her to come to your caravan afterwards. Is that true?'

'No... yes. Part of it,' he blusters, confused and frightened.

'Inspector Finnegan, my granddad is a very old man and is on medication,' Abby states, extremely concerned for his welfare.

Frank holds his hand up. 'Forgive me; let Jack talk.' He eyeballs the old man once more. 'You were saying?'

'Yes, I gave a young girl two tickets earlier. She loved the show and wanted to bring a friend to see it. I assumed they'd have been accompanied by an adult.'

'And the caravan?'

'I never asked her to come to my caravan. What I said was I had something special for her *in* my caravan. I'm not stupid, Frank. I'd never invite a kiddie into my van.'

'And what was this special thing you had for her?'

'At the beginning of the season I had a hundred small dolls commissioned. They're miniatures of the Strawman. I hand a few out at each town we play. I had two left. That's what I was planning to give the little girl and her friend.'

Frank's eyes fall onto Abby. 'Is this true?'

'Of course it is. I'll fetch one.' She disappears into his rundown caravan and returns a moment later with a Strawman doll. 'See,' she says, thrusting it towards Frank.

He studies the effigy, then focuses on Jack. 'And did you see the little girl, Rosie, after tonight's performance?'

Jack shakes his head vehemently. 'No! Honest to God. If truth be told, I'd forgotten all about her.'

Abby fixes Frank with a severe glare. 'Inspector Finnegan, I can vouch for my father's movements tonight. He finished the show about seven-forty. I then walked with him to his caravan and stoked the fire as he climbed into bed. An hour later, I returned with some supper for him and poured him a shot of whisky. We said goodnight, and I heard him secure his door when I left. As I said, he's a very old man and not in the best of health,' she adds stroking her grandfather's shoulders.

'It's true, Frank. After my supper and another shot or two of whisky, I was dead to the world. It was only when the police came thumping on my door that I suspected something was amiss. Then not long after, that lot turned up,' he says with fearful eyes as he nods at the drunken mob.

'Right, get him inside and make him a hot drink before he develops hypothermia,' he instructs Abby.

'And what about them?' she hisses. 'I fear for granddad's safety.'

'Don't you worry about them. I'll take care of it. And put some more wood on the fire. Oh, and Miss Henderson, if you could visit the station at the earliest opportunity with a list of all your personnel and relevant background checks.'

'Certainly,' she says as she takes Jack's arm and leads him away.

Frank returns to Keith and relates Jack's version of events.

'And you believe him?' Keith spits.

'At the moment, I've no reason to doubt him.'

'He's lying!'

'In times like these we all want a scapegoat. Trust me, I've been there. Just look at it logically, Keith. With thousands of the public milling about, and over fifty circus personnel, don't you think someone would have noticed a distinctive old man with a wooden leg escorting a young girl to his caravan? And his granddaughter has vouched for his movements after the show.'

Keith snorts. 'I bet she bloody has! That means bugger all.'

'Keith, I've known Jack a long time. He's eccentric, but he's not a child abductor. All circus personnel need a DBS check.'

'What the hell's A DBS check?'

'Disclosure and Barring Service. They're required by law to be vetted to make sure they have no prior convictions involving minors. Now, if you want to help, then I suggest you disperse your gang and tell them to go home and catch some sleep. Have the police been to your house to get statements?'

'Yes,' he nods, his mind a million miles away.

'And the neighbour?'

'Yes.'

'Right. Leave it to the police until first light. If she hasn't turned up by then, we'll put out a call for public volunteers to help in the search. The best thing you can do is go home and be with your daughter and Jenny. If they haven't done it already, compile a list of Rosie's friends. Ring, call, text anyone who knows Rosie and put the word out. Maybe she bumped into a mate at the circus and went back to their house.'

Ashen faced, he stares at Frank. 'Be honest with me, Frank. It's not looking good, is it?'

It's a tough question. If Rosie left her friend's house at six-thirty, she's now been missing over five and a half hours. Frank knows the statistics only too well. Abducted children who are later found murdered are usually killed within the first three hours. How can he tell his old friend the truth?

'One must never give up hope, Keith.' Frank instantly regrets his supine platitude.

Keith forcefully grabs the collar of Frank's long overcoat, but without anger. 'Don't bullshit me, Frank. The truth?'

Frank closes his eyes and wishes he was anywhere else in the world. 'If Rosie has been taken, the chances are... slim.' His last word slips from his mouth, barely audible. 'But if she's become lost, then we'll likely find her alive and well.'

Keith releases his grip. 'Thanks. I guess I knew,' he replies, deeply troubled, deflated.

'I wouldn't relay the information to Jenny or Scarlet, though.'

'No. Of course not.' He turns and addresses the small crowd, 'All right, lads! Home time. Let the police do their work.'

Frank watches the crowd begrudgingly disperse and melt away into the fog, as Zac and Prisha amble towards him.

'Right, let's get this show on the road. Prisha, head to the station and initiate a full-scale Child Rescue Alert. Inform the coastguard of the events. There's always the remote possibility she somehow ended up in the drink. Although, I'm not sure they'll launch a lifeboat tonight. Not with this fog and no eyewitness to say she went in the water. Get onto HQ and get every available officer over here. All leave cancelled. And compile a list of child sex offenders within a fifty-mile radius then send out officers to interview them.'

'That's a wide area, Frank,' Prisha advises.

'Yes, I know it bloody is!' he snaps angrily. 'And we'll need a recent photo of Rosie. Distribute it to...'

'... the press, TV, radio, social media platforms along with a description of what she was wearing and her last known movements, along with date and times. I'm onto it, Frank.' She turns on her heels, stops for a moment to have a quick word with a uniform, then heads towards a patrol car.

'And Prisha!' Frank shouts after her.

'Yes! Get Dinkel onto the CCTV footage! I've got it covered, Frank!'

Zac stares at her in disbelief. 'She's like a bloody mind reader,' he mutters.

'Hmm... either that or I'm extremely predictable.'

'What do you want me to do?' Zac probes.

'You take charge of the situation here. Conduct a fresh search and interview all the circus staff. Once you've initiated that, head over to the Millers and go over their statements again. Then question Rosie's friend, India, and the brother and mother. Find the route the girls took and where exactly they had the falling out. I also want a list of names of all close family and friends. I know Rosie's biological father is doing time, so Scarlet probably has a partner, maybe ex-partners as well. Check the alibis of everyone, including Keith, Scarlet, and Jenny. Leave no stone unturned. Take a couple of uniformed officers with you. I find they offer a degree of comfort in times like these. And make sure a Family Liaison Officer is on their way. Oh, and anyone who only has a spouse or partner as an alibi, make a note of them. And you'll need to bag Rosie's toothbrush and hairbrush for forensics.'

'Righto, Frank. I'll keep you updated. Are you heading to the station?'

'Not yet. I have to go home.'

'Why?'

Like a flasher on the loose, Frank pulls open his overcoat to reveal a pair of blue and white striped pyjamas. 'That's why.'

17

The living room of the Miller's four-bedroom home is filled with a hush bordering on the sacred. The glow from an orange street light filters through a crack in the red velvet curtains. Prisha idly takes in the interior. The room is clean and tidy enough, if a little threadbare. A typical working-class family who can make ends meet, but don't have a lot of surplus cash at the end of the month for improvements. The matriarch, Jenny Miller silently enters from the kitchen carrying a tray containing three cups of tea. Her face is creased with worry as she places the tray down on a small side table in front of Prisha.

'Thank you,' Prisha says quietly as she picks up a cup and takes a sip.

Scarlet, Rosie's mother, is seated in a chair opposite, nervously flicking at her phone.

'Anything?' Jenny asks.

'Got a text from dad. He and two rugby lads are nearing the West Pier. But no sign of her.'

'And where's Riley?'

'He's searching the huts on West Beach.'

Prisha pulls out her notebook, realising she must tread carefully through this terrain of misery.

'If we could go through a few things,' she begins, gently.

'We've all given statements. I don't know what else you want us to say,' Scarlet barks. 'Why aren't you out looking for her?'

Prisha and Jenny exchange a swift sideways glance. 'We have a team of officers on foot and in cars scouring the town, Scarlet. You gave details of the timeframe to Rosie's disappearance, and what she was wearing, but I'm here to find out more about Rosie's personality rather than the circumstances of last night.'

Jenny takes a seat next to Prisha on the couch as Scarlet puts her phone down.

'Okay. What do you want to know?' she relents, grudgingly.

'Tell me about Rosie. Is she shy, timid, outgoing? Has she any special needs?'

'She's a very bright child,' Jenny replies, rocking forward, nursing her cup of tea. 'Outgoing, definitely not shy.'

'Confident, independent?'

'Yes, I suppose you could say that. She's also very smart. Does exceptionally well at school.'

'Has she ever disappeared before?'

'No. Well, we once lost her in the supermarket, but that was when she was a toddler.'

'Who disciplines her when she does something wrong?'

Jenny looks at her daughter. 'I do,' Scarlet says.

'And is that often?'

'She can be a right handful sometimes, but she's not a bad kid, just... well, you know naughty. Pushes the boundaries.'

'I'd say high-spirited rather than naughty,' Jenny comments.

'Does she play out much?'

Scarlet shrugs. 'If the weather's good, she'll play out on the street with India.'

'It's a nice safe street,' Jenny interjects. 'A cul-de-sac. It's very neighbourly.'

'Does she ever wander further afield?'

Scarlet shakes her head. 'No, not on her own.'

'What about the town? Would Rosie know her way around?'

Mother and daughter stare at each other, unsure. Scarlet winces. 'She obviously knows the landmarks, but if you were to drop her on the promenade and tell her to make her own way home, I don't think she'd know her way back.' Another glance to Jenny. 'What do you think, mam?'

Jenny frowns. 'No, you're right. She's a clever lass, but her sense of direction is not the best.'

Prisha scribbles notes. 'What are Rosie's interests?'

'She enjoys drawing and painting,' Jenny says. 'When Rosie and India are together, they like to put on shows.'

'Shows?'

'Yes, you know... little dance routines and gymnastics to backing-music.'

'Has she ever mentioned what she wants to be when she grows up?'

Scarlet huffs, her patience wearing thin. 'For God's sake! She's eight years old.'

'Scarlet!' Jenny rebukes her daughter before turning to Prisha. 'The latest fad is she wants to join the lifeboat crew when she's old enough. She watched a documentary on it recently. Oh, and possibly a vet.'

'I see,' Prisha says. 'Can she swim?'

'Yes. But I wouldn't say she's a strong swimmer.'

'Water wise?'

'Yes. She knows not to go into the water unless an adult is with her.'

Scarlet rises, her anger bubbling beneath the surface. 'We're wasting time going around in circles. How is all this helping to find my Rosie?'

'I'm trying to form a picture. We have all the facts of when she was last seen and where we think she was heading to, but finding out what type of girl Rosie is may help.' Prisha senses her presence is no longer welcome and slips her notebook away. 'May I take a quick look around her bedroom?'

'Of course,' Jenny says.

18

As the minute hand on the clock hard-heartedly ticks past eight o'clock, Frank crosses the threshold into the busy incident room, his senses immediately swamped by the dissonant squawk of desperation that reverberates around the office. The urgency is tangible, as frantic officers work against time to unravel the mystery behind Rosie Miller's sudden disappearance. An unnerving thirteen hours have elapsed since the eight-year-old was last seen, a speck of innocence against the riotous backdrop of Whitby's frenetic weekend. Frank tilts his head and sniffs. The aroma of coffee, aftershave, perfume, and fresh croissants hides an intruder... the whiff of fear.

Each passing second, each unanswered question, amplifies the dread that gnaws constantly at his gut. An agonising parallel unfolds; the haunting spectre of his own daughter's unresolved disappearance, a wound untouched by time's healing hand, even after all these years. It remains a private torment known only to a select few.

The approaching tempest of an unthinkable tragedy slices through him. His eyes flicker across to Prisha and Zac standing near the whiteboard in hushed conversation. It brings him a modicum of strength. If ever he needed Prisha to experience one of her lightbulb moments… then it's now. Drawing a deep breath, and with an almighty effort, he subdues his own sense of trepidation, knowing the task at hand is critical. Now is not the time for morbid introspection. His duty is to be a beacon of hope, to stoke determination where despair attempts to settle. But in his heart of hearts, he already suspects… it may be too late for Rosie.

Advancing to the front of the room, he positions himself before the "smart" interactive whiteboard and allows himself a smile as he notices a sticker in the top right-hand corner. Some wag has already rechristened it Watson in deference to Sherlock's long-suffering partner.

'Okay team, hush, please. Time for the briefing. There'll be more officers drifting in throughout the day, but for those of you already here, I'd like to thank you all. As major incidents go, it doesn't get any bigger than a missing child. All of us must push hard; work as a team; information share…but… we are not cyborgs. We will need rest, sustenance, and sleep at some point. You're no good to the investigation, nor Rosie Miller, if you're only firing on two cylinders. Individually, you all know what your limits are—don't go beyond them. Okay, I'll hand you over to DI Kumar. Prisha?'

She steps forward, and with a deftness which puzzles Frank, she immediately populates the whiteboard with photos, street maps, and bullet point summaries simply by using a finger to drag objects from the left-hand panel.

'We'll start with what we know: the timeline. Questions at the end, please. The missing girl, eight-year-old Rosie Miller, lives at 12 Ashton Grove, Whitby, with her mother, maternal grandparents, and her uncle. Her best friend, India Anderson, lives across the road at 21 Ashton Grove. Unbeknownst to her family, earlier in the day, Rosie was given two free tickets to the nighttime performance of a children's play, The Strawman Cometh, showing at the circus. At around 6:30 pm last night, Rosie and India left 21 Ashton Grove, and headed towards the circus. Before they reached the circus, India got cold feet. According to India's mother, Zara Anderson, India is a bit on the cautious side, whereas from all accounts, Rosie is a bit of a handful, fearless, a risk taker, and also highly intelligent.'

A DC drafted in from York raises his hand. 'How long did it take the girls to get from Ashton Grove to the path near the circus?'

Prisha points at the map again. 'It's less than a mile. I had a PC walk it out at normal pace and it takes about fifteen minutes. If Rosie continued on alone to the circus, she would have arrived there about 6:45—6:50 pm, ten to fifteen minutes before the show began.'

'That's bloody good timing for an eight-year-old,' the constable states doubtfully.

'As I said, Rosie is above average intelligence for her age.'

'You said the girls had a falling out or a tiff. What about?'

'Rosie is into all things scary, spooky, even gory. India is more timid. Rosie kept raving about the Strawman play. She'd been at the matinee performance with her grandfather earlier in the day. As the girls neared the circus, India lost her nerve and said she was going home. Rosie called her a scaredy cat and said she had better not tell anyone where Rosie was, otherwise she'd never talk to her again. At that point, the girls parted company and India ran back home.'

The DC raises another question. 'Do we have any prime suspects yet?'

Prisha fixes him with a withering stare. 'I said questions at the end. It's important for me explain what we have in a methodical and logical manner. If you keep interrupting, we end up jumping about all over the shop.'

The DC rolls his eyes and mutters, 'Pardon me for breathing.'

'And less of the attitude. This isn't about your ego, it's about a little girl who may be in grave danger. Now, where was I?'

The DC, suitably chastised, withers in his chair.

Frank nods. 'Timeline,' he prompts.

Prisha smiles. 'Thanks. In a moment, DS Stoker will run footage from various home security cameras, which caught glimpses of the two girls on their route. So, to recap, we know what time Rosie left India's house and we know approximately what time she *neared* the circus. I emphasised the word neared because none of the circus performers have given a conclusive ID on Rosie being there last night. But that's hardly surprising as a lot of kids were wearing Halloween masks. But it raises the question; did she even make it to the circus?

'Rosie Miller was wearing a black knee-length puffer jacket, black jeans, and black Adidas Superstar trainers. She had a distinctive yellow scrunchie in her hair, forming a shoulder-length ponytail, and according to her mother, she hates having the hood up on her coat, even when it rains. Before you ask, this is an example of a scrunchie.' She taps at the board and a professional advertising image of a bunch of yellow scrunchies appears on screen. 'India

Anderson was wearing similar clothes. Dark blue puffer jacket, blue jeans, black and white Adidas Superstars, but no ponytail, no hair tie. India's hair is shorter. Over to you, Zac.'

Zac takes over the whiteboard, and with the same dexterity as Prisha, drags and drops a row of files onto the main screen, much to Frank's chagrin.

'Bloody kids,' he mutters under his breath.

Zac begins as grainy footage rolls. 'Two separate shots of the girls passing home security systems on Ashton Grove. One at 6:33 pm, the other at 6:34 pm.' The footage lasts mere seconds, but the girls are unmistakable. 'Next, we have three instances as they stride at a good pace up Love Lane. 6:38, 6:40, and 6:42 pm. Rosie's yellow scrunchie and ponytail are very distinctive in those images. And lastly, one shot of them on Mulgrave Road at 6:45 pm. It's about another twenty seconds to the path that leads to the public land where the circus is. And the same camera on Mulgrave Road captures India Anderson returning at 6:47 pm. She's tracked all the way back to Ashton Grove, passing the first camera at 7:01 pm.'

Prisha steps forward. 'This confirms India Anderson's account of what happened last night is right on the money. The times, the route they took, where and when they parted. So, let's not become sidetracked wondering if we can believe the testimony of an eight-year-old. Next: no prime suspect... yet,' she states, throwing the rotund DC a sideways glance. 'But plenty of persons of interest.'

A few muted groans echo around the packed room. There is a lexicon of words and phrases the police trot out robot fashion either to hide the fact they are stumbling in the dark, or to not divulge too much information about a case as they near a breakthrough. Person of interest is one such phrase.

'Scarlet, Keith, and Jenny Miller... mother and grandparents respectively, all spent the night at home in Ashton Grove. The house belongs to Keith and Jenny, and Scarlet has lived there ever since she fell pregnant with Rosie. They all agree on the time that Rosie went across the road to India's house—6 pm. Jenny watched from her front door to make sure Rosie went straight to India's. They've all been questioned separately, and their stories are completely in sync. Understandably, they are very distraught. Riley Miller also lives at the address. He's the son of Keith and Jenny, younger brother of Scarlet, and uncle to Rosie. He's an up-and-coming rugby star and on Saturday he was playing his last game for Whitby, an away game in Darlington. After the victory, the team went on a pub crawl around the town. He was alerted to Rosie's disappearance at 10 pm last night, at which point he and his teammates boarded the team bus and returned to Whitby, getting dropped off at the circus, where he met Keith Miller and some of his friends. Hence, the ruckus. Take thirty rugby lads, a skinful of ale, and too much testosterone and it's a recipe for trouble.' She pauses and has a sip of water, before facing her attentive audience. 'Nobody is ruled out of an investigation until the end, but I think we can put the Miller clan firmly on the back-burner for the time being. Onto the significant persons of interest.

'First cab off the rank—John Bishop, aged twenty-seven from Kettleness. Scarlet Miller has been in a relationship with John Bishop for three months. Scarlet calls the romance, semi-serious. John works on the trawlers. According to all the Millers he seems a decent enough lad. Well groomed, polite, considerate. Gets on well with Rosie.

'Next is the ex-boyfriend—Mitch Garvey, aged thirty. They split over a year ago having been in an on-again, off-again relationship for two years. Mitch is a chef at The Jackdaw fish restaurant in Whitby. Scarlet Miller said they grew apart, whereas Jenny Miller hinted Mitch was a control freak and he and Rosie didn't get along. Mitch thought the family spoilt her.

'Lastly, we have Rosie's biological father—Blake Dufton. Same age as Scarlet Miller—twenty-six. He disappeared from the Miller's lives when he found out Scarlet was pregnant with Rosie, eight years ago. A bad lad, from all accounts. The Millers assumed he was doing time for breaking and entering and GBH. He received an eight-year sentence and was a guest of HMP Leeds… formerly known as Armley Jail. However, guess what? He was released last week on parole, and not only that, but as part of his parole conditions he presented himself to Scarborough Police Station yesterday afternoon at 3 pm. This information has only recently come to light.'

Muted whispering and knowing looks are exchanged between officers.

Prisha allows them a moment of speculation. 'John Bishop and Mitch Garvey are downstairs in separate interview rooms as I speak. DS Stoker and I will question them as soon as this briefing is over. As for the biological father, Blake Dufton, we are now searching for him. We need to bring him in, and quickly. According to the Millers, Rosie has never met her dad, but occasionally asks about him, and she has a photograph of him on her bedside table. Blake Dufton has made many requests over the years to meet with his daughter. All requests were denied.'

Prisha glances at the clock on the wall. 'Questions?'

A young female DC raises her arm. 'Ma'am, the biological father, Blake Dufton; what are your feelings about the development? Could it be a positive? He may have taken Rosie, but he's unlikely to do her any harm, is he?'

Prisha splays her hands out. 'We're still waiting to speak to Dufton's probation officer to find out what sort of person he is. But first up, Rosie being abducted by her biological father is merely one line of enquiry at this stage; and secondly, we have absolutely no idea what his motive or long-term aim is if it transpires he has taken Rosie. Yes, it could be benign, and he simply wants time with her. Or he could well be consumed with rage at being denied access all these years and wants to teach the Miller family a lesson. There's no love lost between Dufton and the Millers. Especially the granddad, Keith Miller.' She points at an officer at the back of the room. 'Yes?'

'I heard there is another ongoing case. You are currently searching for a sex offender in the area. Could there be a connection?'

Prisha waggles her cheeks from side to side. She has already contemplated the possibility, for about ten seconds, before discounting it. 'There is nothing to link the cases at the moment. Our suspected rapist targets mature women in their homes late at night. From a psychological standpoint, it would be unusual for a sex offender to change their victim demographic or modus operandi. They typically have a specific victim preference which could be linked to age, gender, physical characteristics, and so on. However, this does not mean it is impossible. I'm sure many of us have come across child sex offenders who had previous convictions against adults, and vice versa. It's rare, but as I said, not impossible. So, let's not discount it, nor become transfixed with it. Next.'

'Did the search of the circus tents and caravans and vehicles yield anything of significance?'

'Not yet. Sniffer dogs should arrive in the next hour or so. However, they could give us a false positive as Rosie was at the circus a few hours earlier with her grandfather for the matinee performance of the Strawman. Next.'

'You implied Rosie may never have reached the circus. Why?'

'Because we have searched the entire circus area twice and interviewed all staff and performers, and no one can categorically identify her as being there last night. When the ticket attendant for the Strawman show was presented with a recent photo of Rosie, she remembered her from the afternoon performance, but not from the nighttime show.'

'Why?'

'Rosie asked the attendant what the pay was like working for a circus, to which she'd replied—if you're good at juggling money—you can get by. Rosie giggled at her response. And another thing: there's a notice outside the marquee which states that an adult must accompany all children under the age of twelve.'

'It's possible Rosie tagged along behind a family, pretending to be part of the group.'

'Yes, it is possible,' Prisha confirms, losing patience fast. What she's yearning for is to interview her main "person of interest", not answer endless questions, possible scenarios and countless what ifs. She pulls the plug on her involvement. 'Right, I'll hand you back over to DCI Finnegan.'

Frank stands next to the whiteboard and surveys his team, sensing Prisha's frustration.

'Thank you, DI Kumar. Let's move things swiftly along. I'm sure none of you want to be sitting here listening to me. Zac, how did you and DS Dinkel go with the CCTV footage? Any sightings of suspicious, shady characters knocking about last night?'

Zac raises his eyebrows, pulls out his notebook and studies it. 'Aye, one or two, boss.'

'Would you care to elaborate?'

'We counted twelve Count Draculas, seven Frankensteins, three Mary Shelleys, a coven of witches, at least ten Mr Darcys, a handful of Lord Byrons, nine Charles Dickens, one Ebenezer Scrooge, a dozen Jack the Rippers, and a pair of Bob Cratchits on the loose. Not forgetting the Ghost of Christmas Past and two lone werewolves—one with a bad case of the mange. Oh, and one Batman and Robin,' he adds as an afterthought. 'I think they must have caught the wrong train. There was a Comic-Con event over in Manchester this weekend. But apart from that, nothing much to report, Frank. A relatively quiet Saturday night by Whitby standards.'

He's greeted with an expulsion of laughter and sniggers, a welcome relief valve to the oppressive tension.

Frank grins. 'Most amusing, sergeant. But seriously?'

Zac shakes his head. 'Apart from verifying India Anderson's timeline of events, I can't give you much else. Conditions were not good, Frank. Nighttime, then the fog drifted in. There is one aspect Dinkel is chasing up, but it's a long shot at the moment.'

Frank scans the office for Dinkel. Eventually his eyes fall upon him tucked away at the back of the room. 'Ah, there you are Dinkel. How's the public responded to our appeal for information?'

'Quite overwhelming, sir,' a disembodied voice responds from the back, instigating a flurry of head-turning.

'Don't tell us from back there, lad! Get yourself up here and address everyone properly,' Frank replies, slightly annoyed.

Dinkel clumsily makes his way to the front of the room, clattering into chairs and bumping one officer, causing him to spill his coffee.

'Christ mate! Thanks a bloody lot.'

'Apologies,' Dinkel responds, taking up his position next to Frank, visibly jittery.

'Go ahead, lad. Let's hear what you've got to say,' Frank prompts.

Clearing his throat, Dinkel begins. 'Yes, Mr Finnegan, sir. Ahem, we've had over a hundred calls, many of which claim to have seen Rosie Miller. Unfortunately, most of the reports appear to be erroneous. People from as far afield as Cornwall allege to have spotted a girl matching Rosie's description last night. We've also had a lot of names provided to us, and a few clairvoyants and mystics believing they know where she's being held captive.'

Frank rubs at the back of his neck. 'Hell fire,' he murmurs. He holds his hand up. 'As you all know, the public can be our greatest ally, and sometimes they can be our biggest waste of resources. Public appeals attract the well-meaning, the misguided, the vengeful, the attention-seekers, and the insane. However, we must investigate every sighting, and name put forward in connection with the case. Dinkel, you need to use due diligence to sort the wheat from the chaff.'

'Already onto it, boss. I've devised a traffic light system. Red for urgent follow up; orange for later follow up; and green to be chased up once we've exhausted red and orange.'

Frank's jowls harden as he nods thoughtfully. 'Well done, constable. Excellent work.'

This little commendation visibly lifts the young officer. 'Thank you, sir.'

Frank's serious expression draws a hush and undivided attention. 'Last few words then everyone back to work. We all deal with a lot of shit. It's the job we've chosen. No one held a gun to our head. We do it because we want to make a difference, and God knows, some days it feels like we're paddling a canoe up a river of shit; muggings, shootings, stabbings, decomposed bodies, suicides. It never ends. We won't wake up one day, pull the curtains back, and declare—that's it, job done. No more crime. It's never easy, nor is it for the faint-hearted. But I'm sure most of you will agree, a missing child is our worst nightmare. I know what you will all be thinking. Rosie was last seen by her friend at 6:45 pm last night.' He glances at the clock. 'It's now 8:09 am. I won't lie to you; it's not looking good. But we must never drop our heads; we must believe in a positive outcome. Sometimes, miracles do occur. All it takes is one positive sighting; one name; one crucial piece of evidence.' He notices Prisha and Zac hovering at the doorway, eager to make their way downstairs to the interview rooms. 'Okay, everyone knows their roles. There's a coach waiting outside to take members of the search team to the recreation ground near to where Rosie was last seen. There should be up to two hundred public volunteers waiting for us. Teams of twenty, led by a detective plus a uniformed officer. You all have the specs. We move through Whitby, west to east. Every street, every garden, every alleyway, every spare bit of land to be searched. We knock on every door, show the occupants a photo of Rosie and ask to search their gardens, garages, sheds. We can't insist upon it. But if anyone refuses, then make damn sure you get their name and address, and we'll obtain search warrants. I usually find the public is more than amenable in these situations. And remember; we're not interested in knocked-off goods, drug labs, violent relationships... we're after a precious eight-year-old girl. Anything untoward, make a note, and we *will* follow up at a later date.' His eyes flit across the faces in front of him. He straightens his back, chest expands. 'As I said before, we do this job to make a difference.' Voice softens. 'Let's make a difference for the Millers. That's it—briefing over. And good luck, everyone.'

As he briskly strides towards Zac and Prisha, the office pulses with a rush of vibrant, constructive vigour. His once razor-sharp analytical acumen may have diminished with the years, but his knack for instilling confidence in his team remains as potent as ever.

'Boss?' Prisha questions, hand gripping the handle of the door as though her life depended on it.

'The interviews with Mitch Garvey and John Bishop; the clock is against us. This is not a game of cat and mouse trying to catch a killer after the event. Rosie could still be alive. No pussyfooting around. No mind games. Go hard and fast. Put them under the pump and throw everything at them. Find out where they were last night between seven and ten. They're either involved, or they are not involved. End of. We need to find Rosie alive. *Understood*?'

'Yes, boss,' Prisha and Zac reply in determined unison.

'Go on then!' he yells, unleashing his attack dogs. 'What are you bloody waiting for?'

19

John Bishop relaxes as he finishes recounting his movements on Saturday night. Prisha smiles.

To the unguarded, her smile may be interpreted as caring, understanding… she gets it. Shit happens, right? Life happens. But that winsome, toothy smile is a honey trap. Sweet, syrupy. Come here, little fly and sip on nectar.

Bishop is careless. She hates careless. If you're going to bullshit about your alibi, then at least make an effort, for God's sake! Words are overrated. Body language, on the other hand…

As he told of his whereabouts from the previous night, he gazed up and to the right. A sure sign someone is not telling the truth in her book. Also, the huffing and puffing. The false annoyance at being questioned. The hands resting nonchalantly on the table, as if to prove he's unruffled, and yet, the fingers of each hand entwined with each other, creating a barrier, a defence, protection.

She glances at the clock on the wall. Wonders if she'll develop RSI in her neck. Her eyes flit back onto the moribund solicitor, then across to John Bishop.

She puckers her lips. 'How long have you been in a relationship with Scarlet Miller?'

Stretches his right arm, lifts his left shoulder. Tense. 'About three months.'

'Is it serious?'

'It's early days, but yeah, we're a good match.'

'And what about Rosie?'

Concern, puzzlement. 'What about Rosie?'

'Do you get along?'

Shrugs. 'Yeah, we get along. She's a live wire.' A half smile on reflection.

'So I've heard. Can be a bit of a handful by all accounts. High-spirited. Endless energy. Inquisitive. Daring.'

'Yes. I suppose.'

A curve ball out of the blue. 'Where is Rosie?'

Apparent shock. Did she not believe his alibi? Hands unlock. Arms fold. 'I've no idea. If I knew where she was, I'd have said, wouldn't I?' A definite hint of petulance.

'Possibly... unless you've done something to her.'

Another huff. Arms unfold. Rests them back on the table, palms up, pleading.

'Look, I understand what you're doing. When something happens, you always start with close family members and friends. I've seen enough cop shows to understand that. But I've told you where I was. I don't know what else to say.'

'Let's go over it again. You were with Scarlet for a few hours yesterday afternoon at the Millers' place. You left around five. You got home, took a shower, then went to your mate's house, Wilko—Tom Wilkinson, who lives on Ruswarp Lane. You arrived about six and stayed in, watched the footy, had a catch up. Received a text from Scarlet at about 10 pm telling you Rosie was missing. You went back to the Millers on Ashton Grove, then made your way to the circus where a small crowd was gathering.'

'That's right.'

'Call him.'

Alarm. 'What?'

'You're here voluntarily. You still have your phone on you. Call Tom Wilkinson.'

Mild panic. 'I... I don't have his number.'

Prisha rolls her eyes. 'Oh dear. This is going south at a rate of knots for you, John. Your best mate—Wilko, and you don't have his number. Not to worry,' she says, pulling her mobile out. 'I spoke with Scarlet earlier and she gave me Wilko's number. I'll call him,' she explains, tapping at her screen.

John Bishop leans in towards his solicitor. 'I don't think I want to do this anymore. Can we stop?' he whispers.

Prisha rises as her call is answered. Places it on speaker. 'Is that Mr Wilkinson, Tom Wilkinson?'

'Yeah. Who's this?' A soft Geordie accent.

'I'm Detective Inspector Kumar, North Yorkshire CID. I'm part of the investigating team searching for a missing girl called Rosie Miller.'

'Rosie Miller? Scarlet Miller's daughter?'

'Yes, that's correct.'

The solicitor attempts an intervention. 'Inspector Kumar, my client voluntarily attended this interview to assist in your inquiries. He has now decided he does not wish to continue with the interview.'

Prisha holds her hand up. 'Mr Wilkinson, can you tell me your whereabouts last night between the times of 6 pm and 10 pm?'

'What? You don't suspect...'

'Your whereabouts last night?' she repeats forcefully.

'I was up here.'

'Where's here?'

'Sunderland. My mam's fiftieth birthday. I came up Friday night.'

The solicitor rises and leans across the table. 'Inspector! As this attendance is voluntary, Mr Bishop is free to leave unless you have grounds for arrest. If you think you have such reasons, please explain them now.'

Prisha blanks him. 'Is there anyone who can corroborate your whereabouts last night, Mr Wilkinson?'

'Aye. All my family. We had a big knees-up at my mam and dad's place. At least fifty people. It kicked off about six and went until the early hours.'

'When was the last time you saw John Bishop?'

The solicitor is red in the face. 'Inspector, I've informed you my client wishes to end this voluntary interview and leave the premises. It is both inappropriate and unprofessional to ignore his request!'

'I caught up with John about a week ago. Why? Oh, hang on, I get it...'

'Thanks for your time, Mr Wilkinson,' she says, ending the call and glaring at John Bishop.

'As my client's legal representative, I ask you to respect his rights and terminate this interview!'

Completely ignoring the brief, she bellows, 'Stop playing games, John! Where were you last night?'

Bishop squirms in his seat and drops his head into his hands, but says nothing.

'Inspector Kumar! My client's rights are being violated!'

She rounds on him. 'And what about the rights of eight-year-old Rosie Miller? What about her rights!' Her fiery eyes bore into John Bishop. 'Last chance before I arrest you in connection with the disappearance of Rosie Miller. Where were you last night?'

The wet blanket of a solicitor is on the verge of bursting. 'If you persist in this unwarranted hectoring and intimidation of my client, then you leave me no other choice than to lodge a formal complaint with the…'

Prisha slams her palms hard into the table. 'Enough of this bullshit! John Bishop, I am arresting…'

John leaps from his chair. 'All right, all right! I'll tell you where I was!'

20

With the formalities over, Zac stares at Mitch Garvey, weighing him up. He has a cocky demeanour. Sure of himself. A big lad. Obviously works out.

In his soft Scottish brogue, Zac begins. 'You understand why you're here, Mitch?'

He nods. 'Yeah. It's about the missing girl, Rose Miller. As I used to go out with Scarlet Miller, you suspect I had something to do with Rosie's disappearance.'

'I don't suspect you of anything at the moment. You came in here voluntarily, and I thank you for that. In situations like these, it's important for the police to eliminate as many people as quickly as possible. That way, we can concentrate our resources on finding the real perpetrator.'

'You're talking as if someone has abducted her. Anything could have happened to the lass.'

The hairs on the back of Zac's neck tingle. *Odd thing to say.* 'Such as?'

A flicker of a grimace across his face. 'I don't know. She could have had an accident. Fallen into the sea. Got lost. Who knows?'

'When did you split up with Scarlet Miller?'

Shrugs. 'About a year ago.'

'Mind telling me why?'

'Not at all. It had run its course. Sometimes it's better to end a relationship than let it fester.'

'The relationship wasn't going well?'

Another shrug. 'We'd started to argue more often. It wasn't fun anymore.'

'Nothing to do with your controlling behaviour?'

Surprise followed by recollection. 'Oh, I see. You been speaking to the old battle-axe?'

'Who?'

'You know who... Scarlet's mum, Jenny Miller. She always had it in for me from day one.'

'She said you were critical of the clothes Scarlet wore on the rare occasions she had a night out with the girls.'

Tilts his head to one side. 'She dressed like a tart. Short skirts, high-heels, tits hanging out.'

'And what had that got to do with you... how she dressed?'

'Because she looked like a slut. I know how men think. See a girl like that out on the town and they all think they're in for an easy lay.'

'Ah, I see. So, the problem isn't the woman. The problem lies with men.'

Confused, he patently does not appreciate the concept. 'What the fuck are you on about? I came in here to help; not get a lecture on gender issues.'

'How did you interact with Rosie?'

'Spoilt brat if you ask me.'

'In what way?'

'Had Scarlet, Jenny and even Keith wrapped around her little finger. Got whatever she wanted. Manipulative.'

'It's fair to say you didn't get along, then?'

'I tolerated her. But no, she rubbed me up the wrong way, and she knew it. She knew how to pull the strings and press the buttons, did that one.'

'Interesting... you said—she knew, and did that one.'

'So?'

'You spoke of her in the past tense.'

'You're trying to trip me up. Can we hurry this along as I have better things to do?'

'Tell me your movements yesterday between 6 pm and 10 pm.'

Deep sigh. Picks at the cuticle on his right thumb. 'Went to work at three...'

'You're a chef at The Jackdaw fish restaurant on the promenade?'

'Yes. Arrived at three, worked my shift. Finished at eleven then met up with some mates and we headed over the bridge to the old town and hit the pubs.'

'You didn't see Rosie at all yesterday?'

'No. Of course I bloody didn't. Why would I?'

'You said you were at work from 3 pm until 11 pm?'

'That's right.'

'You didn't leave the restaurant at any time?'

Shifts uneasily. 'No. I was there all night. It was busy, flat out.'

Zac taps at the table with his finger. 'Hmm... that's not what your manager told me. She said you ducked out for forty minutes. Left at 6:30, arrived back around 7:10.'

Thinks. 'Oh aye, that's right. I nipped up to my mother's place on Windsor Terrace. She's suffering from shingles. I've been calling in each night to make her something to eat, draw the curtains, put her electric blanket on, that sort of stuff.'

'You're a good lad, aren't you?'

'I think the world of my mam. She sacrificed a lot for me.'

'That's mothers for you. Did you have your phone with you?'

The question throws him. Pauses... a dead giveaway. 'Phone?' he replies, buying time.

'Yeah, you know, those rectangular things. You tap a number, and it lets you speak to other people with phones. They come in handy. Well?'

'Erm... no. I left it in the kitchen at The Jackdaw.'

'I see. I have a problem with your account, Mitch. The quickest way to get to Windsor Terrace is to turn right outside the restaurant and head along the promenade. Yet none of the CCTV cameras picked you up going that way.'

'I went the back way. Cut up through Pier Lane onto Cliff Street. Bypass the crowds. It was heaving last night with the Goth Weekend and what not.'

Zac smiles. 'Really?'

'Aye, really,' Mitch snaps.

'Then why do we have CCTV footage of you entering Fun Time amusement arcade at 6:36 pm? That's the opposite direction to Windsor Terrace. A five-minute stroll from The Jackdaw.'

'Wasn't me.'

Zac pulls a photo from a folder on the table and pushes it across to Mitch. 'Unless you have a doppelgänger, then I'm pretty certain it's you. You're still wearing your chef uniform with the little Jackdaw emblem on the arm. Oh, and Mr Patel was working in the change kiosk last night. He recognised you. Says you're a frequent visitor, have been for years.'

Considers his options. Huffs. 'Okay, so what? I nipped out for a quick smoke and twenty minutes in the amusements before it got busy in the restaurant. No crime in that, is there?'

'No, there's no crime in that. Then why the cock and bull story about visiting your sick mother?'

'I didn't want the manager to find out.'

Zac stifles a laugh. 'That's the problem with lies, Mitch. Once someone picks away at the thread, you have to backtrack and change your story. That's why the best liars have good memories and always keep as close to the truth as possible. I don't blame you for visiting the arcades. I'm a bit of a sucker for them myself. Takes me back to my childhood. It's amazing to think that in this day and age, those old slot machines, the penny pusher, and those crappy little horses that whizz around a racetrack can still hold such an appeal. But they do. A magnet for kids.'

'They have a charm.'

'Mr Patel said he saw you chatting to a young girl in the arcade.'

Alarm. 'What? No, that's not true.'

He pulls out another photo and slides it across the table. 'The big fella on the left... that's you. The young girl has her back to the camera but is looking up into your face. Ring any bells?'

'Okay, look, yes, a young lass came up to me and asked if I could give her a quid as she'd spent her money. I felt sorry for her and gave her a two-pound coin, and that was it. Didn't see her again.'

'This is like déjà vu. Back to the lies again. Why didn't you say that originally?'

'Because I know what you lot are like. You're looking for Rosie and would assume that me talking to a girl of similar age in the arcades somehow makes me guilty.'

Another photo is retrieved from the file and slid across to Mitch Garvey. 'This shows you speaking on your phone in the arcade. Which is odd because a moment ago you said you left your phone in the kitchen of The Jackdaw.'

'I forgot, that's all.'

Zac shakes his head, perplexed. 'Christ, I've met some woeful liars in my time, but you take the proverbial fucking biscuit! You couldn't lie straight in an iron-lung. How can I believe anything you say? What are you trying to hide, Mitch?'

'Nothing.'

Zac glances at his wristwatch. 'Okay, you're not willing to cooperate and I haven't got time to sit here playing guessing games. Do you understand how serious this is? A wee girl went missing last night. A girl, you know. You openly admitted you didn't like her.'

'I never said I didn't like her. I said she was a spoilt brat, and we didn't get along.'

'So, you did like her?'

'What? No! I know what you're implying. I'm no fucking paedo.'

'Do you even care about her welfare?'

'Of course I do. I don't want anything bad to have happened to her. She may have been a little shit, but I wouldn't wish harm upon her, or on any kid, for that matter.'

'And there you go again... past tense. She may *have been* a little shit. Not *is* a little shit. Right, here's the deal, Mitch, and I hope you make the right decision. You either tell me the truth from the beginning, otherwise I will arrest you in connection with Rosie's disappearance. Even if it turns out you had nothing to do with it, being arrested in connection with a missing girl leaves a bad smell. It will filter out into the community. Smells like that linger, cling to your clothes. Suddenly your friends stop calling. People turn the other way when they see you in the street. Your employer decides you're not cutting the mustard at your job. Mud sticks. Alternatively, you come clean, and you walk out of here, cleared of any wrongdoing. It was simply the police eliminating individuals who had a connection with the Miller family. The public would understand that. Just routine.' Silence ensues as both men stare at each other. 'What's it to be? Your choice, but I haven't time to fuck around.'

Mitch licks his lips, shoots a glance at his mute solicitor. 'Okay, but this is confidential, right? If I tell you the truth, then you can't use it against me?'

'I don't make promises I cannae keep, sunshine. Now, stop fucking around and tell me what really happened last night!'

21

Frank sips on his cup of tea as Zac and Prisha enter his office, both sporting glum faces.

'I can tell by your expressions you haven't had a win. Prisha, you go first. John Bishop, the current boyfriend; what's his story?'

They both take seats, weary, dispirited. 'He tried to give me the runaround, Frank. He fed me some rubbish about being at his mates last night. I rang his friend who has been in Sunderland since Friday. I gave Bishop a mouthful, and a few veiled threats then he told the truth.'

'Which is?'

'He's been having an affair.'

'Why didn't he tell you about the affair from the get-go?' Frank asks, puzzled.

Prisha rubs her tongue back and forth over her front teeth. 'A delicate matter,' she says in a hushed voice, glancing nervously over her shoulder into the incident room. 'A bit close to home, boss.'

'Go on.'

'Sergeant Andrew Howard, from uniform. He worked here for a while before relocating to Scarborough.'

'Yes. Tall lad, good copper. Straight as a die. He's been drafted in as part of the search team. I was speaking with him earlier.' He scowls. 'Wait... hang on, you're not telling me he and Bishop have been...'

'No. But John Bishop has been slipping it to Andrew's wife whenever the sarge is on nightshift. Bishop was predictably reluctant to tell the truth in case it got out.'

'And have you verified this with Sergeant Howard's missus?'

She nods, eyes wide. 'Oh, yes. Had a very embarrassing chat with her ten minutes ago. To say she's distraught is an understatement. I gave her my word that I, we, would not divulge information about the affair. It's a private matter. What John Bishop told me in the interview room was strictly confidential. Despite my assurances, she wasn't convinced and assumes the information will leak out soon enough.'

Frank twists his neck, emitting a satisfying crack. 'Slap my blue arse. What is wrong with the world? No one can seem to keep their undergarments on these days,' he mutters, staring out of the window.

Zac throws Prisha a grin and mouths the words—undergarments. She stifles a laugh.

'I must admit, I feel a little sorry for her,' Prisha reflects.

'Well, don't!' Frank snaps. 'You reap what you sow. The only one I feel sorry for is Sergeant Howard. Poor bugger. There he is, working nights, putting life and limb at risk for the safety of the public and his missus is playing hide the sausage with another fella, who is *currently* in a supposed relationship with Scarlet Miller. Isn't life complex enough? Why do people do these things?'

Prisha puckers her lips and shoots Zac a glance. 'Anyway, we can scrub John Bishop off our persons of interest list.'

'Hmm...' Frank growls, decidedly unhappy about many things. 'Go on, Zac. What have you got?'

'Not dissimilar to Prisha, really. Another toe-rag lying to save his skin. Mitch Garvey was at The Jackdaw restaurant last night working his shift in the kitchen from 3 to 11 pm. Except, he snuck out for forty minutes between 6:30 and 7:10 pm.'

Frank freezes. 'That's right in our timeframe for when Rosie disappeared.'

'Hold your horses, Frank. Mitch Garvey spun me a web of lies. Although, it wasn't really a web, more like a string bag. Had more holes in it than Julius Caesar on the Ides of March. He said he went to visit his sick mother, but he didn't. He hung around in Fun Time amusement arcade waiting for his dealer to turn up. Apparently, after his shift ends on a weekend, he likes to hit the town with his mates and take a little speed to liven things up. He's a casual user and only buys from the same dealer he's used for years. The dealer was running late, but eventually showed up at Fun City. He's a low-level pusher from Scarborough, and we have him on CCTV handing something to Mitch Garvey at 7:02 pm. Mitch reciprocates by handing over a fifty, then they both leave the arcade a few minutes apart.'

Frank pulls at the loose skin under his chin. 'I suppose it's good we've removed them from the radar. So, the Miller family is out of the picture as Scarlet, Jenny, and Keith were all at home together. Riley Miller was in Darlington with his rugby team, and the current and ex-boyfriend have sound alibis. Where does that leave us?'

Prisha leans forward. 'The biological father, Blake Dufton, is looking more and more promising. Any news on him, Frank?'

He shakes his head. 'No. Not yet.'

'Dinkel was working on something,' Zac adds. 'I need to check in with him to see if he's made any progress.'

Frank squints. 'Aye, you mentioned that in the briefing. What is he chasing up?'

'A car caught on camera on Belle Vue Terrace last evening.'

'Belle Vue Terrace? That's about what... five minutes from Mulgrave Road, where the girls went their separate ways?'

'Aye. Not even five minutes.'

'Was the car acting suspiciously?'

'Not the car, as such. It's an inanimate object, Frank.'

'Very funny.'

'But yeah, something was off. Slowly driving back and forth. Parking up. Driving away, disappearing, then returning a few minutes later.'

'Pimps, drug dealers, casing a joint or stalking someone, perhaps. ID on the vehicle?'

'No. Looks like a white Fiesta or Corolla. A hatchback. Couldn't get a number plate. Dinkel was trying to obtain more CCTV footage to get a positive ID on the car. Might be nothing to do with Rosie's disappearance, though.'

'Worth checking out all the same. Every lead, no matter how innocuous, must be chased up if only to eliminate it.'

'Yes, boss.'

Frank checks his wristwatch. 'Hell, I'm late,' he states as he jumps to his feet and grabs his coat.

'Where are you going?' Prisha questions.

Coat halfway on, he stops and stares at her. 'Over to the Millers. Give them an update. It will not be fun, but I thought it only appropriate considering Keith's an old pal of mine. After that, I'll head to the recreation reserve to see how the search is progressing.'

Prisha frowns. 'Where exactly is Superintendent Banks? She's noticeable by her absence.'

Fastening his buttons, he replies, 'She was on a weekend golfing trip in Scotland. On her way back down as we speak. Should be here within the hour... more's the pity. I could do without her officious, soulless do-it-by-the-book mantra. Anyway, never mind about her. Prisha, Zac, get me something, anything, and soon.'

They watch on with mixed feelings as Frank hurries through the incident room.

'Poor bastard,' Zac murmurs. 'He's been through this before. Christ only knows what's going on in his head.'

Prisha is more pragmatic. 'Do *you* think Rosie is already dead?'

Zac strokes his long locks back over his head. 'Put it this way, Prisha, if I was a betting man...'

'Which you are.'

'I'd want good odds to put money on finding her alive.'

As Prisha considers his words, an unbidden memory flashes through her mind: the vivid imagery of the last time she played tennis, resurfacing with startling clarity. The randomness of the recollection puzzles her, but she swiftly dismisses the stray thought, refocusing on the task at hand.

'Hmm...'

Zac pulls at the door handle. 'What about you?'

'I think she's still alive.'

Puzzled, he turns. 'Really? You know the stats when a kiddie goes missing. The percentages aren't good. I know that, Frank knows that, and you know that. Rosie, poor, wee lassie, probably died sometime between 7 and 10 pm last night... at the hands of some sicko.'

'Don't say that. I know the stats,' she snaps.

He's surprised at her emotional reaction, which is unlike Prisha. 'What is it?'

She ponders for a moment. 'Not sure. It's just...'

'Go on, spit it out.'

'I have this picture I've painted of her in my mind from all the information we've collated and speaking to her mother and grandma. There's something about Rosie, which is different.'

'Such as?'

'She's a fighter. A survivor. She's been before.'

Zac is baffled. 'Been before! What the hell does that mean?'

'It was something my Nani used to say about me when I was young. She thought I'd lived before.'

'Reincarnation?' Zac states in a mocking tone.

'Call it what you will. I don't give it a name. And, for your information, I don't believe in all that nonsense either, but...'

'But what?'

'I have a gut-feeling Rosie is still alive. She has too much spirit to have left her family so soon.'

Zac groans. 'Fuck me drunk. Obviously, you do believe in that bullshit,' he comments as he exits.

'No, I don't,' she murmurs to a blank plasterboard wall. 'I know Rosie is still with us. But where the hell is she?'

22

Dinkel is completely absorbed in his work in the corner of the incident room as Zac taps him on the shoulder, causing him to jump out of his skin.

'You're a wee bit jittery, sunshine,' Zac remarks, smiling.

Dinkel holds his hand over his chest. 'You scared me to death.'

Zac pulls up a chair. 'Any progress on the mystery vehicle? We can't waste too much time on it.'

He nods enthusiastically. 'Yes. Feast your eyes on this,' he says, nodding at the screen. 'I've reviewed the footage of the car on Bell Vue Terrace. As you've seen already, the car is first spotted at 6:15 pm, then briefly at 6:18, 6:22, then again at 6:30 and 6:32 before it disappears. Now take a look at the CCTV footage from St Hilda Terrace. A similar vehicle is seen heading easterly at 6:35. At the roundabout, it takes the second exit onto Stakesby Road—time 6:38. And it appears there's only one occupant. Hard to say for certain, but the driver appears to be male. Three minutes later, it takes a left turn onto...'

'Ashton Grove, the street where the Millers live,' Zac whispers, as his heart thumps into his chest.

'Ashton Grove is not a long street, eight hundred feet, max, and a cul-de-sac. Now look at this,' he says, pulling up fresh footage. 'This is the same home security footage from 6 Ashton Grove, which captured the girls heading towards the circus last night. The car passes by at exactly 7:10.'

'What the hell was he doing for thirty minutes on Ashton Grove?' Zac murmurs. 'What about a number plate? It may be the same car, but we can't ID it from those images.'

Dinkel holds his finger up. 'Aha! Wait and see. The vehicle turns left back onto Stakesby Road, which joins Castle Road. On the corner is a Shell petrol station. As the car passes the garage, another car pulls out and illuminates the number plate.' Dinkel zooms in on the plate. 'ZD10DNY. A 2010 Ford Fiesta registered to Carson Colby, aged twenty-nine.'

'Carson Colby. Are you taking the piss? He sounds like a Wild West outlaw. Address?'

'Number two, Manor House Road, Robin Hood's Bay.'

'Any previous?'

Dinkel shakes his head. 'Nothing sinister. Received a speeding ticket a few years back. Doing forty in a thirty zone.'

Zac is perplexed. 'Is that it?'

'Yep. I double checked.'

'Right, I need an arrest and search warrant.'

'I've already lined a magistrate up.'

Zac rises and gazes down at Dinkel, the officer who replaced his fallen colleague, Jason Cartwright. 'Dinkel, I'm beginning to warm to you. We'll make a copper out of you yet. Right, what are we waiting for?'

'You want me to come with you?' Dinkel gasps, astounded at the proposition, considering Zac's antipathy towards him since his arrival at Whitby five months ago.

'Aye, of course I do. Let's pay a visit to Billy the Kid from Robin Hood's Bay.'

'You mean Carson Colby, right?' Dinkel questions with an element of doubt.

23

Zac drops through the gears and pulls up a couple of houses back from the suspect's address.

'Nice area,' he says, surveying the well-to-do semi-detached houses in a pleasant street in the small seaside hamlet of Robin Hood's Bay. His eyes drift across to the fields behind the buildings and the Methodist church opposite. He waits until the patrol car, containing two uniformed officers, turns onto the quiet road, and hangs back as per his instructions.

'What if he resists arrest?' Dinkel enquires nervously.

Zac gazes at him as though he's a cockroach. 'Then you put on your boxing gloves. Resisting arrest.'

Dinkel doesn't like the sound of that one little bit. 'You mean... use force?'

'Aye. Too right, sunshine.'

'But what if he's innocent?'

'Well...' Zac considers the question for a moment. 'No harm done in the long run.' He studies Dinkel again. 'You transferred from York, yeah?'

'That's correct,' Dinkel confirms.

'Before you joined CID, you had five years in uniform?'

'That's right.'

Zac grimaces. 'Then you must have encountered all sorts of trouble on nightshift. Why your reticence now?'

Dinkel jiggles his head from side to side. 'For some reason, I was mainly office bound. You know, chasing up descriptions of perpetrators, CCTV, re-reading witness statements. I didn't get out much. Although, I remember a weekend when there was a big FA Cup quarter final between Sunderland and Newcastle...' he pauses as he recollects. 'Or maybe it was Middlesbrough V Hartlepool... or was it...'

'Dinkel?'

'What?'

'Shut up.'

As they exit the unmarked vehicle, Zac waves to the patrol car behind, indicating for them to keep back until further notice. He receives a nod from one of the two officers in the car. As they amble towards the address, Zac spots a man, in his late twenties, in the front garden, positioning a post-hole digger at the edge of the house.

Strewn out over the lawn are bags of dry concrete, power cords, drills, saws, plus a large stack of wooden decking boards. There's an old model BMW sedan parked in the driveway, but no white Ford Fiesta.

The man momentarily looks up from his arduous work and spots Zac, but doesn't take much heed.

Zac walks alongside the garden wall and pushes at the gate. 'Excuse me, are you Carson Colby?'

Nervous, suspicious, he replies, 'Who wants to know?'

Zac pulls out his warrant card and flashes it at him. 'I do. Detective Stoker, North York...'

He doesn't have time to finish his sentence as the man bolts, heading down a side path leading to the back garden.

'Dinkel, head next door in case he jumps the fence!'

Zac sprints down the side of the house as the suspect scales a fence and runs into a field inhabited by a dozen bemused cows.

'Oi! Come back!' he shouts, realising the futility of his words. With great effort, he throws himself at the panel fence. Cheap pine wood splinters, but he hauls his tall frame over and gives chase. The man is already halfway across the paddock, racing towards a small cluster of trees.

'Sarge!'

Zac glances over his shoulder as Dinkel nears. 'Don't follow me. Do you not understand the basics of pursuit?'

he huffs. 'Get on the radio and tell patrol our suspect is heading towards Thorpe Lane, the main road into town. And tell them to have an officer secure the house. Make sure no one leaves.'

'Roger Whittaker, that, sarge!' Dinkel replies, apparently energised by the chase.

'And Dinkel, head in the direction of the junction with the main road in case he turns left. Change your radio to channel 6 and stay in touch.'

The suspect disappears into the copse as Zac clambers through a barbed wire fence and becomes snagged.

'Fuck it!' he seethes, staring at the rip in his new winter overcoat. Extricating himself, he enters the wood, pushing through branches and shrubs, mud squelching underfoot.

The distant sound of unseen cars is muffled in the low-hanging fog. He spots a figure scampering across the road, but instead of heading right, he hangs a left, which baffles Zac for a moment.

'The knob jockey has taken a left... why? He can only head into the village or the beach.'

He curses himself for his lack of fitness. He's been meaning get back in the gym for over eight months but has never got around to it. His quarry is always in sight, but the distance between them remains unchanged. Zac zips across the road and into the driveway of a semi-detached house. In the back garden, he groans with dismay as the suspect scrambles over another fence and vanishes.

'Shit the bed!' he puffs.

'Oi, what the hell are you playing at?'

Zac throws a glance behind him as an elderly man emerges from the back door.

'Police!' he shouts back, breathing hard. Another flimsy lap panel fence. This time as he mounts the top, a sudden cracking stabs at the air. His body sags as the fence succumbs to the unexpected weight.

'You'll bloody pay for that!' shouts the old man, waving his fist.

Dropping to the other side, he stares at his muddy boots, then pulls at a splinter stinging the fleshy pad of his palm. Wearily, he glances up. It appears Carson Colby, if indeed it is him, is also feeling the pace as he slows to a jog. Zac thinks of Rosie Miller, then his own young boys.

'Come on, Zac. You can do this,' he encourages himself.

With legs full of lead, he ploughs on.

Clicks at his radio, 'Where are you, Dinkel?'

'Not sure. I've never been to Robin Hood's Bay before.'

Zac silently curses him. 'You've got a pair of bloody eyes in your head! Tell me what you see?'

'Erm... there's a car park and a lot of large red brick buildings. One is called the Victoria Hotel.'

'Good. Follow that road and it will lead you down into the old fishing village. I think that's where he's heading. We may be able to cut him off.'

Zac navigates another boggy field, which sucks the last remaining energy from his legs. The only thing pushing him on is the thought that a little girl could be tied up somewhere, terrified, alone. As repulsive as the notion is, it's preferable to the other thought which lingers at the back of his head, unwilling to materialise.

Another small cluster of trees creep from the foggy terrain, as the figure ahead slips out of sight. The screech of a seagull and a blast of briny freshness tells him they are nearing the sea. His skin is moist with sweat and mist.

The man ahead slows to a snail's pace.

'Got you, sunshine,' Zac mutters as he emerges from the dense canopy. His heart sinks as he realises why the suspect has slowed. He's wading, knee high through a beck.

'Oh, give me a break,' he cries as he steps into the bubbling, icy water, running swiftly over smoothed pebbles beneath. The man exits the stream, scrambles up a steep bushy bank, mounts a stone wall, and drops to the other side.

Zac flicks at his radio. 'Dinkel, state your position?'

'On King Street, outside a shop called the Higgledy Pig. Why, where are you?'

'Knee deep in fucking water. Our suspect is now on New Road heading south towards the beach. If you're quick, you should be able to apprehend him on the corner near the old Coastguard Station.' He hears muted voices filter through the radio. 'Who are you talking to?'

'Erm... nobody.'

'Did you hear what I said?'

'Yes. Coastguard Station. On my way in a moment.'

Zac scrabbles his way up the steep embankment, scales the wall and lands on the road as the suspect rounds a bend and vanishes from view.

'Who is this guy? He must have two dozen Duracell batteries stuck up his arse.'

He jogs on, feet squelching, lungs aching. The deserted street is narrow, the single vehicle road hemmed in either side by weathered stone fishing cottages. The aroma of freshly brewed coffee blends with the tantalising smell of fried bacon, wafting on the breeze as he lumbers past a café. His stomach growls with hunger. In the distance, he spots his prey nearing bollards next to the slipway.

'Where's Dinkel?' he pants to himself. He rattles past the Smugglers Ale House, then the toy shop, all the while the fugitive remains elusive, disappearing down the slipway and out of sight. Coming to a halt at the bollards, he takes a moment to catch his breath, the cold air causing his chest to tighten. He continues at a more measured pace down the worn cobbles until he finds himself on the beach. Finally, fortune favours him. The high tide leaves the man cornered with nowhere to flee.

Still no Dinkel.

The suspect stares at the water, then back at Zac, and wades out into the sea.

Zac shakes his head as he nears. 'Don't be bloody stupid, man! It's over. Now come out of the water unless you fancy swimming to Norway.'

'Actually, I think he'd end up in Denmark if he swam east,' Dinkel says as he jogs up behind Zac. 'To reach Norway, he'd have to swim northeast.'

Zac turns and stares at him. 'Thank you, Marco fucking Polo.' He does a double-take as he spots a takeaway coffee in Dinkel's hand. 'You have got to be joking!'

'What?' Dinkel asks, innocently.

'You stopped off for a fucking cup of coffee?'

'It didn't take long. A couple of minutes max. I thought a shot of caffeine would...'

'Shut the fuck up and go apprehend and arrest our suspect.'

Dinkel stares aghast at the rippling waves and the man who is now waist deep.

'I'm not a strong swimmer,' he replies, wavering.

A large rogue wave hits the suspect, plunging him under water. Coughing and spluttering, he staggers to his feet and trudges ungainly back to shore.

'It's a misunderstanding,' he says, coughing out seawater. 'I can explain. I thought it might be dodgy, but I wasn't certain.'

Zac strides up to him. 'Carson Colby?'

'Yes?'

'I'm arresting you in connection with the abduction of Rosie Miller. You do not have to say anything. But it may harm your defence if you do not mention when questioned something which you later rely on in court. Anything you do say may be given in evidence.' He pulls out his handcuffs and spins the man around. 'Now where is she, you snivelling, little haggis fucker?'

24

Joyce Winterbottom waits patiently as Roger, her ageing King Charles spaniel, snuffles around the bottom of a small Hawthorn bush. Partially blind, and riddled with arthritis, his sense of smell is still acute.

'Come along, Roger. You've been sniffing that damn bush for five minutes.' She tugs at the lead and the dog reluctantly totters back onto the gravel path. Progress is painfully slow, but it allows Joyce time to ponder her missions for the day. She has an afternoon tea planned for the Sneaton Neighbourhood Watch committee. And she needs to type a follow up email to the local council about the potholes on the main street, which they still haven't fixed. And there's the jumble sale to arrange at the church hall scheduled for the final Sunday of the month. She's detected a distinct lack of interest in the event, and sometimes wonders if she's the only person in Sneaton who feels a moral obligation to improve the community. As she rounds a bend, she detects the shape of a car in the distance, parked up at the turning circle at the end of the gravel lane.

'Not again,' she hisses with undisguised venom. 'The police promised they'd do regular patrols to stop this from happening. Obviously fobbing me off. Well, we'll see about that.' Walking faster than Roger cares for, she marches up to the car and pulls her phone out. She peers inside the vehicle and makes out the squished-up body of a youngish man, huddled under a woollen blanket, fast asleep in the back seats. She takes a photo of him, the car and lastly, the large sign in front which reads "Sneaton Wood. No Camping. No Overnight Parking. Penalties Apply."

She huffs and turns on her heels. 'The arrogance of some people. Cocking a snook at the laws of the land. Blatant contempt. This country is going to the dogs at a galloping trot!'

25

Zac emerges from No 2 Manor House Road in a foul temper and marches up to the patrol car parked in the driveway. He jumps into the backseat alongside the handcuffed Carson Colby.

'Right, sunshine, let's go over this one more time,' he snarls. 'And none of your bullshit.'

'I'm telling you the truth. I've never heard of a Rosie Miller. You've got your wires crossed. I'm not a bloody kiddy fiddler. I hate those bastards.'

'From the beginning; why did you run?'

'I told you; it's the decking timber. A guy came knocking on the door a few days ago. He said he was a builder and had over ordered on a job and wanted to know if I'd be interested in buying the wood. I sort of suspected he might have been dodgy, but that's aged *oak*. It costs a small fortune. The wife's been nagging me to build a deck for a while. The guy was selling it at half price. It was too good an opportunity to miss out on. When I saw you turn up and flash your badge, I panicked. I thought you were here about the decking.'

'You mean to say I chased you through gardens, over fences, across fields, and through a bloody stream all because of some knocked-off decking?'

'I guess,' he says, sheepishly.

'You're bullshitting me. Where's the Ford Fiesta?'

'Ford Fiesta?'

'Yes! A 2010 Ford Fiesta, number plate ZD10DNY registered to Carson Colby of two, Manor House Road, Robin Hood's Bay.'

'My brother-in-law borrowed it yesterday morning. He's just got out of the nick. He's not a bad lad. He fell in with the wrong crowd. Says he's going straight. He needed wheels for the weekend to find digs and get some work lined up.'

Zac drops his head into his hands. 'Shit,' he whispers. 'This brother-in-law, is he called Blake Dufton by any chance?'

'Yes. How did you know?'

'Because Rosie Miller is his daughter.'

'What?' Carson Colby exclaims, eyes on stalks.

'You're telling me you didn't know he had a daughter?'

'I knew he'd fathered a child years ago, but he's never mentioned her. Not that I've seen much of him for the last five years with him being inside and all.'

'Where's your wife?'

'She's visiting her mother in Manchester. Went by train on Thursday. Due back Monday.'

'And where's Blake now?'

'I wouldn't have a clue. He said he'd return the car on Monday after picking my missus, his sister, up from the train station. He has a valid driver's licence, and I put him on my insurance.'

'Phone number?'

'He didn't have a phone. Said he was going to buy one over the weekend.'

'Fuck, fuck, fuck!'

Zac springs from the car and slams the door aggressively shut as Dinkel and a uniformed officer amble down the house steps.

Dinkel shrugs. 'Checked, double checked, triple checked. Cupboards, under the stairs, loft, shed, under beds, even had a look inside the washing machine. If Rosie was ever here, she's not here now. I dare say when the forensic experts arrive, they may find something.'

Zac grimaces and rubs at his face. 'Get on the radio and cancel forensics. We've wasted enough bloody time on this wild goose chase.'

'What?' Dinkel asks, baffled. 'But...'

'It's not him. Carson leant his car to his brother-in-law yesterday... Blake Dufton.'

'Then why did he run?'

Zac stares at the pile of timber on the lawn. 'He thought we were here about some knocked-off decking. Bloody dipstick!'

'Oh, I see.'

The uniformed officer peers into the back of the patrol car. 'What about Mr Colby, sarge? Are we going to charge him with anything?'

'I'd love to; handling stolen goods, resisting arrest, wasting police time, but we're already under-staffed and overworked. And we have more important tasks at hand, like finding Blake Dufton and Rosie Miller.'

'You want me to release him?'

'Aye, let the cock-muppet go.'

26

PC Jackson is listening to soothing classical music in his patrol car parked up in a layby. Tired and sleepy, he rests his eyes. The roads are unusually quiet, presumably due to the fog, which is only now lifting.

'Control to Tango 240. Control to Tango 240, over.'

PC Jackson groans. 'Shit, what now? I bet there's been a bloody pile up somewhere,' he grumbles as he clicks at his radio transceiver. 'Tango 240. Go ahead, Control. Over.'

'We've had a report of a car parked up at Sneaton Woods. Looks like it's been there overnight. Can you investigate? Over.'

Jackson shakes his head dismissively. 'Roger, Control. Who reported it, Joyce Winterbottom, by any chance? Over.'

There's a brief snigger. 'Roger, that. Over.'

'On my way. Tango 240 out.' He pulls onto the main road, cursing. 'Is this the best use of police time? Some poor bugger probably parked up last night because of the foggy conditions.'

The patrol car inches along the gravel lane until it's directly behind the Ford Fiesta. PC Jackson stares at the number plate and picks up his transceiver.

'Tango 240 to Control, request a repeat of earlier vehicle details; the Ford Fiesta acting suspiciously in Whitby last night? Over.'

'Control to Tango 240, vehicle identified as a white Ford Fiesta, registration ZD10DNY. Over,' the operator responds.

'Vehicle located in Sneaton Wood. About to investigate,' Jackson affirms, 'Known danger level of the driver or occupants? Over.'

'Unknown at this time, Tango 240. Proceed with caution. Over and out.'

27

Frank enters the incident room and inwardly groans as he spots Superintendent Anne Banks and Zac standing in the doorway to his office. She immediately waves him over.

'This is all I need,' he mumbles to himself.

'How are the Millers bearing up?' she asks as he approaches.

'Scarlet and Jenny Miller are putting on a brave face. As for Keith... well, he's a shadow of his former self,' Frank replies, downcast, gazing at the worn carpet.

'And the search?'

'It's well underway. The Search and Rescue Team is leading it with over two hundred public volunteers. They started up near the golf club and are sweeping west to east across town. They'll be door knocking every house, searching every garden, shed, garage, wheelie bin, and spare bit of land.'

'What about thermal imaging?'

Frank shakes his head. 'Too foggy to get a chopper in the air at the moment. The fog has lifted a little, but I think it's set in for the day. To be honest, Anne, it's more of a public reassurance campaign than anything else. I have a bad feeling about this one.'

'There's been developments while you were out. Zac?' she says as she slips behind Frank's desk and drops into his chair.

'We have our prime suspect downstairs. Prisha's about to interview him.'

'Go on?' Frank says, glancing at Zac.

'The car being driven suspiciously; it belongs to a Carson Colby from Robin Hood's Bay. Carson is married to Julie Carson, formerly Julie Dufton.'

'Don't tell me; the sister of Blake Dufton?' Frank states, joining the dots.

'Correct. Carson loaned his Fiesta to Blake Dufton yesterday morning. Blake reckoned he wanted to spend the weekend looking for digs and trying to line up some work. However, thanks to some diligent work by Dinkel, he tracked the car from CCTV footage. It was spotted on Ashton Grove for thirty minutes between 6:40 and 7:10 pm last night.'

'Hell fire! Then it's possible Rosie returned home and never went to the circus.'

Zac raises his eyebrows 'That's one theory.'

Superintendent Banks frowns. 'What have the Millers got to say about Blake Dufton?'

'They don't have the time of day for him, especially Keith. Apparently, Blake made requests to Scarlet asking to see Rosie while he was inside.'

'And?'

'She never replied. Threw the letters in the bin.'

'And what about Rosie? Has she shown any interest in getting to know her father?'

'According to the Millers, she asks about him occasionally, more out of curiosity than a yearning to know him.'

'Hmm... okay, this is good progress. I think we have our man. The question is... what has he done with Rosie?'

'Let's not jump the gun, Anne.'

'Nonsense, Frank. Blake Dufton had the motive, means and opportunity. I need a result and I need it quickly before this thing blows up into a national news story. And on a positive note, I can't imagine an estranged father harming his own daughter.'

'Payback?' Frank suggests. 'What about the car, any clues?' he says, turning to Zac.

'Macdonalds wrappers in the passenger footwell. Meal for one. A few things in the glove box, which I assume belong to Juile Carson. Pair of women's gloves, earphones, lipstick, hair tie. A woollen blanket in the back seat. And in the boot a new claw hammer, a new pair of heavy-duty gardening gloves and a cloth bag.'

Puzzlement etches over Frank's face. 'Hell, I don't like the sound of that. Any blood on the hammer?'

Zac shakes his head. 'Not to the naked eye. The car is with forensics as we speak.'

Anne rises and smooths down her skirt. 'I have a media conference lined up for three this afternoon. I want some news by then, Frank. Hopefully, good news. We could certainly do with some around this place.' She heads to the door, then stops. 'Any progress on the suspected rapist?'

'What? Oh, no. Prisha's working it but has obviously focused her attention on finding Rosie Miller.'

Anne pouts, pulling a stern expression. 'Hmm... well, don't let it slide too long. This is CID. We can multitask, you know. Right, keep me informed of any developments. I need to speak with the Chief Constable and let him know the latest situation.'

Both men gaze in silence as she strides briskly through the office.

'Multitask,' Frank repeats, the word laced with disdain. 'I sometimes wonder what planet she's on.' He flops into his chair and stares through the window at the gloomy weather. 'I was supposed to be spending the weekend with my niece,' he murmurs regretfully. 'What was Blake Dufton told when he was arrested?'

'It was patrol who picked him up at Sneaton Wood. Arrested for parking illegally overnight. He was told we wanted to question him in regard to suspicious activity from last night.'

Frank nods thoughtfully. 'Good. He doesn't know we're onto him about Rosie, then?'

'Not directly. If he took the girl, then I'm sure he's put two and two together.'

'Have you secured the area at Sneaton Wood?'

Zac's shoulders rise as he puffs out air. 'Yes, but we're running out of resources, Frank. We won't be able to comb the area until the Search and Rescue Team have finished in Whitby.'

Frank's eyes swivel, focussing on the incident room and the chaotic hustle and bustle. Officers leaving, officers arriving. Constant chatter, phones ringing, people exchanging pieces of paper, and Dinkel updating the interactive whiteboard like an expert. Frank's never been a fan of big teams being thrown together for a major incident. There's too much white noise, literally and figuratively. To him, it's a case of the right hand not knowing what the left hand is doing. He could manage a team half the size and obtain results quicker. His desk phone rings, ending his rumination.

'DCI Finnegan.'

'Frank, you're not going to like this?' the desk sergeant states, an element of apprehension in his voice.

Frank swallows hard, anticipating the worst. 'Go on,' he whispers, as he throws Zac a fearful gaze.

'A nines came in a few minutes ago.'

A glug of adrenalin fires through his bloodstream. 'And?'

'A body has been found up on West Cliff, where the circus is.'

Feeling faint, his vision becomes blurry. 'Oh, sweet mercy... please don't tell me it's a girl?'

'No. A white male. Details are sketchy, but it's an adult.'

'Thank Christ for that!' he exclaims. 'Ahem, sorry, that came out wrong.'

A wry chuckle echoes down the line. 'Yeah, I know what you mean, Frank.'

'Okay, sergeant. Thanks for that. I'm on my way,' he declares, jumping to his feet.

'What is it, boss?' Zac asks as Frank makes his way out of the office.

'The body of an adult male has been found up near the circus. Come on, look lively! Don't you know how to multitask?'

28

With the formalities over, Prisha offers Blake Dufton a flicker of a smile to put him at ease. She studies him, not yet certain how she's going to play it. In cases like this, every second counts. If she goes in hard too early, he could clam up altogether and go down the "no comment" route. Her eyes drift onto the duty solicitor, who looks about as enthused as a dead haddock. It's nobody's definition of fun to be entombed in a police interview room on a weekend. Her focus returns to Blake: a handsome lad with a quiet demeanour, softly spoken. He doesn't look like the sort of person who would hurt a child. But appearances are made to deceive.

Flicks open a folder on the table. Peers at the notes inside. 'I see you've recently been released on parole, Blake?'

'Yeah. A few days ago.'

She reflects and nods. 'You were doing an eight stretch for grievous bodily harm and breaking and entering. Are you prone to violence?'

Screws his face up. 'No.'

'Then why the charge for GBH?'

'Look, I readily admit to breaking into the post office, but I never hit the old guy.'

Prisha glances at the notes again. 'You mean the postmaster, Mr Cleaver? Fifty-eight-years old. A fractured skull. Struck with a heavy-duty flashlight. Suffered memory loss. He and his wife retired from the post office not long after the attack. Hardly surprising, considering the traumatic event. I bet he still suffers nightmares. Funny how your fingerprints were on the torch that whacked Mr Cleaver over the head.'

Blake examines Prisha's emotionless face and reclines in his chair. 'I held the torch earlier as Johnny was breaking in through the back door. Once inside, he took hold of the torch.'

'Ah, yes, your accomplice, Johnny Moon. How come his fingerprints weren't on the torch?'

'He was wearing gloves. Shows how bloody stupid I was, doesn't it?'

'Not wearing gloves or robbing a post office?'

He snorts. 'Both.'

'Yet Johnny said it was you who struck Mr Cleaver.'

'Yeah, well, Johnny Moon is a fucking liar. I'd never hit an old guy.'

'I can understand your resentment. He received three years for breaking and entering. Only served eighteen months, whereas you lost five years of your life.'

He shrugs. 'Look, what's going on here? What's the big deal? I parked up in a wood that doesn't allow overnight parking. Hardly the crime of the century, is it?'

'The Ford Fiesta; tell me about it?'

'I explained all this to the arresting officer. The car belongs to my sister, Julie Colby, although it might be registered in her husband's name—Carson Colby. They live in Robin Hood's Bay. I borrowed it yesterday for the weekend. I wanted some time alone, to have a look at the job ads, and see if I could find a share house.'

'The car was seen being driven suspiciously in Whitby last night between 6:15 and 7:15 pm. Care to tell me what you were doing?'

'I wasn't doing anything,' he states, glancing behind Prisha at a blank wall.

'Stop, start. Parking up. Driving around the same spot near Bell Vue Terrace. Almost like you were searching for something... or someone.'

'I was looking for an overnight parking spot. I'd tried getting a bed-and-breakfast but everywhere was chockers, what with the Goth Weekend and all.'

'It's a twenty-minute drive to your sister's place in Robin Hood's Bay. Why didn't you head there? Far more comfortable than sleeping rough in a car.'

'Look, I've spent five years cooped up in a tiny cell with various dodgy guys. I wanted... needed some time alone. Time to think. My own company. You could never understand.'

Peruses her notes again, calm, measured. 'I believe you have a daughter?'

Eyes flicker. 'Yes. So?' he says, with a hint of regret and bemusement.

'Rosie Miller. Eight years old. When did you last see her?'

Eyes close. 'I've never seen her,' he murmurs, appearing ashamed.

Silence as she stares at him. Signals of guilt manifest in all but the true psychopaths.

Something's wrong.

'Why have you never met her? Not interested?'

Heaves and sits up straight. Suddenly looks older. 'They won't let me.'

'They?'

'The Millers. Rosie's mother, Scarlet; her parents, Jenny, and Keith. They think I'm bad through and through. I'm not. I did some stupid bloody things when I was a kid.'

'Have you tried to get in touch?'

Nods, reflectively. 'I sent letters over the years.'

'Rosie was three when you went inside. How come you didn't see her before then?'

'Because I was young, a dickhead. Into drugs and drink. I never wanted Scarlet to have the kid. Told her to have an abortion, but she wouldn't. Some say prison makes people worse, but not in my case. It taught me a valuable lesson.'

'Which was?'

'Life and freedom are bloody precious. I had a lot of thinking time. Made me recognise where I'd gone wrong. I never want to end up back inside. I thought about Rosie, and her growing up without a father. Prison made me grow up. I have to be responsible for my life, and for my actions, and that includes Rosie. I just want a relationship with her, to get to know my own flesh and blood, to be there for her when she needs me.'

Prisha claps her hands together. 'Bravo! That all sounds very nice. The sort of crap a Parole Board love to hear. A feel-good story. Reflection, acknowledgment of your sins, followed by redemption. It almost brought a tear to my eye. Is there an encore?'

Face hardens. 'It's true. I've changed.'

'Of course you have,' she replies, taking three photographs from her folder and sliding them across the table. 'That's why we found a claw hammer, a pair of gardening gloves and a cloth bag in the boot of the car. What were you planning to do with them?'

Folds his arms. Stares at the photos. 'Who says they're mine?'

'Because the receipt in the bag has a date and time stamp from yesterday afternoon. Bought from Wilkinsons in Scarborough.'

Trapped. Thinks quickly. 'Carson was building a deck. I thought I'd help him out when I returned the car on Monday. There are a lot of nails in a deck.'

Prisha pauses, momentarily distracted. Mentally, she's transported to the vicinity of Belle Vue Terrace. Doubts enter her thoughts. Decides to hit him hard, then call a recess. Give him time to worry.

'I take it you haven't listened to the local news during the last twelve hours?'

Eyes scrunch. Puzzlement. 'No. Why? What's happened?'

'Yesterday evening, a child went missing around 6:45 pm. Last seen heading towards the circus at the far end of West Cliff.'

Shuffles. Swallows. 'Shit, no, I hadn't heard. Has the kid been found yet?'

He said kid... not her. 'No. And the clock's ticking.'

Reflects and has a lightbulb moment. 'Hang on a minute... is this what it's about? Is this why I'm here?' Panic rising.

'Belle Vue Terrace is only a four-minute drive from the circus.'

'No, no, no! I had nothing to do with it! This is crap. Why the hell would I take a kid?'

Casually flicks through her notes again, gently easing towards the killer blow. 'At 6:40 pm, the Fiesta you were driving turned onto Ashton Grove. You were there for at least thirty minutes.'

'So?'

'Don't treat me like a bloody fool, Blake. I haven't got time for this shit. Ashton Grove is where the Millers live. I know that and you know that. Why did you go to Ashton Grove?'

Fingers intertwine. 'I was hoping I might see her,' he mumbles, barely audible.

'Sorry, can you repeat that?'

'I said I was hoping to see her.'

'Who?'

'Rosie, who bloody else would I be talking about?'

'So, you were going to knock on the Miller's door?'

'No. I was hoping she may have been playing in the street. Or maybe her head would pop up in her bedroom window. She *is* my daughter. I have a right to see her.'

'We'll take a quick break in a moment, but before we do, answer me this; did you see or talk to Rosie yesterday evening?'

'No! Look what's going on here? Why do you keep asking about Rosie?'

'Because the girl who went missing last night... *was* Rosie Miller.'

Prisha re-enters the interview room and performs the formalities. Blake Dufton is in a state of high agitation.

'You've got to release me so I can search for my daughter,' he pleads.

'And how are you going to do that? You don't even know what she looks like.'

'You must have a photo. I can help. It's my right. She's my flesh and blood.'

'You want to help?'

'Yes!'

'Then tell me where she is?'

'For God's sake! You don't believe I'd harm my own daughter, do you?' he shouts.

'Did Rosie return to Ashton Grove last night while you were parked up outside her house?'

'No!'

'Did you speak to her? Coax her into your car? Drive off?'

'No! I'm telling you the truth. I want out of here. You can't keep me,' he says, rising from his seat.

'SIT DOWN!' Prisha bellows.

The solicitor places a hand on Blake's arm. He responds by dropping back into his chair.

'I can keep you here for at least the next twenty-four hours, longer if I so choose. And I intend to unless you start telling the truth. Let's go back to the hammer, the gloves, the bag. Why did you have them? And don't spin me the tale about helping your brother-in-law with the deck.'

'It's true. That's why I bought them.'

'Do you even care about Rosie?' she sighs.

'Of course I do. I love her.'

'How can you love someone you've never met?'

'I don't know. I feel a connection to her. I want to make up for lost time.'

'Okay, then help me out,' she asks in a soft, friendly tone.

'How?'

'Stop wasting my bloody time!' She slaps the table with her palm, making him and his solicitor jump. 'The longer I sit here listening to your bullshit, the less time I have to find Rosie alive! Now, the hammer, gloves, bag; what were you planning to do with them?'

He pushes back in his seat and groans, on the brink of tears. 'It was because of Rosie I didn't do it. I intended to, but then I thought of her, and I experienced this enormous feeling of inner strength.'

'You're making no sense. You said you didn't do it. Do what?'

'The jeweller's shop near Belle Vue Terrace! I was planning to do a dirty smash and grab. Smash the window, use the claw on the hammer to pull the glass out, and grab whatever was on display. That's why I had the gloves and the bag. I knew the police would be at full stretch policing the town because of the Goth Weekend. But I didn't go through with it. I couldn't do it because at the last moment I thought of Rosie. She's something worth living for. She's all I have left. Now please, let me leave so I can search for my girl?' he pleads as tears roll down his cheeks.

Shit! It's not him. He has nothing to do with it.

29

Frank carefully navigates the car through the chaos of the congested Whitby streets. His frustration and concern are evident in his tone as he grizzles in Zac's ear.

'What the hell is happening, Zac?'

Confused, Zac replies, 'What do you mean?'

'A few days ago, all we had to worry about was the usual drug dealers, car thefts, and the odd break-in. Now we have a missing youngster, a potential rapist on the prowl, and a dead body.'

'The body may not be suspicious. No point jumping to conclusions.'

'So much for a relaxing weekend with my niece. It's all gone tits up. This bloody Goth festival doesn't help matters, either.'

They park up, exit the car, and button their coats against the biting wind swirling in from the sea. A small crowd of circus performers are congregated outside the marquee where The Scarecrow Cometh show took place. They are subdued and appear in a state of shock. Zac spots PC Pembroke waving at them from the caravans and vehicles situated away from the main site. They stride briskly over to her.

'Nice bit of overtime for you, Kylie,' Frank remarks.

She flashes an apologetic smile. 'It all comes in handy, sir. Although, I'd rather be at home with a good book in front of the fire.'

'Let's walk and talk. What have we got?'

'An elderly gentleman named Jack Henderson, also known as...'

'Ginger Jack,' Frank whispers, halting abruptly. 'Oh, hell. What happened?'

'It appears he fell and hit his head on the wood stove. He has a big gash to the right side of his forehead, and possibly blood splatter on the edge of the fire, although it's hard to tell.'

'Why?'

'The stove is still hot, and it's baked on. It might not be blood.'

He continues walking and asks, 'Who discovered the body?'

'His granddaughter, Abby Henderson. She banged on the side of the caravan, his usual wake-up call. When she hadn't seen him an hour later, she went inside and found his body.'

They arrive at the grubby caravan cordoned off with police tape.

'Are forensics on their way?' Frank asks.

'Yes. I tried you first, Frank. But I couldn't get hold of you, so I went straight to Superintendent Banks, who authorised it. Charlene Marsden said she'd have her forensic team up here within the hour.'

'Excellent work, Kylie. Grab another uniformed officer and question the circus performers. And get their real names. I don't want any Coco the Clowns or The Great Gandalf appearing on the interview sheet. If you spot Abby Henderson, ask her to come and see me.'

'Will do, boss.'

'By the way, how was Abby? Upset?'

Kylie ponders the question. 'She wasn't distraught, but neither was she performing the can-can. Stunned is the word I'd use.'

Frank and Zac hastily don protective body suits.

'Zac, give Bennett Whipple a call and ask him to get his arse up here pronto.'

Zac stares at him in dismay. 'Do I have to? Old Raspberry is a royal pain in the freckle at the best of times. You know how he reacts when he's called out on a weekend.'

'If he gives you any blather, tell him I gave the order. I'm hoping and praying this is an unfortunate accident, but after the angry mob turned up here last night, well, it's too much of a coincidence for my liking. And I don't believe in...'

'Coincidences,' Zac replies, annoyed and dispirited, as he pulls out his mobile.

Frank cautiously pushes at the caravan door, enters, and evaluates the scene. The crumpled body of Ginger Jack is lying across the floor, next to the wood burner, which still contains glowing embers. The old man's eyes are open. He's fully clothed, still in his dirty green trench coat, his wooden leg a few inches away, near the sink, detached from his stump. A poker is in his right hand, gripped by white, bloodless fingers. The gash to his head is about two inches long, clotted blood hardened into a scab.

'Oh, Jack, Jack, Jack,' Frank murmurs wistfully, a wave of empathy washing over him. 'What the devil happened here, old lad?' For a moment he becomes distracted as he listens to Zac arguing with the irascible doctor on the phone from outside the caravan.

'I appreciate you look forward to your weekends off, Doctor Whipple,' Zac replies, raising his voice. 'I *also* enjoy the weekends with my wife and children. Unfortunately, our chosen profession occasionally intrudes upon those simple pleasures. Now, DCI Finnegan wants you up here at the circus on the West Cliff as soon as is humanly possible, and he won't take no for an answer. I'm sorry... I didn't quite catch that? Oh, I see. It was a Nigerian word. Okay, thank you. See you soon, Doctor Whipple.'

As Zac enters the caravan, he bangs his head on the lintel of the doorway.

'Fuck me blind!' he cries.

'Mind your head,' Frank says with little concern, still scanning the interior. 'I take it Whipple is not in the best of moods?'

Zac rubs furiously at his forehead. 'No! I think he called me a twat in Nigerian. Although, I can't be certain.'

'Another addition to your extensive lexicology, sergeant. However, Nigeria is a linguistically diverse country, Zac, with hundreds of different languages. The official spoken lingo is English, adopted from the colonial rule. How long will Whipple be?'

'He's at least six-foot five, Frank. I don't think he'll grow much taller at his age.'

'Most amusing.'

'He's already in town. Christmas shopping. So, a few minutes away.'

Frank's puzzlement is obvious. 'Christmas shopping? He's a bit eager, isn't he? I don't do my Christmas shopping until Christmas Eve. Daft bugger.'

Zac pulls at his white protective suit. 'Hell, it's bloody warm in here.'

Frank cautiously places his fingers on top of the stove, then immediately removes them.

'Aye. The wood burner is still hot to the touch.'

'What's your first impressions?' Zac asks, gently massaging his forehead.

'I think Kylie's initial assessment is on the money. It appears the old lad got up in the middle of the night, either to stoke the fire or take a piss, and his wooden leg came off, lost his balance, and hit the edge of the stove, hard.' He picks up a small glass tumbler from the draining board and sniffs it. 'Plus, he had a whisky or two before bed. Even so, let's keep an open mind.'

Zac stoops and picks up an object off the floor. 'Hey, an old-fashioned wooden clothes peg,' he states, holding it aloft.

Frank stares at the object. 'Hell, I haven't seen a dolly peg for nigh on thirty years. It's missing a leg.'

'A bit like its owner,' Zac remarks with a smirk.

'You're on fire today, lad.'

'As you always say, if you don't laugh, you'd curl up in a ball and cry.'

Frank crouches, painfully groaning as he does so. 'Here's the broken part,' he mutters, clasping a slender piece of wood. Rising, he closes the caravan door and gazes at the hasp and latch. 'Not the greatest security system I've ever seen. Obviously, he slid the peg through the hasp as a makeshift bolt.'

'Which means someone forced the door and broke the peg.'

'Possibly. But we don't know that for certain. The peg may have been broken for some time.'

'Would he have anything of any value in here? Maybe the takings from the circus?'

'Nah. I was sitting with him only twenty-four hours ago eating a sausage sandwich. He had nothing of value. His granddaughter looks after the money side of things, and most of it is handled electronically.'

A deep bass rumble resonates from outside. 'Detective Chief Inspector Finnegan!'

'And here comes the Easter Bunny,' Zac mutters as he pulls open the van door. 'In here, doctor,' he yells. 'Time to get the dictionary out,' he notes drily.

The daylight is briefly thwarted as Whipple's towering frame lumbers into view. Already donned in full protective gear, he carries a doctor's bag in one giant mitt. Frank casts his eye over him. He's often wondered why Whipple bothers with a hair mask, as his gargantuan noggin is as smooth as a billiard ball. The doctor doesn't appear to be in the best of moods as he slogs forwards, chuntering in Yoruba, a southwestern Nigerian language.

'This is most disagreeable, inspector. Most disagreeable, indeed. In the cyclone of my demanding week, I yearn for golden moments of respite, akin to a weary warrior seeking refuge from the chaos of battle. The weekend is my sacred sanctuary, a temple where I can finally nurse my soul back to health, like a heroic knight tending to the wounds of his noble steed. With great zeal, I protect these precious hours, for they are my rejuvenating elixir, my joyous escape from the ravages of the week's tumultuous tribulations.'

'Come again?' Frank replies, throwing a deaf one.

As Doctor Bennett Whipple lumbers into the caravan, he smacks his head on the lintel with a resounding thwack, shaking the entire structure.

'Ode oshi! Sweet mamma!' he exclaims, staggering forward, almost poleaxed.

'Mind your noggin,' Frank advises as Zac watches on with a satisfying smirk.

Bennett collapses onto a bench seat and rubs vigorously at his brow, and a rapidly rising bump.

'A hematoma has already materialised on my metopic suture,' he murmurs, his weekend going from bad to worse.

'Nasty,' Frank commiserates, resisting a smile.

'I have heard the expression—seeing stars—but I have never actually experienced it. But now, I am bedazzled by phosphenes and overwhelmed with pre-syncope more commonly associated with aortic stenosis and hypertrophic cardiomyopathy.'

'It was a hefty blow. Zac did the same thing a moment ago. But in his case, where there's no sense, there's no feeling. However, doctor, we have a dead body on our hands,' Frank says, nodding at the lifeless form of Ginger Jack.

'One moment, inspector. I can feel the onset of a severe bout of hyperopia.'

Frank winces. 'That's a disaster waiting to happen. The nearest public convenience is some distance away, Bennett.'

'It's blurred vision, inspector. Blurred vision!' he bellows.

'Okay, calm down. No need to shout.'

Whipple struggles to his feet, shoulders, and head stooped to avoid the ceiling. He tries to squeeze past Frank, but as neither man could be described as svelte, there's a moment when their stomachs meet, ensuring an impasse of massive proportions. Like ancient dinosaurs trapped in a cave, they labour to move forwards, backwards, or sideways. Frank is hard up against the sink and bench-top, whereas Whipple is wedged with his back to the pantry door. All the while, Zac watches on in growing amusement as a serious bout of huffing and puffing ensues.

'Inspector, if you could move slightly to the left, it may help,' Whipple suggests, wheezing like a pair of rusty old bellows.

'No, I think you need to sidle left.'

'That's impossible. I'm immobile. This is a most egregious and ignominious calamity,' Whipple grunts, as a bead of sweat rolls off his forehead.

'Aye. It's not my idea of fun, either,' Frank puffs, wrinkling his nose. 'Did you have garlic for dinner last night, doctor?' he enquires as both men's cheeks touch, creating a rasping sound as stubble meets stubble, rather like Velcro being ripped apart.

'Mrs Whipple cooked forty clove garlic chicken. A gastronomic delight,' he pants.

'You don't say.'

'Indeed, I do. Chicken is a high-grade protein with a low fat content. With the progression of senescence in the male homo-sapien, it is sagacious to reduce the intake of saturated fats. And of course, the benefits of garlic have been well known for millennia, to wit: garlic, or allium sativum, to give it the Latin name, exhibits potent anti-microbial, anti-inflammatory, and antioxidant properties due to its key bioactive constituent, allicin, making it beneficial for cardiovascular health, immune support, and overall well-being.' He ends with a gasp.

'There is too much of a good thing, though, Doc. Forty cloves is overkill.'

'Au contraire, inspector, au contraire.'

Grinning like a village idiot on Fentanyl, Zac pulls out his phone.

'No need to call the fire brigade just yet, Zac. I'm sure we can extricate ourselves,' Frank advises.

'I wasn't calling them. I'm getting a photo of this,' he replies, chuckling. 'Two pigs in a ginnel!'

Whipple grimaces in obvious discomfort.

'What's the matter, Bennett? Are you in pain?' Frank enquires on noticing Whipple's contorted expression.

'Indeed, I am, inspector,' he wheezes. 'The door handle of the cupboard is impinging upon my intergluteal cleft, which in turn is generating excessive throbbing in my inferior gluteal arteries and sciatic nerve.'

'Count your blessings, Bennett. If you were two inches shorter, that doorknob would be impinging on your rusty bullet hole. Zac, stop pissing about and help us out!'

Zac puts his phone away and grabs Frank's outstretched hand. He gives it a good yank. It has little effect.

'Sweet merciful shite! You big Scottish troglodyte! You nearly had my arm out of its bloody socket!'

'Sorry, Frank.'

Whipple blinks rapidly as faintness washes over him. Beads of sweat drip from his pale jowls, despite his dark skin colour. He refuses to keel over. It would be undignified.

Stoic to the end, he remarks, 'I can assure you, inspector, the glenoid cavity of the scapula is a most robust ball and socket joint, and the probabilities of your upper humerus disengaging are slim to none.'

'Is that right?' Frank snarls. 'It wasn't your bloody arm the buffoon yanked at!'

'What about if you both try sucking your guts in?' Zac suggests.

Whipple glares at him. 'Whilst Inspector Finnegan is obviously suffering from abdominal adiposity, and an accumulation of visceral fat causing gastrointestinal distension, I can assure you, sergeant, I am in the optimal weight range for my height. As Mrs Whipple often glowingly remarks as I exit the shower, I possess the body of a god.'

'Aye—Buddha. To be honest, neither of you are shy of a battered sausage or four.'

With one last Herculean effort, the impasse is broken as both men stagger free, panting with the exertion.

Whipple pulls a pristine white handkerchief from his pocket and dabs at his sweaty face.

'The temperature in this mobile establishment has escalated to an oppressively sweltering degree,' he remarks with a contorted expression of distress.

Frank rubs his forehead on the back of his sleeve, red-faced, sucking in garlic and sweat infused air.

'It's that bloody wood stove. It certainly pumps out the heat. Now, if you could get down to business, doctor, it would be appreciated.'

Whipple regains his composure somewhat, and studies the body. 'The cadaver is a transtibial amputee,' he states, dropping ungainly to his haunches. 'Inspecting the residual limb, I would say amputation occurred many years ago.'

Frank shakes his head. 'Yes, we are aware of the missing leg, Doc. If you could focus on the rest of the body, it may speed things along.'

Whipple would normally rile against such instructions… but not today. He wants out.

'The victim exhibits a significant laceration, lateral to the frontal bone, possibly caused by a forceful impact against a hard, potentially sharp edge. No immediate signs of skull fracture, however, there is potential for underlying neurological damage. Further examination is required for comorbidity determination.'

Frank winces. 'Erm… meaning?'

Whipple rises gingerly, and wearily, to his feet. 'You wish me to extrapolate upon my rudimentary initial assessment?'

'If you could.'

'Very well. If this were a children's parlour game of Guess the Mode of Demise, I would ascertain the individual has fallen and hit his cranium against the side of the combustion heater, causing death by traumatic brain injury, or a brain haemorrhage. Either scenario would disrupt vital functions such as breathing, heart rate, or blood pressure, leading to immediate cessation of life. Satisfied, inspector?'

'Not quite. One last thing…'

Whipple emits an enormous sigh. 'Time of death… inspector?'

'You read my mind, Doc.'

'Your mind is a veritable open book written by an adolescent, inspector. Rigor Mortis has not yet set in. But as the ambient temperature is exceedingly warm in this abode, it may have postponed the onset of muscular stiffening. However, his flesh is cool to the touch, surprisingly so, and he is exhibiting signs of post-mortem hypostasis identifiable by a purplish-red discoloration of the skin. This is caused by gravity pulling blood to the lowest points of the body.'

'And the time of death?' Frank prompts.

Whipple shakes his massive melon as he heads to the door. 'Two to eight hours ago. I will furnish you with my final expert assessment post the post-mortem, which will not be occurring this weekend!' he bellows.

'Okay. Keep your wig on,' Frank calls out as the hulking figure of Doctor Whipple lumbers away. He ponders for a moment. 'Post the post-mortem? That's a first.'

'Aye. They broke the mould when he was born, thank fuck. There's only enough room for one Whipple in this world.'

'Quite literally. How does a man of his size get through the day?'

Zac stares at his boss. 'Probably the same way you do.'

'Not funny, Zac. Not funny.'

'Humour is subjective, Frank.'

'Come on, let's hear Abby Henderson's version of events.'

30

Frank massages his eyes with the fleshy part of his palms.

'What a bloody weekend?' he yawns wearily.

'What's your thoughts on Abby Henderson?' Zac asks as he takes a seat and slurps on a long-black.

'I believe she loved her grandad, and had no motive for doing him in. She already owns fifty-one per cent of the circus.'

'What about the broken peg?'

'As Abby said, sometimes he used it as a bolt to secure the door, sometimes he forgot.'

'But surely, he'd have used it last night after the mob turned up baying for his blood?'

'There's no toilet in his caravan, Zac. I dare say the old lad would get up in the night and take a leak from the doorway. Maybe he forgot to slip the peg back through the hasp. Easy mistake, especially after a few shots of whisky. Let's wait and see what forensics come back with. I'm hoping it was an unfortunate accident, for everyone's sake.

Our focus must be on Rosie Miller. The death of Jack Henderson can go on the backburner for now.' He lifts his head and gazes through the window into the incident room. 'Ah, here comes Prisha. Let's see how she got on with Blake Dufton.'

Prisha enters the office and takes a seat next to Zac.

'How'd you go with Blake Dufton? Have you nailed him?'

Prisha's chest heaves, followed by a long slow expulsion of air. 'It's not him, Frank?'

The chair creaks alarmingly as he pushes into the backrest. 'What?'

'It's not him.'

'It has to be him! He's our only serious suspect!'

'You're not listening, Frank. I'm telling you; Blake Dufton knows nothing about Rosie Miller's disappearance. In fact, he's extremely distraught.'

Frank lowers his voice to a slow, deep baritone. 'Please tell me you haven't let him go?'

'Yes. I have no grounds for holding him.'

He leaps to his feet. 'Jesus H Christ on a bike, Prisha! What the hell are you playing at? He was on her street last night around the time she went missing. It's got to be him! Who else could it be? There are no other suspects! You should have consulted with me on this one, damn you.'

'Calm down, Frank,' Zac advises.

He rounds on him. 'Don't tell me to calm down! We've a young lass who has been missing for nearly eighteen hours; a random rapist on the loose, and now a dead body at the circus to investigate. I think I'm entitled to be a little agitated, don't you? And now, to cap it all, Jessica Fletcher here has let our prime suspect walk out of the station without a care in the world!'

'You'll pop a roid if you're not careful,' Zac advises.

Frank rubs at the side of his temple with his fingertips, pulls a packet of paracetamol from his desk drawer, and pops four pills into his mouth. He scans the desk for water, but on seeing none, grabs a cup of tepid tea and washes the tablets down with the dregs.

Unruffled, Prisha turns to Zac. 'What's this about a dead body at the circus?' she whispers.

'Ginger Jack. Found dead in his caravan.'

'Suspicious?'

'Doesn't appear so, but early days. A large gash to his head. Forensics are up there now.'

Frank stands at the window with his back to them. He pulls a double teapot, hands on hips.

'I'm sorry for my outburst, Prisha. It was uncalled for. It's this case...'

'No need to apologise, Frank. We all need to let off steam occasionally.'

'What were your reasons for letting him go, and what about him behaving suspiciously last night?' he asks, turning to her.

'He was acting suspiciously because he was planning on a quick smash and grab at the jewellers on the corner of Bell Vue Terrace. Hence, the hammer, gloves, and bag. He had a change of heart when he thought about Rosie. I genuinely believe he wants to form a connection with her. He then drove to Ashton Grove in the forlorn hope he may catch a glimpse of the daughter he's never seen.'

'And you one hundred per cent believe him?'

'Yes. When I told him Rosie was missing, he was bereft.'

'Some of these buggers are good actors.'

'No way. I had doubts about him almost straight away. I think prison has scared the bejeezus out of him and he doesn't want to go back there.'

'And yet he was on the brink of robbing a jeweller's shop. You could have charged him with going equipped.'

Prisha raises her eyebrows. 'Come off it, Frank! The chances of obtaining a conviction would be decidedly slim. If he'd been apprehended last night, then yes, it could be reasonably argued the *intent* was there to commit a burglary. But, the day after, *and* an admission of a change of heart, well, that blurs the lines. And what would be the point? It wastes precious time, and a guy who is out on parole could find himself back inside.'

'Exactly! Dufton is a bad egg. The sooner he goes back inside, the better.'

'I don't believe he is bad. He did one stupid thing five years ago, for which he's done his penance. I believe he's changed. We all have impulses. It's whether we act upon them that lands us in trouble. He had a choice, and he made the right decision this time. Nothing to say he won't do something stupid in the future, but I'm convinced he has nothing to do with Rosie's disappearance.'

'I hope you're right, for both our sakes. The Super has already made her mind up about him. She likely persuaded the chief constable of Blake Dufton's guilt, as well. So, where does that leave us?' he says, his eyes focusing on Zac. 'What about known child sex offenders?'

'We've interviewed thirty of them so far and they all have alibis,' Zac replies, as he strokes his stubble.

'Any of them have previous convictions for abduction?'

Zac puts his coffee down, pulls his notepad out and flicks through the pages. 'Yeah. A John Bramble from Pickering.'

'Right, bring the bugger in. I don't care if he has an alibi or not. Let's put him under the pump.'

Zac shakes his head. 'He's not involved, Frank. He's in his late-eighties, in a wheelchair and needs oxygen four times a day.'

With the wind knocked out of him, Frank flops back into his chair. 'This is a nightmare,' he whispers. 'We have nothing. We've eliminated all close family, boyfriend, ex-boyfriend, the biological father, and sex offenders.'

Zac cracks his knuckles. 'We only checked the sex offenders within the fifty-mile radius. What about outsiders? There's an influx of ten to fifteen thousand people for the Halloween Goth Weekend. Many will have come from all over the country, or abroad.'

'Christ! And how are we supposed to manage that? Set up roadblocks around the exits out of town and question each and every one of them in the hope one is a paedophile from another part of the country. Anyway, if she has been abducted by one of those bastards, he'll be long gone by now. He's hardly likely to hang around the scene of the crime, is he?'

'Might not be male,' Zac says.

'I'm going on the stats. Ninety-five per cent of child sex offences are carried out by males. We've reached an impasse. Where to now?'

His eyes swivel from Prisha to Zac, then back again. Both glance at each other sheepishly, for once, devoid of ideas.

'Not sure,' Prisha mumbles, feeling exhausted.

He glances at his wristwatch and acknowledges their tiredness. 'Right, Prisha, tell anyone who has been working here since midnight to knock off for six hours and get some shut-eye. And that includes you and Zac.'

'Wait, boss!' she interjects as he strides into the lively incident room, fumbling in his trouser pocket for his car keys.

He raises a hand to quell her. 'My decision is final. You both need rest. And once I've updated the Super, I'll be doing the same. There are plenty of experienced officers to hold the fort for a few hours while we're away.' He stops and studies a piece of crumpled paper retrieved from his pocket, a touch of confusion crossing his face. 'Hmm... that seems like a lifetime ago,' he mumbles. He scrunches Ginger Jack's racing tips into a ball and launches it towards a rubbish bin under Prisha's desk. The projectile bounces off the bin and lands on her keyboard.

'Nearly,' Zac says, smothering a yawn.

Frank's mobile rings. He pulls it from his pocket and answers without even looking at the caller's name.

'Finnegan?' he says, his tone jaded, defeated. His eyes bulge. 'I hope this isn't some sort of sick joke. No, of course you wouldn't. Sorry, Charlene.' He hangs up and stares at Zac and Prisha as if he's seen a ghost.

'What is it, Frank?' Prisha asks, alarmed by his demeanour.

'That was Charlene Marsden from forensics. They've found something in Ginger Jack's caravan,' he states in a mild state of shock.

'What?'

He steadies himself on a desk. 'A yellow scrunchie. There are hair strands attached. They'll run tests on it, but they won't have the results until later this evening.'

'Shite,' Zac murmurs. 'How did we get this one so wrong?'

With the blood drained from his face, Frank gazes back and forth between Prisha and Zac.

'We've been busy chasing shadows when all along, the most obvious suspect was dancing in our spotlight. There's none as blind as them that refuse to see.'

'Should we pull in Abby Henderson? After all, she was the one who vouched for her grandfather's movements after the Strawman show last night,' Zac suggests.

Frank strokes his cheek. 'No. Not until it's been verified the scrunchie belongs to Rosie.'

'Where was the scrunchie found?' Prisha enquires, puzzled.

'In Jack's caravan. Stuffed down the plughole in the sink.'

Prisha's lips pucker as her eyebrows dart downwards. 'Hmm...'

31

The powerful spray cascades off her face, runs down her shoulders, sleeks from waist and buttocks, then drizzles onto the shower floor, where the suds corral into an exuberant exodus as they rush towards the plughole. Her eyes are fascinated with the watery dance, the symbolism not lost on her. The heated embrace of the water has drawn her in for longer than planned. With only a meagre three hours of fractured sleep under her belt, the warmth has done little to rejuvenate her. Instead, it has only amplified her drowsiness, wrapping her in a soporific cocoon.

'There's only one thing for it, Prisha,' she encourages herself, bracing for the experience whilst turning the hot water tap to the off position. The shock is instantaneous as she counts, rather quickly, to thirty. Fists clenched, elbows tucked into her waist, she curses as she shuts off the water.

The torture ends, but the aftermath lingers as she shivers in the brightly lit bathroom. The weariness forcefully ejected, her mind clears. Exiting the shower, she grabs a fluffy towel and vigorously rubs herself down as she ponders the last forty-eight hours.

Wrestling for her undivided attention is the Rosie Miller case. She hangs the towel up and stares at herself in the long rectangular mirror on the bathroom wall. Speaking aloud, as she tends to do when alone, she replies to her own questions.

'Okay, Prisha, what's your bedrock, the cornerstone of your detective work? Simple... human nature. We are creatures of habit. Our actions may seem incomprehensible, chaotic, without order, no rhyme or reason to a casual observer, but that's never the case. Even a madman has a routine, a system. Ginger Jack has been with the circus since he was fifteen. He has no criminal record, not even a caution. Why, at his age, would he suddenly change his behaviour and harm a little girl? The truth is... he wouldn't. Then what about the yellow scrunchie found in his caravan? Well... if it is Rosie's, which I'm sure it is, the question should be—how did it get there, or more pertinently, who put it there? Is someone framing Ginger Jack, and if so, who would benefit from his demise? Or are they trying to divert attention from themselves and muddy the waters?'

She moisturises, pulls her clothes on, fixes her hair, and leans in closer to the mirror.

'And then there's Frank. He shouldn't be even on the case. It's way too close to home for him to make rational judgements. Why hasn't Anne Banks intervened?' She curtails her introspection. 'Never mind about Frank. What you must focus on is what's happened to Rosie Miller. You have this, Prisha, you have this,' she whispers. 'Find the answers to the riddles... and please let the little girl be alive.'

She high-fives herself in the reflection, immediately cringes at the action, then exits the bathroom, not before issuing herself a chastisement, 'You dickhead!'

Pausing at the front door, she grapples with her conscience. Retrieving her mobile, she stares at the four missed calls from Adam and the two text messages, "Are you okay?" and "Call me?" She has been busy, but not too busy to type a ten second text reply.

Grasping the nettle, she hits the call button and bites her bottom lip.

'Hi.' He sounds distant, clearly annoyed.

'It's me,' she replies, suddenly devoid of anything to say.

'Yes, I know it's you. I have your photo on my phone. I'm out on the tractor. How are you?'

'Good. About last night, or was it early this morning? Anyway, I'm sure you've heard about the missing girl, and I should have had the courtesy to call or at least send a text message, but, well, I don't know. Shit! I'm crap at this relationship thing. This is how it is, Adam. For whatever reason, I always put my job first, and that's how it will always be. I understand if it's not for you. I'm not sure I'd want to play second fiddle...'

'Can I...'

'... to someone's job. Never sure where they are or when they'll call. It would be a nightmare, hanging around waiting. I said it wouldn't work. We're too different. Polar opposites and...'

'Prisha!' he yells down the line.

'What?' she mumbles, overcome with contrition.

'I understand. I was calling to see how you were holding up. I'm just finishing up on the farm for the day. Would you like me to come over?'

'What? No. I mean, I'm about to head back to the station. I grabbed a few hours sleep but I need to return to work. I'm not sure how long I'll be there or what time I'll knock off.'

'That's fine. I was going to offer to come and make a meal. Then when you do finish, at least you can zap it in the microwave. I make a mean chilli con carne. I can take tomorrow morning off, not that I'm expecting to spend any time with you. I know you'll be busy.'

Puzzlement creases her features. 'Why?'

'Why!' He yelps, a mixture of amusement and incredulity. 'Because that's what people do when they care for someone.'

'Care?'

'Yes, care. I don't have the balls to use the L word yet in case it freaks you out. But when you have feelings for another person, then it's normal to want to help them out when they're under stress. Well?'

Her heart rate accelerates, indicating her genuine emotions, while logic tells her his proposal is a bad idea. The hush takes an eternity.

'Erm...' is all she can muster.

'Okay, I get it. Listen, call me when you have some downtime. I'll be waiting for you. And look after yourself. Bye, Prisha.'

'No, wait! Yes, come over. I'll leave the key under the wheelie bin. And, well, thanks. You've cheered me up.'

A kindly chuckle echoes through the ether. 'We have progress. I'll see you anon.'

'Bye, Adam.' She wriggles her mouth from side to side, contemplating what's occurred. 'Is this what I want?' She checks her watch and yanks at the front door. 'Hell! I don't know what I want!'

32

A thin wisp of steam drifts from the takeaway coffee cup and evaporates into the stuffy air of the incident room. Prisha, weary and groggy from her disrupted sleep pattern, falls into a reverie. The steady hum of activity from the few remaining officers tells her they are no nearer to finding Rosie Miller. A fresh lead, a clue, a cohesive and credible statement from a member of the public would ignite the atmosphere. It would create an electrical charge, energising everyone. But there is no charge. Instead, there's the lethargic click-clack of computer keyboards, idle chat about knock-off times, tough decisions about what takeaway meals will be bought on the way home. Overall, a vibe of defeated lassitude which circulates like a virus.

She glances at her wristwatch—5:30 PM. Twenty-three hours since the little girl vanished. Taking a sip of coffee, she indulges in a moment of pleasure, inhaling the aroma, experiencing bitterness, relishing a satisfying warmth on her tongue.

'That is *so* good,' she murmurs to herself as she takes another mouthful.

Picking up a ball of scrunched up paper from her keyboard, she rolls it around and around in her hand, enjoying the roughness on her palm. There's still no sign of Frank or Zac. A few seconds pass until her eyes wander over to Dinkel, who is busy at the interactive whiteboard. He's like an obsessive puppy with a new toy. Annoying, in a childlike way. But she is slowly warming to him. Perhaps in another hundred years she'll actually like him. He'll never be a James Bond, Jack Reacher, or John Luther, but then, who is? However, maybe, *just maybe*, he has a few characteristics of Poirot—minus the prideful arrogance. Dinkel is analytical and dedicated. He's a number cruncher, not an action man. For the current investigation, Dinkel has the pivotal role of receiver, a leap of faith on Frank's part. As the name suggests, the receiver diligently receives and scrutinises all incoming documentation, ensuring its accuracy while identifying urgent matters for immediate attention.

She studies him as she remembers the task she gave him yesterday. 'Hmm...'

Another slow gulp of coffee, caffeine acting like an elixir. Rising, she saunters over to the whiteboard.

'What's the go, Dinkel?' she says, startling him.

'Oh, uploading the latest info, boss.'

'How are you feeling?' she asks.

The question baffles him. 'Feeling? I'm feeling fine. Why?'

'Full of vim and vigour? Brain re-charged and raring to go?'

He pulls a face, as though he's committed an indiscretion. 'Erm... yes. I'm good to go.'

'Good.'

'Good?'

'The little job I gave you yesterday morning—the unsolved rapes—did you enter all the details into the whiteboard?'

He flashes his pearly whites. 'Yes, I did.' Frowns. 'I wasn't sure what to name the folder, so I went with case number, crime type, followed by the victim's name. Therefore, 74338, Sexual Assault, Hannah Turnbull, but we can easily rename it if you want?'

'No, that's fine,' she replies, trying to contain her impatience.

'And...' he declares with a hint of satisfaction, 'I believe I've identified other victims by the same perpetrator.'

She pulls up a chair. 'Go on.'

Dinkel rapidly drags and drops photos with accompanying names onto the board.

'The witness statements from the victims of rape, or attempted rape, have an uncannily familiar description of their attacker. And they're all quite recent. Male, white, tall, and thin. All assaulted in their homes late at night. And two of them also mention a smell, similar to what Hannah described in your report.'

'Really?'

He taps at two photos on the board. 'Prudence Walker said it was similar to furniture polish, but with a hint of sweetness. Whereas Alice Carmody described it more like a scented candle, you know, resembling bees' wax but with a very faint smell of coconut or possibly vanilla, and an underlying chemical aroma, if that makes sense.'

'Interesting,' Prisha ponders. 'Hannah said it smelt like an antiques shop or church which could indicate bees' wax. What about DNA from semen samples?'

'There are no semen samples. The attacker wears a condom.'

'How very noble of him. That could complicate matters. What about hair, fingerprints, or fibres from the attacker?'

'Nothing. All we have are matching footprints from two of the assaults. Lifted from the lawn.' Grimacing, Dinkel wobbles his head from side to side. 'And to obfuscate the matter even further, the attacks happened all over the country.' He drags another item from the left of the board onto the main screen and a map of England materialises, littered with nine red dots. 'Well, I say all over the country. That's not quite true. As you can see, mainly in the southeast, and some further up north on the east coast, which I find odd.'

Prisha nods. 'Yes, it is peculiar,' she says, studying the crime map. 'Most rapists have a certain area they operate in. They know the quiet spots, the street layouts. They are notoriously territorial, and yet, this is a scattergun approach, seemingly random.'

'Could be a taxi driver, or a delivery driver?'

'Hmm... possibly. Anything else?'

'Yes. Five of the women reported they had underwear stolen from their washing line a day or so before the attacks. Oh, and some of the local press and tabloids have run stories on the assaults and labelled the attacker, the Stick Man. I assume because he's tall and thin... and a man. Although, having read some of the reporting, they have made many sloppy errors in regard to locations and timelines.'

Prisha shrugs. 'Par for the course.'

'And that's as far as I got, ma'am, I'm afraid. I put it on hold once the search for the missing girl began.'

'Don't apologise, Dinkel. You've made a great start. An excellent piece of methodical police work. I'm impressed,' she says, rising and moving closer to the board. 'Patterns,' she murmurs.

'Ma'am?'

'Patterns, Dinkel. Repetitions, arrangements, configurations. Nothing is truly random. Whether it be the actions of a serial rapist, or mass murderer, or even the way *you* peel an apple and slice it into sixteenths before eating it, which, by the way, is damned irritating. Everything comes down to patterns. It's our job to unveil the hidden thread that links the pieces together.'

'Synchronicity?'

'Exactly. So, what *do* we know? Descriptions of the attacker match. The modus operandi is the same; women of similar age, living alone, late at night. Steals underwear a night or two before. Obviously, does some reconnaissance beforehand.'

'Probably to make sure the woman lives alone and doesn't have a dog.'

'Correct. A smell similar to beeswax. Attack sites dotted all over the place, and a set of footprints. It's not much to go on. Any ideas, Dinkel?'

He studies the photos of the victims, the dates the attacks took place, then glances at the red markers on the map. Fidgeting nervously, he shrugs. 'Nothing's jumping out at me, ma'am.'

'No. Nor me,' she responds, her index finger tracing the various attack sites on the board.

Dinkel coughs. 'Ahem...'

'Something on your mind, Dinkel?'

'It's been some time since I've eaten. Would you mind if I slipped out to grab some food?' he asks hesitantly.

She barely registers his request, her attention still on the whiteboard. 'What? Oh no, go ahead. Take forty minutes. We have a long night ahead and you need to keep your strength up,' she acknowledges.

'Cheers, boss,' he replies, relief evident in his voice. Grabbing his jacket, he rushes to the door as Prisha continues to scrutinise the puzzle in front of her.

'If our guy is a taxi driver,' she whispers to herself, 'then he's landed some very lucrative fares exclusively on the east coast. But what about stealing underwear beforehand? That doesn't add up for a taxi driver. Their fares *are* truly random, whereas a delivery driver or courier would have a set route or area. But this guy zigzags into at least five different counties and some are small towns, only connected by B roads. Why wouldn't he stick to cities or large towns? This is not the mould of a typical serial rapist. And the dates are odd. There must be some logical sequence in there somewhere... but where?'

She settles back into the comfort of her desk chair, staring at the map on the board. As her mind races, she absentmindedly toys with the crumpled ball of paper, twirling it between her fingers, thinking, thinking, thinking.

'Come on... it's there, Prisha. Why can't you see it?'

33

With Dinkel contentedly munching on a steak and mushroom pie, Prisha's mind returns to the missing girl. She wanders over to him as flakes of pastry fall onto the grubby carpet.

'You're the receiver, Dinkel. Every single piece of information comes through you. Correct?'

'Ma'am,' he agrees.

'You have a list of all the people who work for the circus?'

'Yes.'

'And they all gave statements as to their whereabouts when Rosie went missing, and what they saw or didn't see last night?'

'Yes.'

'Then let's go through them... one by one. Systematically, yeah?' She turns to head back to her desk.

He beams. Christmas has come early. 'Spiffing idea, ma'am!'

She spins around and glares at him. 'Spiffing? Are you taking the piss? This isn't the nineteen-thirties and we're not Jeeves and Wooster. Although sometimes I feel like Jeeves. Come on, let's get on with it.'

Her comment flies right over the top of Dinkel's head as he hastily stuffs the last remnant of pie into his mouth and moves to the whiteboard.

He taps at the board. 'Right, the Rosie Miller case,' he states as he drags folders back and forth. 'Statement, statements,' he murmurs. 'Okay, got them. Where do you want to begin?'

'I don't care,' Prisha says turning to a clean page in a notebook and grabbing a pen.

'How about alphabetically with their last names?'

'Whatevs. Just get on with it.'

Prisha makes notes as Dinkel reads aloud the statements taken from the circus performers and staff. As he finishes Prisha huffs as she flicks back and forth through her notepad.

'It doesn't make it easier that some performers have multiple names. Take Kronsky the Clown for example. Not only does he perform as a clown but he's also an acrobat called The Great Alphonso, but his real name is Jakob Kowalski from Warsaw.' She throws her pen down in disgust. 'And you've checked all the names against the PNC?'

'Yes. I put them all into the database.'

'And?' she questions. Sometimes it's like pulling teeth with Dinkel.

'Nothing of any note. Traffic offences, shoplifting, public intoxication, trespass. Oh, and one guy who exposed himself outside a girl's school when he was fifteen. He was handed a caution. But that was twenty years ago.'

'What sort of girl's school?'

'Ma'am?'

'Primary, secondary?'

Dinkel winces signifying his misgivings. 'It didn't specify.'

'Christ, what's wrong with some officers when filing their reports?'

'Maybe it was knocking off time. You know what people are like.'

'What's the guy's name who exposed himself?'

'Slippery Pete, the contortionist, and Muscles Magoo when he plays a comic strong man.'

'Real name!'

Dinkel hurriedly taps at the whiteboard, 'Erm... Peter Murphy. Aged thirty-five. Originally from Dublin.'

Prisha frowns and flicks through the pages of her notebook one more time. 'Hang on a minute... where's the illusionist?' It's more of a thought bubble than a question.

'Illusionist?'

'Yes... His show was cancelled last night. He had a cold. I poked my head into the tent last night and he and his assistant were packing up. What *was* his name? Nostradamus, Nostradamus,' she mumbles as the cogs in her brain tick over. 'Samson Durat! But his assistant called him Kevin.'

Dinkel taps at the whiteboard. 'No record of a Samson Durat, ma'am. Or a Kevin, or an illusionist, or a Nostradamus for that matter.'

Prisha rises slowly, deep in contemplation. A harsh buzz throws her connective thoughts into disarray as she pulls her phone out and taps the answer button.

'DI Kumar, speaking?' she says as she notices Zac enter the incident room looking like he's been dragged through a hedge backwards.

'Inspector Kumar, it's Hannah Turnbull.'

For a split second, Prisha's mind is a spinning tombola until she remembers about the prowler and attempted rape. 'Ah, Hannah. How are you doing?'

'Okay. Considering,' she replies, her voice indicating otherwise.

'What can I do for you?' Prisha asks, shrinking inside, knowing she has bigger fish to fry, despite the seriousness of Hannah's assault.

'You said I should call you if I remembered anything else about the ...' she pauses. '...about the attack.'

Silence. Prisha waits a moment. 'Yes?' she encourages.

'I think I recall something. I'm not sure though. And I've heard about the missing girl, so I don't want to waste your time, but...'

Prisha grits her teeth, her paper-thin patience dissipating by the second. 'Yes?' She manages her one-word reply with grace, belying her true feelings.

'When he lifted his hand off my mouth...'

More silence.

Prisha's fingers curl into her palm. 'Yes. Go on?' A slight flinty edge to her voice.

'He... well, I think he had a tattoo on his wrist. His right wrist. On the inside.'

'Really? And can you remember what the tattoo looked like?'

'Yes... I think so.'

'Think so, or know so, Hannah?' Patience melts away. 'It's important!'

Tentative. Sniffles. 'I'm pretty certain.'

Good enough. 'Give me the details, Hannah.'

34

The diminutive pot-bellied wood-burner sputters defiantly in the dismal quiet, its hissing and crackling an accompaniment to Frank's deliberate prodding of the stubborn embers. He wrenches the damper wide open, feeding the fire's insatiable hunger for oxygen, yet the shed door hangs slightly askance, betraying its duty to keep the chill out. The relentless North Sea zephyr infiltrating his austere sanctuary ruthlessly steals away any comfort the tiny hearth might offer.

Relinquishing himself to the welcoming grip of his weathered armchair, he finds his gaze enslaved by the desolate expanse of earth of the allotment beyond the doorway. The barren soil mirrors the rawness of his emotions, weary and devoid of life. St Mary's melancholic bell resonates through the mist-shrouded twilight, inscribing the passage of time onto the damp, whispering wind.

His mind turns over, akin to the roiling fog. Grim spectres materialise in the gloaming, murmuring of sinister misdeeds and the inevitable consequences. The solitude of his space, once a refuge, now curdles around him like a prison cell. The bell tolls again, a mournful soundtrack to his contemplation.

Not again, Frank... not again.

The stove continues its futile battle against the cold as he ruminates, a lone figure under the weight of a relentless and inescapable foreboding.

'History repeats,' he mumbles to himself.

The latch to the allotment gate clicks interrupting his desolate brooding. Familiar voices grow louder, momentarily relieving his troubled mind.

'Ah! I thought I'd find you here, old man. I rang your mobile, and it went to voicemail.'

'Sorry, love. I saw the missed call, but I needed a bit of thinking time. How did you know I'd be here?'

Meera pulls a disappointed pout. 'I rang the station, and they said you weren't there. And you weren't at home either, so I knew there's only one place you'd be—your allotment. You were supposed to be getting some rest.'

'I had a sleep,' he replies, smiling warmly at his niece by Meera's side.

'Hmm... how long?' Meera questions with a hefty dose of disbelief.

'Oh, I don't know. An hour or two.'

'Here, Uncle Frank,' Emily says, passing him a large cardboard cup. 'It's cream of tomato. I know it's your favourite soup. And some crusty bread,' she adds, pulling a paper bag from her pocket.

'You're a little angel,' he says, taking the offerings.

Meera gazes around the tiny shed with an air of disapproval. 'Any news?' she enquires in a gentler manner.

'No. I'd have been contacted if there was.' He dips the bread into the soup and takes a bite. 'Hell, that's good.'

'And how long are you intending to be at the station tonight?'

'As long as it takes.'

Meera sighs. 'Frank, you need to look after yourself. Don't burn yourself out. You'll be no use to anyone, and with your dicky heart...'

'My heart's fine,' Frank mumbles as he munches solemnly, then takes a slurp of soup. 'I can sacrifice a few hours' sleep and the odd meal if it means finding her.'

'Do you think the missing girl is going to be all right, Uncle Frank?' Emily asks with wide-eyed innocence.

Despite his forty years of experience telling him otherwise, he puts on his warmest smile.

'Aye, I'm sure we'll find her alive and well. Probably a little adventure that went wrong. That's all.'

His words visibly brighten Emily. 'If anyone can find her, you can, Uncle Frank.'

If only that were true, he thinks.

He notices a pendant hanging around her neck. 'Did you buy that today?'

She drops her head and lifts the locket towards him, grinning. 'Yes. Got it from the little market near the bridge. Do you like it?'

He nods. 'It's very nice. But what the hell is it?' he says, staring at the three intertwining circles of silver.

'It's a Borromean Ring. All three rings are interconnected, but if you remove one, then the other two fall apart.'

Frank raises an eyebrow as his eyes flit to Meera, then back to Emily. 'I see,' he replies, his tone radiating doubt. 'And what's it supposed to signify?'

'It's about interconnectedness. Mind, body, and spirit. Remove any one of them and the others cease to exist. A lot of circus performers wear them as symbols of their expertise—dedication, practice, and understanding.'

Frank chuckles. 'Number three, cup of tea.'

Emily wrinkles her nose up. 'What?'

Meera rolls her eyes. 'Ignore your Uncle Frank. He's trying to be funny. Right, come on girl, you've fair worn me out. I'm ready to put my feet up.'

'Did you have a good time last night?' Frank asks as his wife and niece turn to leave.

Emily nods her head enthusiastically. 'Yes. It was supercool. We didn't spend too long at the circus as the illusionist's show was cancelled.'

'Oh, that's a shame,' Frank says, becoming distracted as he sips the soup. 'And why was it cancelled?'

She frowns. 'Not sure. We saw his van leaving, and the marquee where he was supposed to be performing had a cancelled sign outside. Anyway, the atmosphere along the promenade and up Church Street was fantastic. Can I come again next year?'

'You can come anytime you want, my love. And don't leave it a year. They hold the Goth festival twice a year. Next one will be in the Spring. And I promise... on your next visit I'll spend more time with you. It's just...'

She leans in and pecks him on the cheek. 'You don't have to explain, Uncle Frank. I know how important your job is. I'll say goodbye now in case I don't see you before I go tomorrow.'

'Okay, love. Take care.'

Meera also plants a kiss on his cheek. 'I'll plate you something up, Frank, and leave it in the fridge. You can reheat it in the microwave when you get home. Whatever time that may be. And remember, I'm heading to Birmingham with Emily tomorrow. So, if I don't see you, all my love.'

'Oh, aye. I forgot about that. How long are you going for?'

Meera pouts and turns to Emily. 'He never listens to a word I say.' Her eyes return to her husband. 'A week. I have five pre-made meals in the freezer, so don't be living off fish and chips and takeaways. Do you hear me?'

'Yes, love.'

'Good. I'll call you each night about seven... yes?' she says, turning on her heels.

'Aye. Seven. Bye Emily, bye Meera.'

'Bye, Uncle Frank.'

Frank's gaze is riveted on their diminishing forms as he grapples with an onslaught of emotions that threaten to consume him: the biting sting of guilt, the hollow echo of sadness, and a primal, underlying terror of what the future holds.

He finishes the soup, painfully rises to his feet, closes the damper on the fire, locks the shed, and lumbers down the allotment path towards the gate.

'Come on, Frank, old lad. Let's find the little lass for the sake of the family. Dead or alive, it's the not knowing which is the ever-present tormentor.'

35

Frank removes his coat, slings it onto the hatstand and takes a seat, barely glancing at the three officers, Prisha, Zac, and Dinkel, standing in front of his desk.

'Okay, updates. What have we got?'

Prisha throws a sideways glance at Zac. 'I received a call from Hannah Turnbull not long ago, Frank.'

His eyes narrow to a squint as he drums his fingers on the desk. 'Hannah Turnbull?'

'The woman who had a prowler on Thursday evening followed by the break-in and sexual assault on Friday night.'

The fog in his brain lifts, replaced by a spark of recognition. 'Hannah Turnbull,' he repeats, as if to cement the memory. 'Has she information relating to Rosie Miller?' he quizzes expectantly.

Prisha sways on her heels, shifting weight from one to the other. 'Well, no. But...'

Frank's jowls harden as he holds his hand up. 'For God's sake Prisha! I know it's a serious case, but I've told you we *must* prioritise. Our number one objective at the moment is finding Rosie Miller. We must focus our minds. Do I make myself clear?' he barks.

A quick glance ricochets between Zac and Dinkel as Prisha flinches, a red flush creeping up her neck. 'Yes, boss. I have been focussed. I just...'

'Zac, what about known child sex offenders in the area? Any developments?' he demands, cutting her off.

Zac squints. 'Ahem, Frank, I told you before,' he says, slightly embarrassed for his boss. 'We've checked them all out within a fifty-mile radius and they all have rock-solid alibis.'

'Then widen the bloody area!' Frank yells.

Zac shuffles awkwardly. 'Frank, do you know how many child sex offenders are in the country? Just last year alone, there were over a hundred-thousand sexual offences recorded against minors in England and Wales, never mind Scotland. You can double or treble that figure for offences which go unrecorded. Then there's the issue of people changing their name and disappearing off the radar. Not to mention foreign visitors and illegal migrants. We don't have the resources to...'

Frank flies from his seat and pushes his fists into the leather covering of his desk. 'I don't want bloody excuses, Zac!' he bellows, spittle flying from his lips. 'Widen the bloody area! Little girls don't simply vanish into thin air. Someone, somewhere, knows what's happened to her and it's our duty to find the bastard. And when we do, so help me God!' He pauses, exhausted by his outburst, then sags down into his chair, shoulders slumped.

An uneasy silence gains momentum as the officers stare at the bald spot on Frank's crown.

'Go on then. What are you waiting for?' he mumbles.

The three chastised officers reconvene in the incident room.

Zac rubs at his neck. 'I wondered how long before the old Frank returned.'

'You mean the grumpy, dour Yorkshireman?' Prisha comments, thoroughly dejected.

'Yes. He hasn't been this foul-tempered since Meera put him on the salad and tofu diet during summer. I'm worried about him. I fear he's losing the plot, and his memory.'

'He's tired and emotional. That's all.'

She returns to her desk and slumps in her chair. Too many entangled strands of information are fighting over themselves in her head. All she wants to do is put on her running gear, head to the open moors and take off. Staring out of the window her gaze falls upon the twinkling streetlamps illuminating the promenade and harbour. The town is already swollen with people who intend to enjoy the last night of the Goth Weekend. Thinking of Adam, she wonders whether he's at her flat yet. The random reflection brings her unexpected comfort, as she tries to envisage the life as a farmer's wife. Early mornings, enchanting scenery, atmospheric seclusion... at the moment it sounds like bliss. No scum to deal with. No weird, warped creeps. The roughness of the ball of paper she twirls in her hand snaps her back to reality. She stares at it, then unfolds the creases and studies the words.

'Racing tips,' she mutters, recognising Frank's handwriting.

Turns the sheet over and deciphers the neatly typed information. Place names and dates.

Patterns...

As a thread of clarity is born, she meanders towards the whiteboard, drawn by an inner compass guiding her. Brings up the Hannah Turnbull case notes, and the map pinpointing where the attacks occurred. Eyes fall back onto the crumpled piece of paper. Stares in disbelief as a shard of excitement erupts and quickly builds deep in the pit of her stomach.

'Oh, you little beauty. Dinkel!' she screams. 'Scan this and add it to the Hannah Turnbull file,' she says, handing over the sheet.

'What is it?' he says, mildly perplexed as he peers at the racing tips.

'Turn it over.'

His eyes widen to the size of saucers. 'Oh, I see.'

She grabs her coat and hastens to the door. 'I'll be back in twenty,' she declares.

'Where are you going?'

Beaming at him, she replies, 'Isn't it obvious?'

He shakes his head. 'Erm… no.'

'To get a tennis racket and pay a visit to a craft supply shop.'

'Right… of course,' he replies, gawping in befuddlement as she races from the office.

36

Nervous, Prisha pulls Zac to one side and lowers her voice. 'I need your support.'

His eyes narrow. 'You always have my support,' he replies as he takes a sip of strong black coffee.

Prisha throws a furtive peek around the office. 'You're Frank's closest confidant. If you back me, he'll listen to what I have to say.'

'You're making no sense, woman.'

She leans in closer. 'The thing is, I believe you're right... he's not thinking straight, which is understandable, considering what happened to his own daughter, but...'

Zac's chest heaves. 'But what, Prisha? What exactly is it you want me to do?'

'I think I have a breakthrough in the rape case.'

'Okay.'

'And I have a theory about the disappearance of Rosie Miller.'

'Which is?'

'I'll explain it to you, Frank, and Dinkel in a moment. It's tenuous.' She pauses and peers through into Frank's office where he sits in his usual position... staring out of the window, telephone clamped to his ear. 'If Frank goes off his nut, I want you to step in.'

Their eyes lock. Zac's mouth forms a circle. 'Aye, okay. I have your back, but only if what you're saying makes sense. Understand?'

She offers him a weak smile. 'Thanks, Zac. It will.'

Frank's voice booms out as he emerges from his office, ashen faced. 'Heads up, everyone. I've just got off the blower with forensics, and it's not good news. The yellow scrunchie is Rosie Miller's. Hair samples match. Which means it looks like Ginger Jack is our man. Unfortunately, as you're all aware, the bugger's dead. So now, we must focus our minds on what he did with Rosie. Was he working alone? Does he have an accomplice? How did he get rid of her body, and where? I want a team of cadaver dogs up at the site of the circus as soon as. And we need to bring in Abby Henderson for questioning. She could be up to her armpits in this.'

'Wish me luck,' Prisha murmurs to Zac. She straightens and takes a step forward. 'I'm sorry, Frank, but I don't buy it.' Her voice wavers with trepidation.

Clearly outraged by her statement, he marches towards her. 'You don't buy what, exactly?' he snarls.

'Ginger Jack. He's not our man... sir.'

His face reddens. 'I'd love to believe you. I really would. I liked the old guy a lot, but the facts are staring us in the face; he admitted to arranging to meet Rosie after the show. A crucial piece of evidence, the scrunchie, was found in his caravan. He had the opportunity, and I'm assuming the motive was sexual. I don't want to believe it was Jack, any more than you do, but everything points towards him. So, what *exactly* don't you buy, inspector?'

Prisha swallows hard. Frank is no longer the man she has grown extremely fond of. She'd heard the stories around the station when she first arrived. How he was an ogre, a ruthless taskmaster. But since her transfer, she's barely witnessed it. Yes, he can be grouchy, moody, taciturn, but never intimidating. But now she sees what others have encountered over the years: the angry, imposing man of authority.

She can't back down now, as much as she'd like to. Taking a deep breath, she begins.

'The scrunchie is too convenient, Frank. Why would Jack stuff it down the plug hole? He could have thrown it into the fire, and it would never have been found. And think about it logically; he's an eighty-year-old man, with a wooden leg, and not in the greatest of health. How would he be able to spirit away a young girl amidst hundreds, if not thousands, of people milling around the circus without being noticed? We've already searched the site twice and had the sniffer dogs there. It's not him, Frank. Whoever took Rosie planted the scrunchie in Ginger Jack's caravan to divert attention from themself or implicate Jack for their own ulterior motives.'

The human volcano is in danger of erupting. 'Solid police work is based on evidence, motive, means, and opportunity, *not* on flights of fancy,' he growls in his deep baritone.

Prisha nervously glances at Zac, who steps up. 'Hear her out, Frank,' he states in his soft Scottish brogue.

The intervention surprises Frank. A moment's hesitation followed by a sigh. 'Go on then?'

'Dinkel; whiteboard, map,' Prisha orders calmly.

'Ma'am.'

'First of all, Frank, the Hannah Turnball case,' she continues, pulling out a chair for Frank to sit on.

Frank drops his head and rubs at his face, agitated, then slumps into the seat. 'Give me bloody strength. Does nobody listen to me anymore,' he grumbles.

'Frank,' Zac whispers.

Prisha stands at the whiteboard and points at the map.

'Great Yarmouth, twenty-first of April this year, Amy Anderson, forty-four-year-old divorcee. Raped in her bedroom and left terrified. She describes her attacker as a tall, thin man with a peculiar odour about him. He climbed in through a very small window. Departed via the back door.'

She taps at the next note on the board.

'Norwich, May fifth, Kylie Mowbray, thirty-five years old. She awoke to find a man with a knife standing over her. She screamed, and the intruder fled via the back door. Same description; tall and thin.

'May thirtieth, Skegness, Prudence Walker, twenty-eight years old. She woke with a knife to her throat; the intruder pulled her pants down and fled when he noticed she was on her period.

'The next woman, twenty-eight-year-old Alice Carmody, raped at night in her home in Lincoln on July fifth.

'Goole, three weeks later, Joanne Scalby, raped in her bedroom.'

Frank and Zac exchange concerned glances as Prisha continues the itinerary of assaults.

'Is this the guy who some of the press labelled the Stick Man?' Zac queries.

'I believe so,' she replies, racing through the litany of sexual assaults. 'And last but by no means least, Hannah Turnbull from two nights ago here in Whitby. The rapist was unsuccessful, as Hannah was on her period.' With her finger, she traces a red line between all the towns and cities.

'Great Yarmouth, Norwich, Skegness, Lincoln, Goole, Beverly, York, Bridlington and finally, Whitby. As you can see, the attacks zigzag up the east coast.'

Frank rubs thoughtfully at his chin. 'So, we're looking at a serial rapist who mainly operates on the east coast, occasionally venturing inland.'

'A courier?' Zac adds.

'Or a taxi driver?' Frank says.

'I've considered those occupations and discounted them. Look at the linear progression up the coast, coinciding with the dates of the attack.'

'DNA, fingerprints?' Frank queries.

'No. Nothing apart from a set of footprints from two of the assaults. But all the victim's descriptions match. And three of the nine describe a smell, similar to bees' wax.

'And are you certain it's the same guy?' Frank asks.

'As certain as I can be. Five of the victims reported they had underwear stolen from their washing line a day or two before.'

Frank sighs. 'Okay, you've marked out his predatory itinerary. But who is this bugger and how are we going to catch him? From the dates and locations listed, he's expanding his catchment area.'

'That's correct. It's a matter of joining the dots.' She drags another note onto the board. It's a scanned piece of crumpled paper. In spidery writing is scrawled the words:

Black Meg 3:15 Kempton

Yosemite Sam 3:40 Aintree

Frank pulls his head back. 'Hang on, I recognise that. It's the horse tips Ginger Jack gave me yesterday morning.'

Zac grins. 'Did you back them?'

'Aye, I bloody did. Fiver each way.'

'Last of the big spenders. How'd you go... have a win?'

'Did I hell. They both had three bloody legs.'

'Two more than Ginger Jack.'

'Very amusing. So why have you got that on the board?' Frank asks.

Prisha grins. 'Because—' she double taps the image, and it flips over, revealing the other side of the scan. '—it's the Henderson Circus dates for the last six months.'

Frank rises and takes a closer inspection. 'Great Yarmouth, Norwich, Skegness, Lincoln, Goole, Beverley,' he mumbles as he checks the circus dates against the dates of the assaults.

'I'm convinced the rapist is part of Henderson's Circus,' Prisha states triumphantly.

Frank rubs at his chin, deep in thought. 'There are over fifty people associated with that circus. Exclude the females and we have about thirty men to investigate.'

'I've narrowed it down further,' Prisha says with a bounce in her step.

'Go on,' Frank prompts.

'The mode of entry for many of the attacks was via a very narrow opening; pet flaps, tiny bathroom windows, glass louvres removed in some cases. Which means our attacker is very supple, agile, flexible. We know he's over six feet, so I'd rule out acrobats. They're typically a lot shorter.' She pauses in dramatic fashion and picks up a prop from her desk and holds it aloft.

'Unless I'm very much mistaken, I'd say that's a tennis racket,' Zac comments wryly.

'You'll go far, sergeant.' She points at the racket head. 'The length of the racket head is approximately twenty-eight centimetres.'

Frank grimaces. 'What's that in old money?'

'Eleven inches, sir,' Dinkel states as though he's discovered a fifth dimension.

'On Saturday night, I observed a tall skinny man miraculously slip through the head of a tennis racket. He had the ability to dislocate his joints. I believe the serial rapist is the contortionist! He also has a caution from years ago; exposing himself outside a girls' school. His real name is Peter Murphy, originally from Dublin, but he also has a few stage names.' She fixes Frank with a pointed stare. 'And the phone call I received from Hannah earlier...' she pauses, milking the situation.

'Yes?' Frank quizzes.

'She says her attacker had a tattoo on his inner right wrist; three circles intertwined.'

'Well, I'll be,' he gasps. 'Borromean Rings.'

Zac winces. 'What are Borromean Rings?'

'According to my niece, they're a symbol representing interconnectedness; mind, body, spirit. She says a lot of performers identify with them.'

'And lastly,' Prisha states as she pulls a small glass jar from her pocket and hands it around. 'Take a sniff.'

Frank unscrews the lid and sticks his bulbous hooter over it. 'Hmm... a waxy perfume,' he notes as he reads the label. 'Snazaroo Clown White. Okay, I've heard enough. Zac, Prisha, get a search, and arrest warrant, then head up to the circus and bring Peter Murphy in. Turn his caravan inside out. I dare say you're more than likely to find a lot of women's underwear in there. Oh, and keep it low key.

Those circus performers are a tight-knit bunch. We don't want them knowing who we are after lest they tip him off.'

'One more thing, boss. About the Rosie Miller investigation,' Prisha says. 'Me and Dinkel went through all the statements from the performers with a fine-toothed comb, and there's a missing link. The illusionist and his assistant didn't give a statement.'

'That figures. Meera and Emily spotted the illusionist's van leaving last evening well before the ruckus kicked off.'

All four officers exchange glances.

Prisha shudders. 'I saw the illusionist in the marquee. He was packing away his props which included...'

'A trunk large enough for an adult to lie down in,' Frank murmurs, finishing Prisha's sentence.

Zac places his coffee cup on a table. 'The perfect spot to hide a child. I'm guessing those trunks would be sturdy and heavily lined. Almost soundproof.'

'What did this guy look like, Prisha?' Frank asks.

'Middle-aged, short, stocky with a goatee beard and handlebar moustache. Had a stinking head cold, hence the cancellation of the show. He didn't appear suspicious or in a rush to depart, though. He was more weary, exhausted, than anything. Plus, he had a female assistant. It's unusual for a male, female duo to be involved in child abduction.'

Frank grimaces. 'Unusual, but not unheard of. Do the names Ian Brady and Myra Hindley, or Fred and Rose West mean anything to you?'

'Yes, Frank,' she murmurs contritely. 'I was merely thinking aloud.'

'And have you forgotten about our own case not so long ago, when two girls were kidnapped? We're pretty sure it was a joint effort between Tiffany Butler and Mark Bridges.'

Okay, don't bloody rub it in. 'No, I haven't forgotten. Point taken, boss.'

'Right, Dinkel, you can also head up to the circus and pay a visit to Abby Henderson and acquire the details of the illusionist and his assistant; home address and mobile numbers. Get the specifics of his van; numberplate, make, model, colour, and any distinguishing features. Then relay the description of the vehicle to dispatch.'

'Yes, sir!' Dinkel replies.

'Let's bring the illusionist and his assistant in for questioning and have forensics go over all their equipment. It could be totally innocent. But then again...' he tapers off, dark thoughts once again clouding his thinking. He heads back to his office but hesitates in the doorway. 'And well done, Prisha, Dinkel,' he calls back without turning.

37

Zac and Prisha part company with Dinkel, who heads towards the encampment of caravans in search of Abby Henderson.

'Hell fire,' Prisha complains, gazing upon the hordes of people as she and Zac dodge and weave their way through the crowds that have flocked to the circus.

The sound of carnival music and the hustle and bustle of impromptu performers creates a constant discordant hum. There's an air of merriment and intoxicating wonder as random clowns perform to small gatherings of young children accompanied by parents. They deftly blow balloons and turn them into sausage dogs, swords, a bouquet of flowers, and various hats and crowns, then hand them to the mesmerised youngsters. Performers breathing fire, acrobats tumbling then standing on each other's shoulders to create pyramids. A magician takes a spectator's wristwatch, puts it into a white drawstring bag, places it on the ground, then smashes it with a wooden mallet, only for the watch to miraculously appear on the wrist of the magician. As enthralling as the entertainment is, the two detectives only have eyes for one man—the contortionist, Peter Murphy.

'I suggest we split up. We can cover more ground that way,' Prisha suggests.

'Aye, good idea. If you see him, don't tackle him alone. Wait until I'm with you.'

'Okay. I'll radio you if I eyeball him.'

As they go their separate ways, Prisha curses. 'Damn it! There's too much activity.' She refocuses and reimagines the contortionist she saw yesterday evening when she was with Adam. Her stomach aches from hunger. The aroma from a hot dog stand, the nutty whiff of roasting chestnuts, and a sugary scent from the candy floss stall does little to help. She pulls a bottle of water from her pocket, unscrews the cap and takes a hearty glug, while her eyes swivel from left to right, picking out individuals then discounting them; clowns, stilt-walkers, jugglers, a mime artist, fire-eaters, living statues and the incessant sinister echo of a distant Wurlitzer.

After sauntering around a few marquees, she succumbs to her appetite and buys a hot dog, lathered with fried onions, and squirts a healthy daub of mustard over it.

Taking a large bite, she flicks at her radio fastened to the inside of her coat.

'Any luck?' she mumbles through a mouthful of food.

'Not so far. We could quiz Abby Henderson and ask if, and where, Murphy's performing tonight?'

'No. As Frank said, they're a tight-knit crew. We don't know what Abby Henderson's relationship is with him. The last thing we want to do is alert him to our presence, otherwise he'll melt away.'

'Fair enough. What are you eating?' Zac asks.

'Hot dog. Have you noticed how good food tastes when you're starving?' she says, her eyes trailing a group of ageing Goths.

He laughs. 'Thanks for that. My belly thinks my throat's been cut.'

Twenty feet away, she spots a gathering but cannot see what or who is entertaining them.

'Keep in touch.' She finishes the rest of her hot dog and wipes her hands on a serviette and dabs at her mouth. Ambling over to the crowd, she deftly snakes her way into the midst of it. Standing on a small platform is a lanky man, his face masked by a heavy white daub. A long shabby coat, down to his knees, hangs from his skeletal frame. He's performing a mime, which for reasons Prisha cannot fathom, the onlookers find amusing. Attempting to lift a pantomime-style barbell from the ground, he struggles in grotesque fashion, eliciting laughter from his audience. Suddenly, an exaggerated idea appears to strike him as he holds one bony finger aloft and gazes quizzically heavenwards. From his pocket, he withdraws a can labelled spinach written in flamboyant cartoon-style letters. With a dramatic mime, he consumes the invisible contents, tipping it down his lean throat to a drumroll blaring from a speaker.

An anticipatory silence spreads through the onlookers as the seemingly ordinary coat bulges at the seams. It splits and falls away from his frame, revealing an outrageously inflated muscle suit. Flexing his monstrous biceps, the mime artist bends and effortlessly hoists the barbell high into the air, sending a wave of cheerful applause and laughter rippling through the captivated crowd.

Prisha studies him.

'Three intertwining circles,' she murmurs, focussing on his wrist. She surreptitiously taps at her radio as the mime artist performs ostentatious bows, grinning maniacally. 'Zac, I've spotted him,' she whispers, gazing around for a landmark. 'He's between the hall of mirrors tent and the insane asylum marquee. Hurry!' Her attention returns to the mime artist at exactly the moment his gaze locks onto her. He squints, the white clown paint beneath his eyes wrinkling in response.

That's what Hannah Turnbull described... wrinkly bags beneath his eyes.

A shudder of fear reverberates through Prisha as his unyielding gaze deepens, his grimacing smile evaporates, supplanted by a sinister frown. As the audience thins, the performer gestures them back, beckoning them to huddle tightly together. Stooping, he pulls something from an open suitcase laid on the ground. He welcomes the gathering audience with a benevolent grin, only to let his head loll sidelong, bringing his ear down to his shoulder as he smirks at Prisha. A tug at some hidden item culminates in a deafening bang, followed by a pall of dense white smoke. Shrieks of terror intertwine with the thrilling ripple of excitement and a smattering of expletives. Prisha is jostled in the ensuing rush as the crowd bolts away from the stage. By the time her equilibrium is restored, and the haze begins its slow retreat, the mime artist has disappeared.

'Damn it!' she yells, her voice lost in the overwhelming noise of laughter, and mild panic.

Rapidly scanning the area, she picks him up as he ducks inside a tent. She breaks into a trot, shouting at people.

'Excuse me! Coming through! Move! Out of my way!'

Some of the crowd heed her warnings, others are oblivious to it. She slows as she nears the entrance to the tent.

'Oh, just bleeding wonderful.' She stabs at the button on her police radio. 'Zac, our suspect is on the run. He's onto me.'

'Where is he?'

'He's entered Bedlam.'

A moment's pause, followed by a crackle. 'I thought you were off the medication. What the hell is Bedlam?'

'It's a sideshow marquee, with actors. Bedlam is an insane asylum from the Victorian era. He's wearing some sort of inflatable costume.'

'Where is Bedlam? I'm halfway around the big top.'

'It's opposite the hotdog stand. Follow your nose.'

'Right, I'll be there in a mo. Wait for me.'

Prisha has no intention of waiting for anyone. Like a bloodhound, she makes a beeline to the entrance. A woman dressed as a nineteenth century nurse steps forward.

'That'll be ten pounds please, love. Tokens only,' she states.

Prisha flashes her warrant card. 'Police, CID.'

'Oh, aye? That's the third time tonight I've heard that.'

Prisha opens her puffer jacket and points at the police radio, and handcuffs attached to her trouser belt.

'Obstructing the police is an arrestable offence!' she grizzles.

'Okay! Don't get your knickers in a twist. I was only checking,' the woman spits.

The verbal rebuke barely skewers Prisha's consciousness as she plunges headfirst through the entrance of the marquee, bypassing the warning: "Do Not Hit the Actors". Within, gloom prevails, pierced intermittently by the shadowy glow of artificial candles illuminating a path underfoot. Emanating from hidden speakers, a ghoulish symphony of screams, shrieks and disquieting groans underscores a haunting soundtrack of shackles dragging across cold stone floors, with the occasional clank of an iron door slamming shut. With cautious urgency, Prisha navigates the convoluted pathway, its twists and turns conspiring to create a disorienting labyrinth. The canvas walls play host to painstakingly rendered images of Victorian insanity, a grim montage of ward life: rows of cast iron beds, the stark solitude of confinement cells, a rotating chair poised for torture, and the cruel bite of manacles and leather straps.

Compounding the dread, a dank, rotting stench permeates the air, a fetid miasma from a foul-smelling, bygone age.

'And people actually pay a tenner for this,' Prisha mutters, quickening her stride through the oppressive murkiness. She rounds a corner and is confronted by an apparition in a dirty, stained nightdress, her hair an unkempt bramble, arms bearing cruel scars resembling savage claw marks.

With arms outstretched, she pleads a mournful refrain, 'Help me find my baby? My baby.'

'Clear the path, police!' Prisha commands, not the least bit impressed with the harrowing, contrived spectacle.

In a dim enclave, a disturbing scene unfolds: an elderly man, his face contorted in anguish, simultaneously scratches at his face and strikes his back with fervour, using a birch. His mind appears entranced by the words of scripture.

'And I will execute great vengeance upon them with furious rebukes; and they shall know that I am the LORD, when I shall lay my vengeance upon them. And I will make them eat the flesh of their sons and their daughters, and every one shall eat the flesh of his friend in the siege and...'

'Daft old twat,' Prisha murmurs as she stealthily passes him by.

Nearing the entrance to what she discerns as a fake prison door, a crude plastic imitation of wrought iron bars, her eyes fall upon the chilling words above it:

SOLITARY CONFINEMENT.

Inside, four bedraggled customers appear extremely unsettled. A woman clings to her partner in palpable distress, while eerie figures emulating the deranged emerge from murky corners, groaning and weaving erratically, dressed in old-fashioned, full-length nightgowns daubed in brown stains, resembling excrement.

Prisha marches up to the patrons. 'Have any of you seen a tall, thin man come through here?' she barks.

A rotund man of indiscriminate age, adorned in a stereotypical Sherlock Holmes costume, glances nervously at her while he adjusts his deerstalker.

'Are you part, part, part of the act?' he stammers, apprehensive.

'No! I'm not part of the bloody act. I'm the police!'

'Oh, sorry. What was he wearing?'

'He was wearing an inflatable muscle suit.'

Sherlock narrows his gaze. 'You sure you're with the police?' he replies, his eyes filling with dread as half a dozen wretches caterwauling and, in various states of disfigurement, inch forwards. From her peripheral vision,

Prisha spots something incongruous to the setting. A small neon sign.

EMERGENCY EXIT

Pushing past the canvas flap, she emerges into the gloomy night and the hundreds of people enjoying the festivities.

'Damn it!' she curses, her eyes darting around wildly.

The Goths have invaded en masse once again, donning extravagant garb and ostentatious displays, but tonight, they vie with witches, werewolves, and a myriad of creatures pulled straight from the depths of myth and folklore. For some reason, Prisha's gaze ventures to the North Sea on her left. A swift pulse of fear shoots through her veins as she witnesses a rapidly advancing curtain of sea fog heaving towards the shoreline. The madhouse behind her never stirred fear within, but inexplicably, this wholly natural spectacle curdles her blood. The billowing mist also hypnotises an accumulating group of spectators, as it swallows both piers and tumbles over itself into the harbour. Sounds of awe and disbelief reach a crescendo as the crowd's focus shifts from the circus to the frightful display of Mother Nature in all her menacing subterfuge.

She gulps anxiously and spins around.

Spots him skulking away through the caravans of the circus crew.

Taps at her radio.

'Zac, suspect is making his way through the caravans east of the circus heading towards North Promenade. I'm going to track him along the Cleveland Way footpath. He's probably hoping to make it into the main part of town where he can disappear into a narrow street or alleyway.'

'Bloody hell! I'm still searching for the hot dog stand...oh, wait, I can see it. Okay, I'll make my way to North Promenade and follow behind.'

Prisha pushes through the crowd and breaks into a trot until she hits the walking track, which is less crowded. The jog morphs into a sprint. If she can get ahead of the suspect, then if he turns to bolt, he'll run straight into Zac. She zigzags up the paths near the pavilion and rests at the mini-golf course as she scans the crowds of people, trying to pick out a tall, thin man dressed in a rubber muscle suit. She's expecting him to come from the west, but he doesn't materialise. Dispirited, she flops down on a bench and sucks in the icy night air.

A thunderous explosion overhead gives her, and the rest of the hordes, an almighty fright. Immediately she thinks it's a maroon flare once used by the lifeboat services to summon their crew, but that practice has long since been replaced by electronic means. She concludes it was probably a dickhead with an illegal firework. Gazing at the blue smoke that drifts languidly in the sky above Whalebone Arch, her eyes return to the horizontal. Squinting, she rises from the bench.

'That's him,' she murmurs as she picks out the mysterious Stick Man, who is walking at a rapid pace towards the arch. Setting off at a sprint, she relays the information to Zac as her quarry breaks into a jog.

'Zac, Stick Man nearing Whalebone Arch,' she pants.

'Aye, okay. I can see it in the distance.'

Trailing behind, she follows him to the twisting stone steps that lead down onto Khyber Pass. The fog has completely obliterated the eastern part of town and engulfed the river as spindly fingers of mist creep up the side of the harbour walls on the western side and leak onto the streets. She expects that when he reaches the bottom of the steps, he'll hang a left and head towards the West Pier and the dense cloud, but inexplicably, he doesn't... he turns right.

Taps at her radio mic.

'Zac, he's turned right and is heading up Khyber Pass.'

'Okay, I'll head down East Terrace and try to cut him off.'

Panting hard, she increases her pace, keeping him in sight. Shortening the gap between him, she passes the row of seats known as Bram Stoker's Bench, which on a clear day offers magnificent views of Whitby Abbey, but not tonight.

Zac's voice fizzes through the radio. 'Christ, I'm about spent. I need to get to the gym more often. I'm halfway down East Crescent. Is he still on Khyber Pass?'

'Yes. I'm about fifty metres behind him. I don't think he's spotted me. If he keeps going straight on, we'll have him. Approach nonchalantly, as if you're a tourist.'

'Will do.'

'Hang on... shite!'

'Prisha, what is it?' Zac cries in concern.

'He's veered left onto Cliff Street.'

'Okay. Don't go down Cliff Street by yourself. It's narrow, with no exit routes, and you're blocked in on either side by the backs of houses. It's a real bottleneck.'

'I'll be fine. I'm a big girl.'

'You won't be fine! I mean it; wait for me,' he yells.

Despite his warning, Prisha is in no mood to let her suspect slip through the net. She pulls out her torch and slows to a walking pace as she turns left and enters the steep decline of Cliff Street. Zac was right, she thinks, as the backs of houses corral her into a narrow passageway, only wide enough for a single vehicle and with no footpaths. Venturing further down the street, she feels a cold chill wash over her. She flicks the button on the flashlight, which offers a weak, intermittent glow and she instantly knows why—she forgot to replace the batteries. With no streetlights and the half-moon long ago vanquished, she can barely see more than five feet in front of her. She passes a forecourt, set back from the street, where a solitary car is parked, and a few lonely rubbish bins sit alongside.

Then...

She sees it...

... and slows.

Halts.

Rigid.

Stalking menacingly, in the distance, the fog slithers up the street like a ghostly tsunami in slow motion.

'Oh, fuck,' she murmurs.

Having completely lost sight of the Stick Man, uncertainty creeps into her thoughts.

Should I retreat and wait for Zac?

Squinting into the gloom, she instinctively recoils.

Her heart doesn't flutter, it seizes as time itself hovers in suspense.

Swallowing becomes an insurmountable task as a distinct figure emerges from the vaporous shadows.

'Oh, sweet mercy...' she whispers as the fog now licks at her feet, then claws up her legs.

The abomination advances.

Coarse fur shrouds the body.

Snarling teeth.

Bipedal, and yet... its head, that of a rabid hound!

38

Fumbling for her radio, her hands shake so violently she drops it. It clatters to the ground and skids out of sight.

As the fortune teller's warning reverberates around her head, the encroaching fog renders her immobile with fear.

The dreadful creature stops a few feet in front of her, raises its arms and... removes its head.

'You all right, love?' the man asks in a broad Yorkshire accent. 'You look like you've seen a ghost,' he says, breaking into a throaty laugh.

'You stupid bastard!' she screams at him. 'You scared me half to bloody death!'

He takes a step back, contrite. 'Cool it, sweetheart. Calm down. It is the Goth Weekend. You must have seen plenty of werewolves tonight. They're two-a-penny.'

Placing her hands on her knees, she bends and breathes hard. 'Did anyone pass you?' she questions, regaining her composure, somewhat.

'Nah, not on this street. I'm a bit lost, what with the fog and all. And too many pints of Timothy Taylor's,' he adds as an afterthought. 'Does this road lead up to West Cliff and the circus?'

She nods. 'Yeah, keep going and turn right at the top.'

He replaces his canine head and offers a mumbled apology before striding off.

She spots her radio and retrieves it.

'Zac, where are you?'

'About a minute away.'

'A warning; you'll pass a werewolf in a moment. I nearly had a heart attack. I'm about a quarter of the way down Cliff Street.'

'You were supposed to wait! There's no telling you, is there?' he grumbles.

Leaning up against the side of a tall house, exhausted, she wipes moisture from her face, realising her suspect has evaded her.

'Ouch! What the hell is that?' she cries as a sudden sharp pain stabs at her breastbone. She rubs at the site of the discomfort, her fingers feeling a small lump. 'Oh, it's the stupid bloody amulet from the scam artist.'

Just as she considers ripping the chain from her neck, a noise interrupts her. She turns and stares up the street.

'Zac, is that you?' she calls, straining to see anything through the swirling mist.

No reply.

Taps at the radio.

'Zac, where are you now? State your position?'

A muffled voice, distorted by interference. Crackles of static... then nothing.

She inches forward as the same sound visits her again.

A squishy noise, accompanied by a metallic creak, grows louder.

'What the hell is it?' she whispers, barely daring to breathe.

Abruptly, from the depths of obscurity, an unmistakable form takes shape.

'Oh, fuck me!'

It gathers pace, hurtling towards her.

Pivoting on her heels, she races down the narrow lane searching for an escape route... anything, anywhere!

As Zac had forewarned, the street is a cruel canyon of brick, trapped by towering walls, offering no chance of deliverance.

The sinister harmony of squealing rubber and groaning metal intensifies.

The car is nearly upon her.

With terrified eyes darting wildly from side to side, scouring for a flicker of hope, her weary legs thrust her further into the embrace of the impenetrable sea fret.

She spots it. A tenuous lifeline.

With a sudden burst of speed, she leaps onto the drainpipe and desperately shimmies up it as fast as she can.

The vehicle careers into the side of the house, sending a salvo of sparks into the air, then clatters into the ancient, cast iron drainpipe, shattering the bottom half.

The impact is violent, but she clings on as the car, now an agent of chaos, ricochets across the street and bounces off another wall, then carries on down the lane like a demented pinball. From her precarious vantage point, Prisha gazes down as the pale figure of the Stick Man sprints past. The fog gobbles the car up, but an almighty bang telegraphs its immediate cessation as it thumps into an immovable object, out of sight.

Stick Man fades into the mist as Prisha drops to the cold, unyielding road, and collapses in a heap.

'Oh, take me home,' she whimpers, thinking of Adam.

Upon the ominous silence, footsteps encroach.

'Prisha!' Zac calls out.

'And here comes the cavalry,' she murmurs, sitting upright. 'Down here!'

He emerges from the gloom and pulls her to her feet.

'What happened?'

'The prick must have broken into a car, released the handbrake, then pushed it down the hill. Nearly wiped me out. Bastard! He went jogging past a moment ago. I tell you what; I'm fit, but this guy is like the fucking Terminator. He never stops.'

Zac grins. 'He'll be stopping in a minute.'

'Why?'

'I radioed ahead. There's a patrol car and two officers waiting for him at the end of the street. There's no escape. And if he comes back up here, then we'll nab him.'

Prisha cocks her head to one side. 'Be careful what you wish for.'

Stick Man's fake muscular form takes shape as he retraces his steps. Seeing Zac and Prisha advance, he holds his hands up in the air.

'Okay. Game over. You win,' he states, blowing hard in a heavy Irish accent.

'Lay down on the ground with your hands behind your back,' Prisha screams, yanking at her handcuffs. Stick Man obliges and offers no resistance.

'Peter Murphy, I am arresting you on suspicion of breaking and entering and sexual assault. You do not have to say anything. But it may harm your defence if you do not mention when questioned something which you later rely on in court. Anything you do say may be given in evidence.' With overenthusiastic zeal, she violently snaps the handcuffs around his wrists.

Zac hauls him to his feet. 'Okay, Muscles Magoo, we have a nice cold cell waiting for you.' He turns to Prisha, grinning. 'I'm a poet and didn't even know it.'

39

The two uniformed officers navigate the prisoner into the back of the patrol car. With his muscle suit now deflated, Pete Murphy has the appearance of a grossly overweight individual with rolls of sagging flesh.

'We'll take him back to the station and hand him over to the duty sergeant, ma'am.'

'Thanks, constable,' Prisha replies. 'I'm certainly not going to question him tonight. He can wait until tomorrow.'

'Not a problem, ma'am. Can we offer you two a lift anywhere?'

Zac shakes his head. 'No, we're good, thanks.'

The uniformed officers climb into the car, start the engine, and carefully engage in a three-point turn.

'Fancy a drink?' Zac enquires.

She smiles. 'I think our work is done for the night, Sergeant Stoker, so why not? I could murder a few G and Ts.'

'Where do you want to go?' he asks as they amble off together.

'Anywhere that serves alcohol. The nearer the better.'

'What about over the bridge on the east side? It's always a good vibe over there.'

'Sounds good. I'm ravenous,' she adds as her stomach grumbles.

'Me too. How about a couple of drinks followed by a fish and chip supper?'

'Now you're talking.'

The patrol car gives a quick toot-toot as it passes them.

'How do you think he'll play it in the interview tomorrow?'

Prisha rolls her neck to ease the tension of the day. 'Depends on his solicitor. He'll probably go down the no comment route. But we have plenty on him whatever games he wants to play. He's one sick fucker who won't be getting off the hook. I'll make sure of that.'

'Aye, another nutter off the streets,' Zac adds with a certain amount of satisfaction as the brake lights of the patrol car distract Prisha's attention.

She freezes. 'What's going on? Why have they stopped?'

They stare in disbelief as a head and torso emerge from the back window of the police car. Long spindly arms stretch out and grip the roof before effortlessly hoisting the full frame of the Stick Man from the vehicle. He drops deftly to the road, takes a quick look around, then breaks into a sprint as the officer from the front passenger seat emerges from the vehicle and gives chase.

'Oh, give me strength!' Prisha exclaims as she breaks into a jog and rushes towards the car with Zac hot on her heels.

'Will this night never end?' Zac groans. 'My feet are bloody aching.'

Prisha shoots a downward glance at his footwear. 'You should know better, Zac,' she shouts. 'When going to arrest a suspect, always wear running shoes, not boots! Get on the radio and alert all officers that Stick Man is on the run again!' She pokes her head through the passenger-side window and glares at the driver. 'What the bloody hell happened? Why was the back window down?'

'Sorry ma'am. He said he felt like he was going to throw up, then began dry retching. I didn't want to spend the next two hours cleaning vomit off the seats.'

Prisha looks in the back and spots the pair of discarded handcuffs, then slaps her forehead with her palm.

'Oh, Prisha, you stupid bloody idiot! He's a contortionist! Of course he can get out of handcuffs. That's why he asked for the window to be wound down.'

'I'm sorry, ma'am,' the constable repeats, cringing with embarrassment.

'It's not your fault. I should have been in the back, handcuffed to him.'

As Zac barks orders into the police radio, Prisha sets off in pursuit. She soon catches up to the older uniformed officer who gave chase.

'I'm too old for this bloody game,' he wheezes.

As she passes him by, she gasps, 'Keep following. I have a feeling he'll head for the bridge and into the crowds on Church Street for cover.'

He barely has the breath to mumble, 'Yes, ma'am.'

Prisha spots the assailant sprinting over the narrow swing bridge spanning the river. He has a good head start on her and his pace is not letting up. She drinks in mouthfuls of heavy air as the mist rests like a leaden overcoat above. The crowds are still in abundance, but most are well lubricated, and shouting for their assistance would be of little value. In fact, it could produce the opposite effect. As Prisha stamps onto the bridge, Stick Man leaves it behind as he weaves through the crowd. He halts and momentarily stops to look around; left, right, or straight ahead? He bears left.

I knew it. He's heading towards Church Street where it will be chock-a-block.

She musters her last reserves of energy, thinking of the lives he has destroyed. Her pace accelerates as she zigzags past inebriated, party-happy Goths, and older men and women reliving their youth. She tracks him like a sniffer dog as his head bobs up and down like a malfunctioning Jack-in-the-box. He sneaks through the old town square before he veers right onto Church Street.

Does this man never give up?

Prisha is expecting him to enter a pub and melt into the background, then find a back exit to evade capture. But he doesn't. He continues up the same laneway, which ultimately leads to the 199 Steps, St Mary's Church, and Whitby Abbey.

Please, lord, not again!

Nearing the infamous steps, he again pauses and evaluates his options as Prisha bears down on him. Throughout her chase, not one uniformed officer has materialised. She's alone, again. It should faze her, but doesn't. He's nothing more than an opportunistic bully. And this time she knows he's unarmed.

Having reflected, he heads left up Henrietta Street.

Prisha almost laughs with glee, then remembers the recently built accessway that leads off the pier onto the shores of Saltwick Bay to the east, and the beach of Colliers Hope to the west. She presses at her radio for the umpteenth time.

'Zac! Zac!' she screeches.

'Yeah, what?' his weary voice returns.

'Is the tide in or out?'

'In. High tide. Why?'

'Because Stick Man is heading up Henrietta Street. He's trapped. No way onto the beach if the tide's in. His only option is to turn around or proceed to East Pier. We have him. Gather the troops and I'll wait for you. This time, he won't escape. Not over my dead body!'

40

It takes a further ten minutes for a patrol car to navigate the narrow, densely packed laneway full of merry revellers, and arrive at the end of Henrietta Street where Prisha is impatiently waiting.

Zac and three uniformed officers, including PC Pembroke, alight from the vehicle.

'It would have been quicker on foot,' Zac grumbles, pulling the collar up on his jacket.

Prisha, chilled to the bone, ambles forward. 'I saw him jog onto the pier, so we have him. He's got nowhere left to go.' She peers at the two uniformed officers from earlier. 'You two stay here on the pathway. Zac, Kylie, you come with me.'

'Hang on,' Zac says, realising the inherent danger in the pursuit. 'I think we need a few minutes to work through this.'

'Work through what?'

'It's dark, foggy, and freezing conditions and we're walking out onto a pier to apprehend a dangerous man. The first part of the stone pier doesn't have handrails. Then we have to navigate a narrow bridge, single file over the sea, to reach the two-storey wooden pier. He could come at us out of the blue at any time.'

'What do you suggest?' Prisha replies, frustrated by his apprehension.

'He can't go anywhere. Why don't we wait until first light and the fog has cleared?'

'No chance. This guy is a master of extricating himself from tricky situations. We must apprehend him now. I don't want him trying to swim for it.'

'Swim for it! Are you mad? Only a fool would get into the water in these conditions.'

Prisha stares him down. 'Pete Murphy could be looking at a minimum of fifteen years in a twelve by six-foot room. He's desperate, and desperate men do desperate things.'

Zac huffs. 'Okay. Have it your way. But can we at least have a safety talk first?'

'Go on.'

'We walk single file. One of us shines a torch to the right, one to the left, and the front person, I suggest you, shine your torch dead ahead. And we keep to the centre of the pier at all times. No veering off towards the edge. One person at a time to cross the footbridge. There's not much of a swell, but nevertheless, if one of us falls into the drink, I don't anticipate a happy ending. And lastly, if he won't come quietly, then we retreat, and wait for back-up and for the conditions to improve.'

Prisha rubs her tongue over her front teeth. 'Very well,' she agrees turning to one of the patrol officers. 'Constable, hand me your flashlight. My batteries are dead.'

The advancement is painfully slow. Step by careful step, they methodically inch along the rugged stone barricade that paves the way to the dominating lighthouse, adjacent to the footbridge. The three torches cast a fan-shaped beam that, in theory, should light up their path, but the insatiable fog devours the light, yielding only meagre visibility. Leading the team, Prisha strains to discern the way forward, her sight restricted to a few feet ahead.

'So much for a couple of cleansing ales and a fish and chip supper,' Zac reflects morosely.

'Did you have to mention food? I'd almost forgotten about my hunger,' Prisha says. 'Eyes down, there's a slight lip on one of the stones.'

'I have a bad feeling about this,' Kylie whispers, as an unseen wave casually slaps against the pier wall, creating a dark and rhythmic thud — like a drumbeat struck by the hand of the devil.

'In twenty-four-hours you'll be able to laugh about it,' Zac comments, trying to lift the mood.

'Twenty-four hours!' Kylie cries in alarm. 'I'm hoping I'll be able to laugh about it in fifteen minutes.'

Prisha raises her arm. 'Okay, we're nearing the lighthouse. Kylie, you stay here whilst me and Zac go around it. Zac, you take the left side. I'll go right.'

Timidly, they circumnavigate the structure until they come full circle.

'All clear,' Zac states. 'Now for the fun part. Crossing the footbridge.'

'How high is it above the water?' Kylie asks, a tremor in her voice.

'Oh, not high. Twenty feet... when the tide is in. Add another twelve to fifteen feet when the tide's out.'

'Christ,' she hisses. 'I wish I'd never asked. I'm not sure I can do this.'

Prisha touches her on the arm. 'Okay. You stay this side. If he makes a bolt for it and gets past me and Zac, you can tackle him as he comes off the bridge.'

'I think I'll come with you,' Kylie says, her fear of being left alone far greater than traversing the overhead conduit from one hellish place to another.

'That's the spirit. Safety in numbers,' Prisha says, her warm smile barely visible. 'I'll go first, then Kylie.'

With one hand gripping the torch, and the other holding the cold, wet handrail, she steps onto the bridge and shuffles along. The fog, having descended a little closer to the water, has left only her head exposed above the white blanket.

Zac chuckles. 'Fuck me! There's a sight to behold. A walking head.'

'It's quite safe. It's not slippery underfoot,' Prisha calls out. She makes it to the other side and releases her breath. 'Piece of piss,' she shouts. 'Come on, Kylie. You can do it.'

Kylie quivers like a jelly on a plate as she steps onto the walkway. She makes it to the middle with little fuss. Another resounding smack of water hits the pier, sending a sharp crack into the air. Already overwhelmed with anxiety, the unexpected noise gives her a start and she drops her flashlight. Her hands reach out to catch it. Falling to her knees, she juggles with the torch, but it slips from her grasp, hits the deck, and rolls over the edge. No one hears it enter the dark abyss below. A panic attack devours her. It's so intense she loses her voice.

'Kylie, where are you?' Prisha cries out. She receives no reply.

'Kylie?' Zac's voice booms.

'Fuck it! Zac, did she fall over the side?'

'How the fuck would I know? One minute I could see the top of her head, next second, nothing.'

'Where the hell is she? Surely she would have screamed? I'm coming back.'

'No. Stay where you are. I'm coming over. Kylie!'

A pitiful, 'I'm here,' punctures the air.

'Hold tight. I'll be with you in a jiffy.'

'I am holding tight. I've lost my torch.'

Zac finds her laid prone on the boards, desperately clutching onto an upright of the handrail.

'Come on, stand up. You're safe now.'

'I can't.'

'Are you injured?'

'No. I'm rigid with fear.'

'Okay, take a moment. Long, slow breaths. Nice and deep.'

Jittery and shaking uncontrollably, she grips Zac's arm with both hands and pushes herself up. Gripping his waist, they inch forward, all the while Zac issuing forth encouragement.

'You're doing fine. Nearly there. Just another few metres to go.'

They exit the footbridge and Kylie drops to her haunches, breathing hard.

'Why did I ever join the police?' she mumbles.

'It's the most fun you can have with your clothes on,' Zac says with a chuckle. 'You wouldn't experience excitement like this sitting in a solicitor's office, week in week out.'

'I'd gladly swap jobs right now.'

'Are you ready?' Prisha enquires gently.

Kylie rises. 'Yeah. I'm good to go. No torch, mind.'

'Just keep in the middle.'

Their progress is sluggish, and the eery hush of the night does nothing to lift the sense of dread. The only sound is the slosh of water far below, and the regular electronic warning bleep coming from the old harbour watch house at the end of East Pier.

'That siren doesn't fill me full of confidence,' Zac notes. 'Do you remember the last time we were on this pier, Prisha?'

'Yes. We pulled Jack Turner's upside-down body out of the water at the end of the pier with a rope tied around his legs. Don't remind me.'

'And do you remember Frank's little warning ditty his father taught him when he was a lad?'

'No. That little nugget of information must have been discarded while I was being chased up dale and down dale by two psychopathic Russians.'

'If Whalebone Arch thy cannot see, then turn around, I'm warning thee.'

Prisha half laughs. 'Ah, yes. That's right. Frank's dad referred to the first part of the pier as Jawbone Walk. Hold up. I can make out the outline of the watch house,' she whispers as she squints at the small circular structure perched on wooden stilts at the end of the pier.

Zac moves to the front. 'I'll go down the ladder first. Shine your light on me,' he states nervously, edging towards the rusting metal ladders that descend to the concrete base of the pier, a few feet above sea-level. The clank of his boots against the rungs adds to the theatre.

With all three officers safely on the reassuring feel of concrete, Zac, and Prisha scan the pier with their flashlights.

'Peter Murphy!' Prisha calls out. 'Make yourself known. Show yourself and raise your hands in the air.' Nothing. 'Come on, Mr Murphy! You're doing yourself no favours. Now please show yourself. There's nowhere left for you to run.'

'He's a tenacious fucker, isn't he?' Zac states with zero admiration.

Kylie pulls her Taser out. 'Let's get it over and done with,' she says in a hushed tone. 'I want this night to end.'

They advance along the pier a good twenty feet until Zac's torch highlights a shadowy figure standing against a wooden piling a few feet ahead.

'Peter Murphy, stop playing silly buggers. You've put yourself and us in danger with this ridiculous escapade. Now come out, hands above you head, then kneel down.'

He doesn't reply.

They advance towards him, still on guard.

Stick Man grins as a faint hissing sound filters through the mist.

'I'll wipe that bloody smirk from your face if you're not careful,' Zac growls.

'Been nice knowing you,' Stick Man says, with a half laugh as he leapfrogs the guard rail and perches on the edge of the concrete.

'Don't be bloody stupid!' Prisha screams.

He salutes them as he jumps into the sea.

41

Monday 2nd November – 2:06 am

A florid crimson hue has replaced the usual grey demeanour on Superintendent Anne Banks' face. Her hair is still grey. And her ability to project a miasma of greyness has not diminished one iota. However, the fact her cheeks are reddening at an exponential rate, as Prisha recounts the night's activities, points to one thing; her head is in danger of spontaneously exploding, which would not be a pretty sight.

Her hands, scrunched into fists, press hard into the top of the desk as she leans on them as if trying to take her weight. To say she is a ball of incandescent fury is an understatement. Standing in front of her, lined up like ducks in a row, are Frank, Prisha, and Zac. The eventful night has spilled over into the early hours of Monday morning. Another factor that has not filled her with joy.

As Prisha concludes her account, Anne shakes her head for the umpteenth time and closes her eyes, before rising to her full diminutive height, her hands still firmly clenched.

She begins, slowly, measured, but all present know it's a dam wall soon to be breached.

'This must be one of the most cack-handed, reckless, foolhardy, dangerous, and incompetent explanations of attempting to apprehend a suspect I have ever heard. And I've been around a long time.'

'That's a little unfair, ma'am,' Frank interjects. 'I can think of far worse.' Her glare is so severe Frank errs on the side of caution and buttons his lips.

Fixing Prisha with a fierce, penetrating stare, the first chink in the dam wall appears.

'Not only did you put your own life in danger but also that of your fellow officers; DS Stoker, and PC Pembroke, who, may I remind you, is barely out of probation. Talking of which, you, yourself are still under probation. How long since I promoted you to the position of inspector?'

'About eleven months ago, ma'am,' Prisha murmurs, head bowed.

'Hmm... eleven months. MY GOD! WHAT WERE YOU THINKING!' And there goes the dam wall. 'You venture out in pitch darkness, swamped by a heavy sea fog, onto a pier that is notoriously dangerous, parts of which don't even have safety rails! Then to cap it all, your suspect swan dives into the harbour.' She rubs at her face and engages in another bout of headshaking.

'It was more of a jump, ma'am,' Prisha mutters.

'Don't answer back! And how the hell did he escape from the patrol car after your initial arrest?'

'He's a contortionist, ma'am. I'm not sure how he did it, but we've all seen the magic shows.'

'A contortionist. And do we have a definitive ID on this man yet?'

Frank lifts his head. 'Peter Murphy. Thirty-five years old from Dublin. Although, he has several aliases, Anne.'

'Such as?'

Frank immediately regrets mentioning the pseudonyms. 'Ahem... Muscles Magoo is his mime act, I believe; and he's known as Slippery Pete when performing his contortionist routine.'

'And some tabloids have labelled the suspected rapist as the Stick Man,' Zac adds, also realising he may have imparted too much information.

Anne emits a false mocking laugh. 'Sweet mercy! Have I been transported into the pages of the latest Beano annual? Stick Man, Muscles Magoo, Slippery Pete!' she yells in disbelief. 'He gave you lot the runaround, didn't he? Although, I dare say we'll be fishing his body out of the water tomorrow.'

'I'm not so sure, ma'am,' Prisha murmurs. 'He was wearing an inflatable rubber muscle suit. Just before he jumped, I recall hearing a hissing sound. Apparently, compressed air cannisters are hidden in the suit. By holding a button down, air is released to inflate the costume. Ahem... that's according to one of the circus performers I interviewed, ma'am. It would provide buoyancy and also protection against the cold.'

She closes her eyes and sighs as a moment's silence ensues. 'What's happening, Frank?' she mutters, world-weary and tired of her job.

He's puzzled by the question. 'Ma'am?'

'Whitby? It's a small fishing village, Frank. A tourist hub for day-trippers and holidaymakers. In the last year it's become the new Wild West... Dodge City! We no longer pursue our suspects, arrest them, press charges, and put them in front of a jury. Oh no, not in Whitby. We simply kill them!'

'We don't know our suspect is dead, Anne.'

'No, we don't. And at this very moment, six hardy volunteers, all with partners and family, are in the lifeboat searching for him, not to mention the coastguard coordination, and the search and rescue teams combing the shorelines. That's many people putting their lives in danger.' Pausing, she closes her eyes and swivels her head from side to side. 'Oh lord, once the media get hold of this...' she trails off into a private nightmare. 'I can see the headlines now—Slippery Pete Gives Bumbling Cops the Slip.'

Frank winces. 'Not enough alliteration for a tabloid headline, ma'am. What about—Muscles Magoo Makes Mockery of Manhunt!'

An imperceptible smirk glides across the faces of Zac and Prisha, but not so Anne Banks.

If looks could kill, Frank Finnegan would be zipped up in a body bag by now. For about the ten-thousandth time, he makes a mental note *not* to be humorous in front of the superintendent. It's like teaching a pig how to whistle: it wastes your time and annoys the pig.

She unclenches her fists, folds her arms, and sways her head in disbelief. Her withering gaze meets Prisha's eyes.

'Something amusing you, Inspector Kumar?'

'No, ma'am.'

She eyeballs Frank. 'This is an omnishambles of epic proportions. No doubt I'll have the deputy chief constable in my ear later today, if not the chief constable himself. The only saving grace is I was spending the night at a friend's house in Sandsend. If I'd been dragged from my bed in York, then I can assure you—heads would have rolled tonight.' She focuses back on Prisha. 'What is it with you, inspector?'

'Ma'am?'

'You're headstrong, reckless, dangerous. You take unnecessary risks. It's like you're always in a rush. Why?'

Prisha thinks of the fortune teller's words before replying. 'I'm... I'm not sure why, ma'am. I do what I think is the right thing at the time. Dangerous criminals need to be caught. We're not dealing with a shoplifter. This man *rapes* women. He ruins lives. Everything has a knock-on effect, like a ripple in a pond. Once someone commits a serious crime and gets away with it, they become emboldened. I suppose...' she pauses, then drops the subject.

Superintendent Banks is curious. 'Did something happen in your past to make you act this way?'

Prisha sways slightly, redistributing her weight. 'I...' She catches herself in time and clams up.

'Continue,' Anne prompts.

'I was going to say, the reason I take chances, ma'am, is because I *am* in a hurry. A hurry to stop bad people from shattering good people's lives. It only takes minutes for those monsters to commit their deeds. And I need to be as impulsive as them... to stop them.'

A deathly quiet pervades the room. Finally, Superintendent Banks breaks the silence.

'You let emotion overrule logical thought, Prisha. Not a good trait for a police officer. At the very least, you should have consulted with your immediate superior, Frank, to take his advice.' Her eyes drift onto Zac. 'And you, DS Stoker. I'm severely disappointed in you. You're also a senior officer with over ten years' service. You should have known better. What if something should have happened to that young PC, or any of you? You have two young boys and a wife. Did you not stop for a second to think about them?'

'Well... in the heat of the moment...'

'Excuse me, ma'am,' Prisha interrupts, 'I am the senior officer, and it was my call and my call alone. Zac is faultless in this. He advised me against the action we took.'

Anne puffs out her cheeks, then sighs. 'But went along with you anyway, eh? Butch Cassidy and the Sundance Kid. Back to the Wild West. Right, get out of my sight, the both of you. I need twenty-four hours to calm down before I decide if there'll be a formal disciplinary hearing.'

They troop from the Super's tiny office like chastised adolescents. Finally, Anne collapses into her chair, tired, prematurely aged.

Frank clears his throat. 'I think you're being a little unfair, Anne,' he offers gently.

'Really? That's what you always say, Frank. The problem is, you treat your juniors like they're your children. You get too close to them. There's no demarcation of authority. You need to be aloof and come down on them like a ton of bricks when they err.'

Frank bristles. 'Maybe I do treat them like my children. That's my way. They need encouragement and nurturing, not lectures and threats of retribution. Yes, when they get it wrong, I give them a slap on the wrist, then a gentle word to the wise. We're not living in the Victorian age where a misdemeanour should be countered with thirty lashes of the belt. It's been a long time since you were at the coalface, Anne. You leapfrogged from inspector to superintendent. You never had a team to run. As Prisha explained, in a dynamic situation, officers must make split-second decisions. Sometimes they get it wrong, but mostly they get it right.'

'Nonsense. There must be a chain of command. Prisha should have taken your counsel. She didn't. In my book, that's called a lack of respect. She's our very own Calamity Jane, is that one. I rue the day I authorised her transfer request.'

'In my book, that's called independence. Trusting gut instinct, your own judgement.'

'And putting many lives in danger at the same time. You need to have her on a tighter leash, Frank.'

'What's the point of owning a bloodhound if you keep it on a leash? Prisha is one of the best detectives I've ever come across. She may be wilful, and bull-headed. But she's not up against kids nicking sweets from the lolly jar. She deals with murderers, assassins, rapists, and hardened, psychotic, drug addled criminals who have no qualms about putting a bullet or a blade into you. We need more people like her. She should be applauded, not humiliated like a naughty schoolgirl. And by the way, this weekend was supposed to be her first weekend off in over four weeks, because of staffing levels. She puts in more hours than anyone I know. I never hear you carp on about that.'

'Don't overstep the mark, Frank.' They eyeball one another for a moment until the Super turns to other matters. 'And what about the missing girl, Rosie Miller?'

Frank bares his teeth and tilts his head. 'There is a new line of enquiry we are currently investigating.'

She glances up at him. 'You're not speaking to the media now, Frank. Cut the crap and give me the facts.'

'The illusionist and his assistant departed the circus on Saturday night about eight-thirty. His show was cancelled because of ill health.'

'Names?'

'Kevin and Cecilia Parker; husband and wife. Although his stage name is...'

'I'm not interested in his bloody stage name!' she bellows. 'And you suspect the girl may have been taken by these two?'

'It's a possibility and needs checking out.'

'And have you located this illusionist and his wife?'

He squirms. 'Not yet. The manager of the circus, Abby Henderson, the granddaughter of Ginger Jack…'

'Strike me down,' she murmurs.

'… has a contact number for the illusionist's agent. But it's a landline and when we call, it goes to voicemail. It is, or was, the weekend, so I'm guessing the agent won't be back behind his desk until later today.'

'And what about the vehicle?'

'We don't have a numberplate, but we know it's a white Ford Transit with decals… vinyl wrap on the side, depicting an upside-down top hat with rabbits peering out, and a magic wand, and I believe, ahem, a few brightly coloured stars above it. Oh, and also his stage name in large letters—Samson Durat, the World's Greatest Illusionist.'

'Tell me I'm dreaming,' Anne mutters. 'Surely, I'll wake soon and realise this whole thing has been an outlandish nightmare. I did have cheese and crackers for supper.'

'The Roads Policing Unit are aware of the vehicle, Anne. And we've also posted to social media asking for the public's help. But as yet, there's no sign of the van.'

'Don't tell me—it's vanished into thin air?'

'Very droll, ma'am. Apparently, their next performance is in Newcastle on Friday night. So, it's possible they've returned home and parked the van in a garage or lock-up.'

She rises wearily and taps at the desk with her finger. 'I'd laugh if this whole thing wasn't so tragic. A suspected rapist who has twice evaded capture. A little girl who may have been abducted by the world's greatest illusionist. The suspicious death of an old man at the circus.'

'They say bad things come in threes,' Frank says, trying to lift the overbearing atmosphere.

'I'm not in the mood for your quips! You've lost control, Frank. A handful of street performers have run you ragged, and you have lost the respect of your officers.' She stands and grabs her coat. 'I'll be back in the office later today. When I return, I hope for your and your team's sake there's been some positive developments.' She pulls at the door, then stops and turns. 'Time is not on your side, Frank, in more ways than one.'

The door snaps shut.

Frank reflects, wistfully. 'No, time is not on my side. The damned clock is always ticking. As it also ticks for you... ma'am.'

42

Prisha pads from the bathroom into the living room, dabbing at her hair with a damp towel. Another warm shower has temporarily washed away the invisible dirt and filth which falls like space dust when dealing with the seedier side of life. Three rapid bleeps from the microwave indicate her food is ready. Tightening her dressing gown, she flops onto the settee as Adam bustles from the kitchen carrying a tray containing a bowl, spoon, and a mug of steaming tea.

'Here we go,' he says, beaming at Prisha as he hands her the tray.

'You didn't have to stay up.'

'Not a problem. Anyway, I didn't. I watched the football on the TV, then fell asleep on the couch.'

'You could have got into my bed,' she says, shovelling a large spoonful of chilli con carne and rice into her mouth.

'I didn't think it appropriate without you being here.'

She grins. 'You're quite old school in some ways, aren't you?'

He sits down beside her. 'What do you mean?'

She takes a moment to swallow her food. 'Oh, you know, you're very courteous, respectful. In the short time we've been together, I haven't once heard you bag anyone or grizzle about life. You always have a smile on your face and look for the best in every situation. How did you become like that?'

He shrugs. 'Not sure. Can't say I noticed. I am who I am. I suppose growing up on a farm made me appreciate things. You witness the seasons come and go in all their forms. You accept life and death, and I guess I realise we're only here for a short time. The world existed for billions of years before me, and it will exist for billions of years once I'm gone.'

Prisha takes another mouthful of chilli as she contemplates.

Could this be the man? Calm, serene. Not well educated in the traditional sense, yet he possesses a deep knowledge accumulated from experience, by observing the natural world, and human nature. I need a rock in my life. Okay... time out. Slow down, girl, slow down.

'This chilli is delicious. Who taught you how to cook?'

'I learnt the basics from my mother. The rest is self-learnt. It's not rocket science, is it? Practice and taking an interest. I love cooking. I do nothing fancy, mind. The TV and internet are full of cooking shows and videos. Type what you want into a search engine, and you'll get thousands of hits.'

A few minutes pass as Prisha attacks her late-night supper with gusto.

Finally, she asks, 'You haven't asked me about my day?'

'You'll tell me about it when you're good and ready. Anyway, you haven't asked me about mine?'

She sniggers. 'Okay. How was your day?'

'Ploughing fields from six in the morning until seven at night.'

'Do you enjoy it?'

He gazes at the floor. 'I love it. I'm in my own world. I listen to podcasts, music, or sometimes think about nothing, or everything. It's smelly, dirty, noisy, but it is real. Go on then, how was your day?'

She grimaces as she finishes off her food. 'I'd rather not talk about it.'

'Thought so.' He grabs the tray and rises. 'I'm more than happy to sleep down here on the couch.'

Prisha reaches out and touches his arm. 'No. I'd like you to come to bed. We have unfinished business,' she says with a wicked glint in her eye.

Adam raises his eyebrows. 'An offer no sane man could refuse. You go up and I'll give the kitchen a quick tidy, then jump in the shower and I'll see you up there.'

As he towels himself dry, he gazes at his reflection in the mirror. Well-defined muscles glisten with damp. He parts his short-cropped hair into a side parting, a recent, new styling after Prisha mentioned her hair preference for men. There is no hubris, nor obsession, simply a young man who exercises, eats healthily, and has a holistic outlook on life. But his ardour *is* on fire.

Gently stalking up the stairs, he enters the dimly lit bedroom with his blood pumping.

His heart sinks as he stares at the prostrate body tucked up in bed, fast asleep.

Shrugs.

Then smiles.

Plants a kiss on her forehead.

'Poor bugger,' he whispers. 'Give me a farmer's life any day of the week.'

Turning the bedside lamp off, he climbs under fresh crisp linen and pulls the duvet over himself.

He turns, snuggles in and drapes one arm around Prisha's waist.

'Night, love,' he murmurs, kissing the nape of her neck.

He receives no verbal response, but her bottom momentarily wriggles back into him.

43

Nestled in a lay-by near Great Ayton, PC Jackson unscrews the top from his thermos flask for a last sip of lukewarm, sugar-laden tea, while the rain drums a rhythmic, calming lullaby on his windscreen. His shift, a quiet one on the roads, is within its fading hour and headquarters still a casual forty-minute drive away.

Throughout the long night, he's traced a tangled path from quaint hotels to rowdy pubs, sprawling caravan parks to cosy lodges; places that beckon to weary travellers and hardy holidaymakers alike. Yet, through it all, the haunting case of a missing girl, Rosie Miller, has chained itself to the edges of his consciousness, writhing like a relentless nightmare. His own daughter is scarcely a year Rosie's senior, making him all too aware of the raw, searing torment her family must be enduring.

Two more stops still separate him from the end of his shift, but the absurdity of his mission is dawning on him.

Hunting after a white Ford Transit, emblazoned with top hats and rabbits, hoping to find an illusionist and his wife, who may, or may not, be involved in child abduction is stretching the bow to breaking point. If the couple are implicated, they will not parade around in public with such an incongruous vehicle. He's sure of it.

Navigating the patrol car across the A172, he follows the short road that leads to the Bridgetree Hotel. The ivy-covered stone building is lit up as the patrol car approaches. Pulling into the car park to perform a quick reconnaissance, he hits the brakes.

His heart pounds, as if trying to escape the confines of its bony cage.

Blinking rapidly, he clicks at his radio.

Cloaked in the icy grip of North Yorkshire's pre-dawn, Kevin Parker, more famously known as the renowned illusionist Samson Durat, encounters an enigma he's unable to solve despite his professional prowess. With his wife, Cecilia, at his side, he throws her a fretful glance, meeting her equally concerned gaze. Two stern-faced uniformed officers have harried them from the warmth of their hotel bed into the windswept car park, accompanied by bone-chilling rain.

'If you could explain what we've supposed to have done, then maybe we can help you out?' Cecilia's voice shivers through the darkness, her fingers curling protectively over the collar of her long overcoat.

Kevin, his speech thick and muffled with a head cold, mutters resentfully through a crumpled tissue.

'This is outrageous! I demand to know what we are being accused of?'

'You haven't been accused of anything... yet, sir. We suspect your vehicle may have been caught up in some suspicious activity. That's all we're at liberty to disclose at the moment,' PC Jackson's words barely cutting through the rain's persistent murmur.

Parker grimaces. 'Suspicious activity? Poppycock! My van has been parked here since late Saturday night. Just ask any of the hotel staff.'

Jackson's silence weighs heavily in the gloom as they reach the vehicle. The moment of reckoning beckons.

'Van keys, Mr Parker,' PC Jackson commands, his voice as taut as wire stretched to breaking point. The illusionist fumbles for his keys before gingerly placing them onto Jackson's outstretched palm.

'Bloody ridiculous! I'll be lodging a formal complaint.' Parker scowls, hardened by bewilderment and the bitter cold. 'We're not involved in anything sketchy.'

'Kevin, be quiet and play along. We have nothing to hide,' Cecilia mutters wearily.

PC Jackson remains mute, opting to press the fob instead. The van flashes its acknowledgement as he hauls open the rear doors; a Pandora's box of prop mysteries lay within its steel belly. The centrepiece: a coffin-shaped trunk synonymous with the illusionist's performances.

Softly treading into the van's cargo hold, Jackson's gloved fingers graze the lid of the box. It refuses to budge.

Turning towards Parker, he queries, 'It's locked; where's the key?'

'It doesn't have a bloody key!' Parker huffs. 'Feel underneath. There's a button.'

Jackson's hand roams beneath the box, his fingertips locate the cold metal protuberance. Pressing it, he hears a distinct automatic click as a latch is released. He throws a fearful glance at the couple, and his colleague.

Taking a single, shallow breath, he offers up a silent prayer.

Please God, don't let Rosie Miller's lifeless body be inside.

Razor-sharp tension slices the air as he hauls open the lid; an electronic cartoon creak, intended for dramatic effect, adds an unwelcome grisly twist to proceedings. In the frosty dawn, it appears despair and hope are but two sides of the same unfaithful coin.

His eyelids flutter like the wings of a trapped moth.

'*Shit.*'

The whispered profanity lingers like an impostor in the musty atmosphere of the van.

44

The smell wafts up the stairs, an invisible but ambrosial presence. Uninvited, but welcomed, it creeps into the bedroom and tickles Prisha's nostrils, the delectable aroma powerful enough to revive her from a deep, contented sleep. Her eyes flicker open and for a few seconds, she has to think about where she is.

'Mmm... bacon, toast, and freshly brewed coffee, if I'm not mistaken,' she murmurs, her mouth instantly salivating. Lifting herself up on her elbows, she gazes around the room, thinks of breakfast, then Adam, then, like a wrecking ball to the head, remembers Rosie Miller. Anxious, she reaches for her phone, but there are no missed calls or messages. Pondering whether that's good, bad, or simply a case of status quo, she leaps out of bed, grabs her clothes, and dashes downstairs to the bathroom.

Cocooned in a shower cap, protecting her locks from the rushing water, a hint of a smile graces her face as the soft, faraway notes of a radio melody dance their way in from the living room.

'I could get used to this,' she half laughs.

Quickly finishing her morning routine, she slips into her clothes. With a spritz of deodorant, a dab of perfume, and her hair expertly corralled into a ponytail, she makes her way towards the enticing aromas drifting from the kitchen.

'Aha! And here's the latecomer,' Adam declares with a toothy grin as he glances at the clock on the wall.

'It's seven-fifteen,' Prisha states, a tad annoyed at the inference.

'I've normally got half a day in by now. Right, sit yourself down and I'll plate you up,' he replies as he places a steaming hot brew of fresh black coffee on the table. 'How do you like your eggs? Scrambled, fried, or poached?'

'Erm...' she doesn't finish her sentence as her mobile rings. 'Morning, Frank. What? Really? Okay. I'll be there in ten minutes.' Hanging up, she stares into space.

'Bad news?' Adam asks with a downcast anticipatory gaze.

'What? No... well, yes and no. Sorry, I have to go.'

'What about breakfast?'

She glances at the sizzling bacon in the pan. 'Slap some rashers between two slices of bread and I'll eat it on the way,' she explains, pouring her coffee into a travel mug.

Without questioning, Adam follows her commands, carefully sliding the bacon sandwich between a couple of paper napkins. 'Any news about the little girl?' He knows he shouldn't ask.

'Not really. A van seen leaving the circus on Saturday night has been located.'

'And?'

Prisha grabs the sandwich from his hand. 'No sign of Rosie inside. Forensics are on their way now.'

Adam frowns. 'Why, if there's no sign of her?'

Prisha narrows her eyes for a split second until she reminds herself he's a farmer, not a police officer, or even a crime aficionado. 'They can do tests to see if she *was* in the van at any stage.' Leaning in, she kisses him on the lips. 'Sorry to dash.' As she hurries into the living room, she almost calls out—love you! But stops herself in time. 'I'll speak later!' is her replacement farewell.

Adam watches her scurry out of the front door. 'Who in their right mind would choose policing as a profession?'

45

In the antiseptic chill of the mortuary, Frank squints at Doctor Whipple, the luminous autopsy lights glinting off his ebony skin. The immense pathologist looms like a haunting spectre over the cadaver; the unfortunate octogenarian, Ginger Jack, resting on the table. His head sports a sizable wound, raw, unforgiving, a stark contrast against the pallor of the wafer-thin skin.

Doctor Whipple adjusts his mask, the lines of habitual seriousness still noticeable on his face.

'Detective Chief Inspector Finnegan,' he starts in grandiloquent English. 'The significant divergence in the cranium, that is, the extensive gash on the scalp, could be perceived as the primary causative factor of demise. The centrally pivoted gash exhibited on the skull adheres meticulously to the perimeter and characteristics of a metallic object, much akin to the combustible heating apparatus found in the decedent's trans-locatable habitation of a domestic nature.'

Frank's face creases as he scratches at the back of his head. 'You mean the wood burner in his caravan?'

Whipple stares unblinking. 'Affirmative.'

'Ahem, so, the blow to the noggin killed him?'

An uncomfortable pause ensues as Whipple towers over Frank. 'An oversimplified interpretation, as usual, inspector,' Whipple huffs. 'There are other factors at play.' With surgical precision, he begins, 'This man was drowning in Venusian afflictions. Hyperchromic anaemia, severe hepatic steatosis, advanced cirrhosis of the liver, reflective of sustained alcohol abuse. His bronchial tubes, sullied with carcinogens, suggest chronic nicotine usage.'

'Aye, he liked a tipple and a smoke, so he did. But don't we all,' Frank says with a thoughtful sigh.

Doctor Whipple glares disapprovingly before continuing, 'Amongst other things, there is pronounced atherosclerosis, possible stenocardia, myocardial infarction, or ischemic heart disease.'

'Hold your galloping majors, steno-what-dia?' Frank's interruption cuts through Whipple's tidal wave of medical jargon.

'Stenocardia, also known as angina pectoris, is a medical term for chest pain or discomfort.'

'He had a dicky heart?'

'Coronary disease, inspector! Coronary heart disease!' Whipple's voice ricochets off the cold, hard surfaces.

Frank grimaces. 'Okay, calm down, Bennett. No need to shout.'

'The heart struggled because of narrowed arteries. Moreover, there's an aggregation of fatty acids in his bloodstream, a testament to his unhealthy diet. I surmise his exercise regimen was miniscule to non-existent. Evidence of a sedentary lifestyle is overwhelming. Thus, while the head injury appears fatal, I'd argue this man was a ticking-time-bomb of chronic maladies, brewing a lethal concoction of imminent mortal termination.'

'And here I was thinking he slipped and fell,' Frank quips.

Whipple's thunderous frown deepens, forming an almost comically stern facade. The barbs of humour never pierce Whipple's ironclad seriousness.

Whipple lowers his voice to a gravitas that bounces around the mortuary. 'Inspector Finnegan, there's much more to it than a mere slip and fall. Beneath the obvious, a universe of silent killers thrived.'

Frank nods at the body on the slab. 'Are you saying the old lad here played bingo with the reaper, and the head wound wasn't his winning number?'

'One may argue, inspector, it was the icing on the cake,' Whipple responds, turning back to the cadaver, as if hoping to find solace in the lifeless form. 'Also, one's mortality is not a jovial matter.'

'Noted, Doc.' A rare silence ensues, drowned out only by the low hum of the air conditioning system.

'Furthermore,' Whipple begins, returning to his scientific vernacular, 'The visceral adiposity index points towards inactive metabolism...'

'The what index?' Frank raises an eyebrow with begrudging curiosity, trying to keep up with the opaque medical language.

'He was severely overweight, acutely so. His body was accustomed to lethargy due to excessive substance ingestion and lack of movement,' Whipple explains, with an air of sincere sobriety.

'The good book does say sloth and gluttony are part of the six deadly sins,' Frank remarks innocently.

'It's seven deadly sins, inspector, seven,' Whipple corrects, his patience curling at the edges. 'The concept is based on several passages from the Bible, including Proverbs 6:16-19, Galatians 5:19-21, and Colossians 3:5-8. The classification of these sins into a list of seven is attributed to Pope Gregory I in the sixth century. The seven deadly sins, as we know them today, were later elaborated in works of literature, such as Dante Alighieri's Italian narrative poem—The Divine Comedy.'

'You don't say,' Frank murmurs, always amazed and slightly bored by the good doctor's inexhaustible knowledge of useless information. 'It's funny though, because old Jack was still sprightly despite his failing health. He performed two thirty-minute shows a day for the kiddies—The Scarecrow Cometh. Think of it as a cross between Worzel Gummidge and the Texas Chainsaw Massacre. I don't suppose you got a chance to see the show?'

Whipple's nostrils flare violently. 'Indeed, I did not, inspector. My idea of relaxation diverges significantly from the normative societal conventions. When I seek to disengage from the rigours of my profession, I pursue solace within the intellectual depths of literary masterpieces and meticulously crafted medical discourses.' His impossibly straight back becomes even more erect, upholding his imposing frame as he hammers home his point. 'In essence, my leisure is not spent in frivolous distractions but rather in seeking cerebral rejuvenation, in nurturing my grey matter with more sophisticated and high-brow deliberations.'

'I take it you're not a fan of Britain's Got Talent, then?'

Whipple, unamused, continues with his medical prognosis. 'Additionally, the man displayed eminent alopecia areata and early-stage psoriasis, indicating heightened stress levels, commonly found in those with excessive alcohol intake.'

'You mean he was tearing his hair out with worry?' Frank questions again, losing the will to live as he receives the usual stern, dismissive glance.

'Metaphorically, indeed,' Whipple concedes with the slightest roll of his eyes, 'While your chosen mode of expression is... colloquial, it's essentially correct.'

'Sounds like he was living on borrowed time.'

'Correct, inspector. The scalp wound quickened an inevitable demise. But make no mistake, morbidity was a consistent companion in his life's journey. This man was a battlefield; an emblem of fortified self-destruction,' Whipple concludes, his sombre tone filling the room.

'Looks like the bang to the scone may have been a blessing in disguise,' Frank offers, bearing a sympathetic air of resignation.

Doctor Whipple heaves a heavy sigh. 'Indeed. Although death is always an uninvited guest, it is often the most punctual.' He makes his way to the sink, removes his latex gloves, and nudges the taps on with his elbow.

'Righto, well thanks for that, Bennett,' Frank says as he opens the mortuary door, then halts, not entirely sure he got what he came for. 'Ahem, Bennett, just to clarify; Old Jack died because he struck his head on the side of the wood burner... didn't he?'

46

Outside, the creeping mist wraps itself around the police station, its arms encircling and choking the slender neck of hope. Inside, the incident room is a murmur of desolation laden with an air of fatalism. The rumble of the antiquated central heating system and the splat of sporadic rain against the windows occasionally punctuates the uneasy quiet.

The room, typically abuzz with scores of officers piecing together evidence, is stagnant. The majority of the team are out and about chasing shadows, eliminating misreported sightings, verifying alibis, admonishing time wasters and charlatans, and, of course, the perennial door-to-door knocking.

At the rear of the room, under the harsh glow of overhead fluorescent lighting, a map of Whitby, and surrounds, is the only item on the whiteboard. A set of diagonal lines, imposed over the chart, indicates the extensive area already searched. Rosie Miller has vanished without a trace, and as time ticks on, the belief in finding her alive is drowning, as many now suspect may have been her fate in the nearby sea or river.

Amidst the unyielding despondency, Prisha refuses to be swayed by the doom. With the intuition of a hunting falcon with newborn chicks, she scours the map, over and over. Tapping at the board she pulls up the list of suspects and re-reads their interview transcripts. Perplexed, she tries to thread the needle as she stares out of the window at the harbour and the faint outline of the vessels moored on the river.

I've missed something... but what? It's staring me in the face... and yet, why can't I see it?

Zac's gentle Scottish brogue jemmies into her reflections. 'Penny for your thoughts?'

She turns and offers him a whisper of a smile. 'Rosie. Where is she?'

Zac's cheeky grin evaporates as he sips from a cardboard coffee cup. His eyes bypass her and rest on the watery expanse in the distance.

'I'm beginning to be drawn towards the herd. Collective intelligence is not without merit.'

She turns back towards the window and watches a lone seagull as it mews and screeches by.

'No. I don't believe she's drowned. Her mother said she knows not to go near the water when alone.'

'Who says she was alone?'

His words hit home. 'It's possible. It's a good way to get rid of your victim and principal witness. But the town was heaving with people. Someone must have seen her or at least heard a scream if that scenario were true.'

'Gagged, drugged, unconscious, already dead? There are a dozen possibilities.'

'We've searched her home twice, haven't we?'

'Yes. All the rooms, wardrobes, cupboards, loft, shed, under beds, inside wheelie bins. We've gone over it meticulously, as we have her friend's house across the road.'

'Hmm... Right, I'm going back over there.'

'Where?'

'To the Miller's place. Where's Frank, by the way?'

'At the mortuary with Raspberry Whipple.'

'Ginger Jack autopsy?' she quizzes as she grabs her coat.

Zac nods. 'Prisha, go easy with the Millers. According to the Family Liaison Officer, they're at breaking point.'

Prisha pouts as she slips into her overcoat. 'I may be a hard-nosed bitch but I'm not heartless.'

'Just saying.'

Hovering at the threshold of the Miller residence, Prisha engages in a rapid-fire exchange of whispers with the Family Liaison Officer, their words dulled by the heavy fog.

'How are they all doing?' Prisha asks.

The Family Liaison Officer shakes her head, clearly concerned. 'The grandmother, Jenny, spends her entire day lost in obsessive cleaning. I've seen her emptying cupboards, wiping them clean before meticulously rearranging everything. Earlier, I found her silently crying while on her hands and knees, scrubbing the bathroom floor.'

'And Keith, the grandfather?' Prisha continues.

'He oscillates between seething anger and extended periods of disturbing quiet,' she reveals. 'In fact, he stepped out a moment ago to grab some fresh air and stretch the limbs. As for Scarlet, the mother, she relentlessly roams the streets before collapsing back home out of sheer fatigue. She steals a few moments of sleep before heading out again. When night falls, she spends her time poring over old family photographs on her iPad. She's just arrived back, actually. Been out since six.'

'And Riley? Scarlet's brother?'

'Riley is perhaps the most active. He keeps a twice-daily ritual of posting Rosie's picture on Facebook and requests everyone to share it. When not engrossed in social media, he teams up with his rugby pals and combs the streets endlessly in his car.'

'Who else is in the house at the moment, apart from Scarlet?'

'Jenny. Can I ask what you want to talk to them about?'

'Just to pick their brains. See if I can unearth something that may seem irrelevant to them, but may be the vital clue we're looking for.'

Prisha is ushered into the depressing living room where a television splashes images across the screen, but the sound is muted. Seated opposite each other, Scarlet, and Jenny Miller maintain an unreadable and stiff expression on their faces. The silent tension hovering between them is potent.

Through gritted teeth, Scarlet curses. 'This must the tenth time we've been bloody questioned. We have no additional information to offer you. Do you really think one of us has done our Rosie in?'

Jenny swiftly rebukes her daughter. 'Scarlet! No-one's thinking that. The inspector is doing her job. She's trying to assist us.'

'Yeah, right,' she sneers.

Prisha, acutely aware of the palpable strain in the room, tries to alleviate it. 'This won't take long. And not for one minute do we suspect foul play from close family members,' she explains, cloaking her own doubts under reassuring platitudes.

The FLO gradually drifts towards the kitchen. 'A cup of tea would do us all good. I'll get the kettle on.'

Following twenty minutes of unrewarding answers, Prisha draws a line under her questioning, having gleaned no additional knowledge. She lifts herself from the soft couch and brushes out the wrinkles from her trousers.

'Thank you for your time. I understand it's painful for you to go over things again, but...'

Scarlet, still truculent, interrupts. 'But it's all you've got left... isn't it, inspector?'

'Please forgive her, inspector. She's tired,' Jenny states, mortified at her daughter's disrespect.

Scarlet retaliates. 'Don't talk about me as though I'm not here!'

Prisha smiles benignly. 'It's a trying time for all.' Turning to leave, she has one last thought. 'If you don't mind, can I take another quick look around Rosie's bedroom?'

'Of course,' Jenny says, half rising.

'No, please stay where you are. I know where it is.'

With a steady pace, Prisha ascends the stairs, the aged wooden boards beneath the carpet protesting with a rhythmic creak. Upon reaching the landing, she veers right and approaches the small box bedroom overlooking the silent street below. Pushing the door ajar, she hesitates and takes in the decor and furnishings for a second time.

The room is innocent and homely: a single bed resting against the side wall, a modest bedside table standing guard with a whimsical Winnie the Pooh lamp and a noticeably lonely hairbrush. Tucked beneath the window is a humble chest of drawers crowned with captured memories in photo frames. Joyfully vibrant child artwork dots the walls in irregular patterns.

She takes a moment to pick out a picture displaying Rosie's biological father, Blake Dufton. She allows her eyes to examine it in detail before returning it to its prior position. Curiosity leads her to flip open a jewellery box, which releases a familiar, cheeky melody. An overwhelming rush of melancholy overcomes her as she observes the innocent sketches plastered around the room.

'Oh, you poor little mite,' she whispers into the emptiness. 'If you're still out there somewhere, you'll be scared, hungry, cold. And if you're not...' she trails off, reluctant to breathe life into the dreadful possibility. With heavy steps, she retreats towards the doorway, casting a lingering, wistful look around the room.

'Rosie, please, give me a clue, any clue, to help me find you?'

She pulls the door gently shut behind her, as if protecting a sacred memory. An abyss of despair threatens to engulf her entirely. Taking a moment to stifle a sudden tearful sniffle, she composes herself.

She says goodbye to the Millers, then saunters down the garden path towards her car, the usual spring in her step noticeably missing. Lowering herself into the driver's seat, she allows her gaze to fixate on the view through the windscreen, her spirit on the brink of defeat.

'Will this damn gothic fog ever lift? It's bloody oppressive.' Turning the ignition key, the car rumbles into life. She drives to the end of the cul-de-sac, performs a U-turn and heads back past the Miller's house, glancing up at Rosie's window as she hums the tinkling tune from the jewellery box. Her mind drifts to the pictures on Rosie's bedroom walls.

She slams the brakes so hard the car's wheels lock, causing the vehicle to collide with the kerbside in a jarring thump.

'That's it! I think I know where you are, Rosie!'

47

With an air of solemnity, Frank takes a bite of his sausage sandwich, the food offering a contrasting sense of comfort to the dark thoughts playing on his mind. His meeting with Doctor Whipple at the mortuary is no longer a pressing concern, and he's relieved to put the grisly experience behind him, at least for now. As he washes down his food with a gulp of hot tea, he attempts to peer through the opaque fog outside. The boats moored on the river, barely discernible.

The passing of Ginger Jack Henderson, although unfortunate, was deemed an accident, a fact that offers Frank a momentary sense of relief. However, thoughts of Rosie Miller and a potential rapist—whereabouts unknown, possibly at large, or maybe floating in the North Sea—darkens his mood.

Casting a glance at his wristwatch, he silently calculates that the lifeboat will return within the next hour or so for refuelling. The land-based search and rescue team has already expanded the search area for Rosie, and for the rapist. The stark contrast is not lost on him. Innocence and depravity are shown the same respect. Yet—there's still no sighting of a body on the shores. He's had some big wins in the last eighteen months, and a couple of big losses, not the least, one of his officers gunned down.

The shrill ring from his desk phone distracts him from morbid thoughts. 'DCI Finnegan?' he says, answering the call from the desk sergeant.

'Frank, I have a Keith Miller in reception wanting to see you.'

'Oh aye, what about?'

'Didn't say. Said it was a private matter.'

'Okay. I'll be down in five. Put him in interview room two.'

He stuffs the rest of his breakfast into his mouth, takes an almighty glug of tea and strides from his office. He spots Zac and Dinkel in deep conversation near the whiteboard.

'Zac!' he shouts. 'Didn't you say Prisha had gone over to the Miller's place?'

'That's right. About fifteen minutes ago. Why?'

Frank scrunches his nose up. 'Keith Miller's downstairs to see me. Bit odd, that's all.'

Zac shrugs as he and Dinkel refocus on the interactive whiteboard.

Frank pulls up a chair and sits opposite Keith Miller in the interview room and studies him. Traces of his Rugby Union days are etched upon his face; the distinctive boxer's nose and a constellation of minor scars. Once a figure bursting with joie de vivre and taking up space with his brawny presence, Keith now seems nothing more than an echo of himself. The sight of his old companion reduced to this wretched condition deals a heavy blow to Frank.

'Keith—how are you holding up?' Frank begins.

His shoulders briefly rise, then collapse. 'Fair to middling. Keeping it together for the missus and our Scarlet. Helps no one moping around, does it?'

Frank massages his chin. 'If you're here about Rosie, I'm afraid there's nothing new. I'm assuming the Family Liaison Officer updated you about our search for the van that decamped from the circus on Saturday night?'

'Aye,' he replies, gazing at the table.

Frank's brow furrows as he purses his lips. 'Did you see DI Kumar?'

Now it's Keith's turn to be puzzled. 'What?'

'DI Kumar? She was heading over to your place.'

'Oh... no. Our paths must have crossed. Why?'

'She wanted to speak with Scarlet again to go over a few things. See if she missed anything.'

'I see.'

Frank taps at the glass on his wristwatch, a subconscious act.

'So... you wanted to see me?'

Keith wrings his hands together, drops his head and stares at the dull white tabletop.

'It's about the old circus guy, Ginger Jack.'

'What about him?'

He raises his tired eyes. 'It was me.'

'What was you?' Frank replies, perplexed.

'It was me... who killed him.'

48

Prisha taps at the handsome image of Zac, then bangs at the steering wheel with her fist, agitated but energised.

The call connects. 'Yes, Prisha?'

'Zac, it's a long shot but I think I might know where she is.'

'Rosie?'

'Who else!'

'Go on?'

'Her bedroom wall was full of paintings, you know, kid's drawings.'

'And?'

'Every one of them was of a boat, or a yacht, or an ocean liner, or narrowboat. Her jewellery box played a song... Row, Row, Row Your Boat! Don't you see?'

'The marina?'

'Yes. We haven't searched the boats. Get a team together and I'll meet you down there in ten minutes. And organise sniffer dogs.'

'Wait, Prisha, before you go, I've got some other breaking news. I've just come off the phone with Charlene Marsden. Forensics found strands of hair inside the illusionist's escape trunk which match Rosie's hair.'

'You're shitting me?'

'I shit ye not.'

'What about the Parker's? Have they been brought in for questioning?'

'They're on their way now, handcuffed in the back of a patrol car. We had an undercover guy masquerading as a hotel guest monitoring them. The Parker's will arrive in Whitby in about thirty minutes.'

Prisha's mind is a maelstrom. 'It doesn't add up. They don't fit the mould of child abusers.'

'Stranger things have happened at sea.'

'Haha, very amusing. Right, see you at the marina. We'll meet in the car park at Endeavour Wharf opposite the train station in fifteen minutes. Bye.'

The relentless mist, a perennial unwelcome guest, hangs low over the River Esk. Shivering in the damp, Prisha gazes upon the boats moored up in the marina. The bobbing vessels appear shrouded in foreboding and mystery. As more officers arrive to the sound of car doors slamming and a general buzz of concerned voices, Prisha's initial excitement fades away, replaced by fear.

'Ready?' Zac questions as he sidles up to her, zipping up his jacket and lifting his collar.

Her eyes roll sideways. 'Yes. Are the dogs here?'

'On their way.'

'What if…' her voice falters.

'Only three possibilities; she's not here; we find her alive, or we find her…'

'Don't say it.'

'Don't give up hope, not now.' Zac turns and barks his orders at the gathering officers. 'Let's do this methodically! Work from the end of the walkways back towards the main footbridge. I'm assuming most of the boats will be locked, but you may be able to see through port holes. Bang on the hatches and call out Rosie's name, identifying yourself. If the wee lassie is here, she may well be scared. We've been in touch with the marina manager and she's contacting all the boat owners to obtain keys, but that's going to take some time. There's nigh on two hundred and thirty births, in this marina, alone, so let's get to it.'

Prisha steps aside as the team of officers rushes onto the pontoon. She follows hesitantly behind and walks to the furthest platform as fine rain caresses her face. Thinking of the innocent sketches on the bedroom wall and of Rosie's smiling photograph in the Miller's living room does nothing to lift a creeping sense of dread. She gazes upon the assorted vessels in front of her; sailing yachts, cabin cruisers, speedboats, sedate pleasure craft. A mooring rope sways gently to the rhythm of the river, brushing against the hull. Climbing aboard the vessel, she tries the cabin door, but predictably, it's locked.

She raps hard and shouts, 'Rosie, my name is Detective Inspector Kumar from Whitby Police. If you're inside, can you call out, please? Your mum is very worried about you.' Pauses. 'Rosie?'

Nothing.

Ambling around the boat, she peers through the portholes, but there's no sign of life or movement. Clambering back onto the pontoon, she approaches the next vessel, a sailing yacht with swirling blue letters proclaiming the name The Whitby Whisperer. This time there's a small gang plank she walks up as the slosh of water slaps at the boat. Following a similar routine, she calls out Rosie's name as the halyard shackle clinks against the aluminium mast. It's a sound which usually brings a sense of comfort to her, but not today. The rhythmic clanging seems to beat out a melancholic death march. Again, she gazes through portholes but can barely see inside the gloomy interior. Circumnavigating the craft, she stops at the horizontal hatch, which covers the steps down to the cabin. With little hope, she pushes at it, and to her surprise, it rolls back.

'Odd,' she murmurs. 'Anyone home? This is the police!' As the yacht gently sways in the tidal river, she tiptoes down the steps and tries the door handle.

A click, and the door creaks open. 'Hello?' she says in a gentle tone as she takes in the compact functionality of the cabin. To the left, a small galley, equipped with a gas stove, sink, and micro-fridge. Opposite is the navigation station with a tiny desk housing a radio, charts, and other navigation equipment. Further into the cabin are two bench seats opposing each other. Separating them is a built-in table. The area is bedecked with classic ornamental wood trim. Creeping along the teak flooring, she squeezes past the table and pulls at another narrow door.

'Jesus!' she screams. Staggering backwards, her hip catches the edge of the table. She loses her footing and tumbles to the floor with a resounding thump.

49

Frank cradles the crown of his head between his fingertips, opens his eyes, and stares at Keith Miller.

'You daft bugger, Keith. Why did you have to say that?' he whimpers, his voice laced with remorse.

Surprise flits over Keith's gritty features. 'What do you mean?'

'Less than an hour ago, I was at the post-mortem with the pathologist. He categorically stated the cause of death was due to a fall and a blow to the head on the wood burner.'

Keith puckers his lips. 'I see. Words once spoken cannot be unsaid. Can they, Frank?'

'No. They can't. Go on then, let's hear it.'

Keith shuffles in his seat and clears his throat. 'I went back to the circus later that night, well, actually, early Sunday morning about two. I obviously knew which was his caravan and I let myself in. The old lad was asleep on his bed, still fully clothed. There wasn't much light, just a glow from the fire. Looked like he'd been into the scotch. I shook him awake and threatened him.'

'How did you threaten him?'

'I had a small tin of lighter fuel with me and a lighter. Told him that if he didn't tell me what had happened to my little Rosie, then I'd burn the bugger alive. I didn't mean it. I intended to frighten him, that's all. I was desperate, Frank, desperate.'

'Go on.'

'The daft old sod clambered off the bed and...'

A hush descends as the tick of the clock is amplified.

'And what?' Frank eventually prompts.

'He made a grab for the poker and raised it above his head. Then his bloody wooden leg fell off. He went down hard like a sack of shit and cracked his head on the stove. I bent down and knew instantly he was dead. He stared wide-eyed at me. I checked for a pulse, but there wasn't one.' Agitated, he rubs at his face. 'I should have done the right thing and called the police and ambulance, but I panicked. Anyway, it's been weighing heavy on my conscience. You know me Frank: I believe in the rule of law and justice. I didn't *murder* the bugger, but at the very least it's manslaughter. People must be accountable for their actions. You do the crime, you do the time. So here I am.'

Frank nods thoughtfully. 'Aye. Says what he means and means what he says—that's you all right, Keith. As honest as the day is long.' He hesitates as his tongue dislodges a piece of sausage meat from his tooth. 'Couple of things; you said you opened the door and entered the caravan?'

'That's right.'

'It wasn't locked?'

'No.'

'And old Jack grabbed the poker and was about to hit you with it?'

Pauses. 'I'm not sure he was going to hit me with it. I took it as a counterthreat, you know, a warning to back off.'

'I see. Where was the poker?'

'What?'

'You said he grabbed the poker. He must have grabbed it from somewhere.'

'Oh, yes. It was laid on top of the stove. Why the questions, Frank? I've confessed to the crime.'

'Yes, you have.'

He reaches across the table and touches Frank on the arm. 'Please, Frank, for old times' sake do me one favour?' he pleads.

'What?'

'Don't arrest me now. Wait until we find Rosie, one way or another, please I beg you. I'm not a flight risk. I'll come quietly once we know the fate of my little girl.'

'Ease up, Keith. You weren't read a caution or offered a solicitor. This was an informal discussion. Nothing was recorded. Which means you can recant your confession at any time. I'll need to investigate this matter further before an arrest is made. Now, if you want to help move the investigation forward, you can voluntarily provide fingerprints and a DNA sample.'

His eyes dart back and forth over Frank's face. 'There's no point. I was wearing gloves, so there'll be no fingerprints.'

'It's standard police procedure to get DNA and fingerprints from suspects. If I do eventually arrest you, then you'll be obliged to comply.'

He nods thoughtfully. 'Okay. Then am I free to go?'

'Yes. Have you divulged this information to anyone else?'

A shake of the head. 'No. My family has enough on their plate right now. I might not be the sharpest knife in the drawer, but I have my head screwed on right.'

'Good. Keep it to yourself,' Frank replies as he rises from his seat.

Keith throws him a concerned look. 'Now, mind on, Frank, I don't want you turning a blind eye to this. I'll pay my penance when the time is ready.'

Frank pulls his lips back and nods. 'Aye. I dare say you will.'

50

Frank can just about make out the fleet of vessels moored at the marina from his office window. His heart thumps against his chest as he takes in the information. He holds the receiver between his shoulder and ear.

'Okay, Prisha, thanks for the call. As it happens, Keith Miller was here less than ten minutes ago. I'll call around to his place to break the news. Keep in touch.'

Ending the call, he staggers to his chair, flops into it, and closes his eyes as tears flow down his cheeks. He drops his head into his hands and quietly sobs for a few moments. Sniffling and wiping the wetness from his face, he stares at his phone.

'Bugger it. I'll call Keith Miller now and put him out of his misery.'

Heavy footsteps clomp down the steps to the cabin.

'Hell's bloody bells!' Zac curses as he bangs his head on the lintel of the doorway. 'That's the second time in less than forty-eight hours,' he exclaims, rubbing at his forehead.

Rosie fails to suppress a giggle.

'That's what happens for being so tall,' Prisha says with a wink and a grin at Rosie.

'Aye, tell me about it. The world wasnae designed for big people,' he replies as he places two cups of hot chocolate and a paper bag containing four donuts on the table.

'Thank you,' Rosie says, gratefully accepting the food and drink as Prisha divvies out the donuts and takes a bite.

'Not a problem, sweetheart. Right, I'll leave you two alone. The doctor and the child protection officer should be here within ten minutes.'

Prisha and Rosie watch on as he purposefully bends exiting the doorway.

'What doctor?' Rosie asks as she slurps at her hot chocolate.

'The doctor needs to see you, Rosie.'

'But I told you, there's nothing wrong with me.'

'I know. But it's the rules. It will be a lady doctor and she has to make sure you're all right, physically and mentally. Then, after that, I'll drive you home.'

As they both delicately bite into the donuts, girl and woman eyeball each other intensely.

'What are you thinking about?' Rosie asks.

'I'm thinking about the scare you gave me when I opened the bathroom door and saw you staring at me, wielding a bloody great big carving knife.'

'What does wielding mean?'

'Holding.'

'Oh.'

With an army of endorphins racing around her body, Prisha is in a mildly euphoric state.

'If you could have one thing in all the world, what would it be?' Prisha quizzes bearing a cheeky smile, hoping the child doesn't ask for anything too ridiculously expensive.

Rosie leans back in the bench seat. 'That's easy,' she replies, confident in her choice.

'Go on then? What?'

'To see my dad.'

Prisha stops chewing, realising it's not something she can buy her. 'But you don't know your dad.'

Rosie pulls a serious face. 'Exactly. That's why I want to see him.'

Her response is followed by a moment's silence as the calming slosh of water signals a change of tide outside.

Rosie breaks the impasse. 'Mam doesn't know it, but I read all the letters,' she says with an air of nonchalance.

'What letters?'

'The ones my dad started sending to mam about two years ago. One a month. She hid them in the bottom of her knicker drawer, but I found them.'

'I see,' Prisha replies, impressed with Rosie's sharpness.

'In every letter he begged mam to bring me to the prison to see him. He says he's changed.' Stops, considers. 'Can bad people change?'

Prisha scratches at her neck. 'Well... it depends if they're genuinely bad, mentally impaired, or have simply made some very poor decisions.'

'What about my dad? He robbed a post office and clonked some old guy over the head. Is he bad?'

Prisha is, for once, out of her depth. 'From what I've heard, I believe your dad made some silly choices. He didn't stop and think about the consequences.'

Rosie's eyes telegraph confusion. 'Does that mean he is bad or not?'

'Personally, I don't believe he is bad.'

'And you're a police officer, so you should know. I want to be a police officer one day.'

Prisha chuckles. 'Your mam told me you wanted to be part of the lifeboat crew.'

'I do. But that's for volunteers. You don't get paid. How much do you get paid?'

'Not enough. But I enjoy my job... well, parts of it. Like today, finding you alive and well. Nothing can beat that.'

'Are you married?'

'No.'

'Boyfriend or girlfriend?'

'Ahem, yes, I have a boyfriend.'

'Do you love him?'

'That's a very personal question.'

'Well, do you?'

'I think I'm starting to fall in love, yes.'

'He's lucky.'

'Thank you.'

'My pleasure,' she says, bearing an authentic smile. 'Have you told him you're falling in love?'

Prisha wriggles uncomfortably in her seat and coughs. 'I... well, I...'

'You haven't, have you?'

She stares at the young girl, amazed at how she can read people. 'I...'

'Doesn't matter. I can see it's making you embarrassed.' A grimace replaces her curiosity. 'Am I in trouble?' she asks with a serious pout.

Prisha laughs. 'No, you're not in trouble. Everyone has been very worried about you, though. After all, you have been gone a long time,' she explains as Rosie bites into a warm donut.

'How long have I been missing?'

'Since Saturday evening and it's now Monday morning, so quite a while,' she says gently. 'It's been a big adventure. Do you want to tell me what happened on Saturday after you fell out with your friend, India, on the way to the circus?'

Rosie waggles her cheeks from side to side. 'Are you sure I'm not in trouble?'

'Positive.'

'I went to the circus to see Ginger Jack in The Strawman Cometh but this time it wasn't as good because at the end, the scarecrow didn't cut off the little boy's head. They hugged instead. Yuk!'

Prisha quells her urge to laugh. 'And after the show ended, what happened?'

'I waited at the back of the tent as Ginger Jack said he had something to give me. But he didn't turn up.' She appears completely distracted as her attention focuses on the second donut.

'So, what did you do?'

Rosie considers the question carefully with a serious expression. 'Well, this other man came along and started talking to me. He told me Ginger Jack would be ages and asked me if I'd like to see the magic disappearing box.'

'Do you mean the box the illusionist uses in his show?'

'Yeah... that's the word. Illusi, illusion, illusionist,' she says, struggling with the word.

'Then what?'

'The man took me into an empty tent where the magic box was. He asked me if I wanted to get inside the box and see if I could escape from it. At first, I thought it would be fun. But then...' she trails off, slightly disturbed.

'Take your time.'

'But then... I don't know. He gave me the creeps, looking at me all funny. Then he took my scrunchie out and began stroking my hair. I got scared and told him I had to go. He put his hand over my mouth and lifted me into the box and slammed the lid down. Bang!' she shouts, mimicking the sound of the lid being shut. 'It was dark, and I was scared. But I didn't cry,' she says proudly.

'You're a very brave girl. How long were you in the box?'

She shrugs. 'Don't know.'

'And how did you get out of the box?'

'Once I stopped being scared, I thought about the magic box. There's no such thing as magic, is there?' she enquires, unsure.

'No, I don't think there is. It's all trickery.'

'That's what I thought. So, I figured there must be a button or a lever that would open the lid. Even though I couldn't see a thing, I felt with my hands along the wood and touched a button and there was a click. I pushed at the lid, and it opened. Then I climbed out,' she explains calmly as she devours the last of the donut and washes it down with a hearty glug of hot chocolate.

'Clever girl.'

'But when I came outside of the tent, it was thick fog everywhere. Then I saw him, and he saw me.'

'Who?'

'The man who put me in the box, of course. My mum told me that if I'm ever worried or lost, then I should tell a police officer. But I couldn't see one and he came towards me, so I ran, and ran and ran. He nearly caught me, but I hid down a dark alley. I waited forever until I was sure he'd gone. But I didn't know where I was, and it must have been the middle of the night as there were no people around anymore when I came out.'

'How did you end up here on the boat?'

Hesitation creeps across her features as she drops her eyes onto the table. 'I'm definitely not in trouble?' she asks suspiciously.

Prisha smiles warmly. 'No. I'm a police officer. Would I lie to you?'

'There was a small gap in the fence that I squeezed through. Then I went from boat to boat until I found one unlocked. I felt safe here and knew someone would find me, eventually. I might be in trouble with whoever owns the boat, though.'

'Why?'

'Because I ate all the biscuits from their cupboard,' she adds sheepishly. 'My mam says it's wrong to steal.'

'Your mother's right, but I think you borrowed them, not stole them. I'm sure we can replace the biscuits,' Prisha says, grinning. 'It was a very good hiding place, Rosie. The man you talked about, the one who put you in the box and chased you; did you see a woman with him?'

She wrinkles her nose. 'A woman?' she questions, shaking her head vigorously.

'Was the man short, stocky, with a goatee beard and a funny twirly moustache?'

More confusion as she grimaces. 'No. That sounds like the illusionist. His picture was on a poster outside the tent.'

Prisha snaps her head back. ‘Oh! If it wasn’t the illusionist, then who was it?’

‘It was the tall, bendy man.’

51

Like an obnoxious drunk at the bar, the fog reluctantly departs, harried along by an icy wind. It leaves behind grey skies, intermittent sleet, and a mountain of litter blowing angrily in the stiff breeze, a stark reminder of the carnival weekend.

Prisha does a three-sixty surveying the circus site as workers hastily take down marquees, tents, and hook up caravans and food stalls to vehicles.

'The evidence keeps mounting against Stick Man,' she says to Zac and Dinkel, buttoning her parka and drawing the hood over her head. Her gaze follows the group of forensic experts in bunny suits as they leave Pete Murphy's caravan, their work finished.

Zac pulls his woolly hat down further. 'Yep. A stash of knickers and bras found in a hidden compartment of his caravan, along with a hunting knife. All grist to the mill. Not conclusive evidence, but together with the witness statements, and the matching footprints, it should be enough to convince a jury. And let's not forget, false imprisonment of Rosie, escaping from police custody, and the attempted murder of a police officer. He's looking at a long time behind bars. And yet…'

'The bastard is still at large,' Prisha says, finishing his sentence.

Dinkel takes a welcoming sip from a cup of hot chocolate. 'Just because they found his muscle suit on the beach at Colliers Hope doesn't necessarily mean he *didn't* drown at sea.'

Even as her feelings for Dinkel thaw, ever so slightly, she can't help but recognise he's still inexperienced… painfully so, sometimes.

She sighs wearily. 'Dinkel, I've spoken with other performers. Those suits are a nightmare to slip into, and even harder to peel off. As formidable as the North Sea is, I don't think it's capable of dislodging a man from a rubber suit.'

Dinkel frowns and considers her riposte. 'Possibly, but I was merely suggesting…'

'Well, don't. Sup your cocoa like a good boy and shut up,' Zac grumbles. 'You're right, Prisha. The evil prick is still out there and can strike again.' He involuntarily shudders. 'It makes my skin crawl to think what he was intending to do with that little girl.'

'I think we both know exactly what he was going to do with her, and what he intended to do with her afterwards. She'd have been able to identify him. He wouldn't have allowed that to happen. It's a disease. Men like that can never quench their perverse sexual appetites. We must catch him because one thing is guaranteed, he will strike again. Where is he, Zac?'

'He could be anywhere.'

'Do you think he's still in Whitby?'

'If he is, then he's certainly not around here. We've searched the circus performers' caravans yet again. No wonder they're getting shitty. It is possible someone is covering for him, maybe loaned him money, a fresh set of clothes.'

Prisha kicks at the damp grass. 'We don't even have a clean mug shot of him. Every time we've seen him, he's been daubed in face-paint.'

'No, it doesn't help with the public appeal, does it?'

Dinkel drains the dregs from his cup in a noisy and annoying manner. 'Ahh! That was good. But all in all, I'd consider it a win. A little girl found alive and well, unharmed. Wouldn't you say ma'am?'

Prisha fleetingly closes her eyes. 'Job half done, Dinkel. What about the women that pervert has scarred for life? Put yourself in their shoes for a few brief seconds. Late at night, you're in the sanctuary of your own home, your haven, your safe place. Then, when you're fast asleep, you're woken by some scary fucker who's standing over you with a hunting knife threatening to cut your head off if you make a sound. Followed by rape. How would you feel, on a night, climbing into bed? Sweet dreams? I think not. That monster's actions lasted minutes. The repercussions for the victims lasts a lifetime.'

He pulls a face. 'I never thought of it like that,' he murmurs as a distant toot-toot reverberates through the gloomy atmosphere. 'I remember an incident from my schooldays,' Dinkel begins. 'I was accused of stealing another boy's apple. Of course, I hadn't, but some mean-spirited beggar placed an apple core in my desk. The teacher erroneously pointed her finger at me.'

Zac eyeballs him jadedly, accustomed to Dinkel's dull monologues. 'Has this story got a point?'

'Not really.'

'Don't leave me on tenterhooks. I won't be able to sleep tonight until you tell me the ending.'

Dinkel shuffles, regretting he'd ever brought the subject up. 'At lunchtime I ran home and told my mother.'

Zac huffs. 'How old were you? Fifteen?'

'I was five, actually.'

'Scarred for life. You poor little mite. Didn't put you off eating apples though, did it?'

'As I was saying...' Dinkel continues.

The distinct toot-toot pierces the air once more. 'What is that sound?' Prisha asks, perplexed.

Zac performs neck stretches, left to right and back again. 'That's the Flying Scotsman coming into the train station. It was chartered for the Goth Weekend.'

'So, it's picking people up?'

'Yep.'

'Where's the destination?'

'York. Apparently, they serve a decent lunch onboard. I've been meaning to take the missus and kids on it for years, but never got around to it.'

'Why York?' Prisha enquires.

'Because it's a major rail hub. From there you can get a train to just about anywhere in the country.'

Dinkel continues unabated 'It was a sanctuary.'

Zac glowers at him. 'What was a sanctuary?'

'Home.'

'Fuck me quietly,' he grizzles. 'Are you still on about the apple story? Dinkel, if you're going to recall anecdotes, then at least make them interesting or amusing.'

'Pardon me for existing.'

Prisha walks off, hands stuffed deep into her jacket pockets as the back and forth between Zac and Dinkel fades. Random thoughts meander through her head.

She suddenly pivots on her heels.

'Dinkel, I think you have it!'

Zac and Dinkel cease their bickering.

'I do?' Surprised, he turns to Zac and whispers, 'I have what?'

'Fuck knows. But I don't think she's referring to your scintillating repartee.'

Prisha jogs back to the duo. 'You said it, Dinkel; when people are in trouble, they return to their roots for comfort and protection. Stick Man, Pete Murphy is a Dubliner. He could catch a train from York to Manchester airport, then a flight.'

'Or a train directly to Chester, then a train to Holyhead to catch the ferry across to Dublin,' Zac adds.

Prisha is already racing back to the unmarked police car. 'What are you waiting for? Move it!'

52

The car screeches to a halt at a set of traffic lights next to the train station. Prisha and Zac leap from the vehicle.

'Park the car, Dinkel!' Zac shouts as he and Prisha dash across the road and up the station steps.

In contrast to the normally placid scene at Whitby Station, today it's a swirling kaleidoscope of people adorned in colours and patterns, a testament to the end of the Goth Weekend. A frenetic mix of scarlet and black draped amongst Victorian bustles and corsets all fighting to differentiate themselves against the emerald green of the iconic steam train.

The officers weave and dodge their way inside to the platform, where it is even busier with crowds of train spotters waiting in gleeful anticipation for the departure of the Flying Scotsman. Two piercing shrieks clash with the constant heavy pant of the engine, akin to a dinosaur with terminal bronchitis.

The scent of patchouli oil, frankincense, cannabis, and the rustic tang of coal smoke vie with each other, creating an exotic elixir as they invoke a different era.

Prisha spots the stationmaster as he blows his whistle. The train shudders, as screams and cheers erupt from the throng. The iron giant rouses and lumbers into motion as Prisha and Zac run behind, desperately attempting to make it to the door of the last carriage. Reaching out, she grabs at the handle and the door flies open as the train gathers speed.

Leaping aboard, she blows hard. 'Come on, Zac!' she yells as he bumps into a bystander, knocking him off his stride. With long locks flowing and his heavy winter coat trailing in the wind, he recedes into the billowing steam coughed out by the engine.

Playing out like a 1940s black and white film, Prisha's heart sinks as the platform ends and Zac drops to his haunches, shaking his head.

She slams the door shut. 'Shit!' Staring into the carriage at the party atmosphere onboard, the words of Superintendent Banks come to mind.

'You're headstrong, reckless, dangerous. You take unnecessary risks...'

Taking stock, she considers her options. She has no police radio with her and on checking her mobile phone, the zero bars indicate she's in a black-spot for coverage.

The door to the adjoining carriage opens as an old-fashioned conductor emerges, who appears to be eighty if he's a day.

'Ticket's please,' he says in a jolly tone.

Prisha flashes her warrant card. 'I'm trailing a suspect who I think may be onboard.'

His genial demeanour immediately changes. 'Oh, I see. Male or female?'

'Male.'

'Is he a risk to the passengers' safety?'

The last thing she wants is a kerfuffle. 'No, he's not. When's the first stop?'

'York. Non-stop all the way.'

She silently curses. 'Ah, I see. How long?'

'If we make good speed, just shy of two hours.'

'How many staff are onboard?'

'The engineer and fireman, and me. We usually have a guard, but we're short-staffed. Do you require assistance in apprehending your suspect if he is onboard?'

She gives him the once over again and thinks of Superintendent Banks' rebuke. 'No, that won't be necessary. And if you could keep the information to yourself, it would be...'

'Of course, ma'am.' He totters off into the carriage. 'Tickets please!'

She steps aside as another Victorian apparition approaches. This time a woman who bears an uncanny resemblance to Queen Victoria ambles by dressed in a black crinoline dress and sporting a straw bonnet, with a knitted shawl draped around her shoulders.

Prisha touches her gently on the arm and pulls out her ID. 'Could I have a word?'

'What about?' she replies in a broad Yorkshire accent, ruining her regal persona.

'I'm looking for someone, but I don't want him to recognise me. Is there any chance I could borrow your bonnet and shawl for a while?'

'Well...' she queries, hesitant. 'Is he dangerous?'

'At present, I don't consider him a danger to the public, but you should not approach him. Not that I wish to alarm you,' she explains, alarming the woman. 'There are other undercover officers onboard,' she lies to placate her.

'Okay. But you will return them, won't you? As it's a hired outfit?' she says, carefully removing the bonnet and shawl.

'Of course I will. What's your name?'

'Helen.'

'Thank you, Helen.' She quickly dons the hat, pulling it down over her eyes, then wraps the shawl around her shoulders. 'How do I look?'

'Like a dog's breakfast.'

'Thanks.'

'It's not a compliment, love. Good luck.'

Prisha watches on as the woman glides through the carriage, her ridiculously oversized dress flowing behind her.

'How do you even go for a pee in those things?' she murmurs to herself as she steps into the passenger coach and furtively eyeballs the male passengers. The carriage is busy but not quite full, and there's a party atmosphere as groups of friends laugh and joke, some already imbibing cans of beer.

After inspecting the first carriage, she doubles back and proceeds to the next one. Nothing seems amiss at first glance, simply a collection of elaborate costumes and dramatic make-up. There are steam punks, individuals in deerstalkers, women in lacy corsets, their ample bosoms under severe restraint, and a man resembling Jack the Ripper seemingly asleep, his top hat askew, his black cloak draped around him. Approaching the door to the adjoining coach, she pauses and gives the cloaked figure a second look. Curled into himself, his face hidden and turned towards the window, the man rests undisturbed. Her eyes drift onto his Victorian style button boots, impeccably polished.

He can't possibly be asleep already. We've only just set off. Hungover? Perhaps.

His slouched position makes it difficult to gauge his height, but he appears slender. As she returns towards him, she pauses beside his seat. The sleeves of his suit are noticeably short, ending at mid-forearm, revealing a tattoo of three interlocking circles on his wrist.

Got you!

She carries on walking and slips into a seat two rows back on the opposite side of him. His top hat is all she can see, but it's enough. She pulls out her phone, and thanks God the bars have reappeared. Two missed calls from Zac. She decides it would be safer to text rather than call.

He's on the train. Second carriage from the back. Dressed like Jack the Ripper, or a Victorian toff. Top hat, cloak. The train is non-stop to York. Organise a team of officers to be at the station. I'll keep my eye on him, but won't make an arrest until he's off the train. Don't call, only text if you want to speak.

She hits the send button, suddenly experiencing a wave of tiredness. When this is all over, she intends to take a couple of days off and do nothing but sleep.

The rhythmic clickety-clack of the train wheels, the good-natured hum of cheerful voices, and the warmth of the carriage offer no assistance in combating the creeping somnolence.

Her eyelids valiantly flicker up and down, but the battle is futile as eventually they succumb to the inevitable.

Her head jerks forward, waking her from her unintended slumber. Groggy, she rouses and feels the trickle of saliva on the edge of her chin. Pulling a tissue from her pocket, she discreetly dabs away her mild embarrassment and shoots a glance across the carriage. The top hat is in the same position, poking up above the head rest. Outside, stark moorland unfolds, speckled with sheep and cattle, the cold, barren landscape contrasting with the cosy interior of the train. A quick glance at her watch reveals she's only halfway through her trip. Despite her resolve to stay awake, she is oblivious of her gradually drooping eyelids.

The piercing repeated whistles from the locomotive wake her a second time. The mood in the carriage has dramatically changed, and her heart instinctively thumps. She's reassured as she glances at the top hat, still in the same position. The passengers are louder and more animated as the train slows. Prisha leans across to a young woman who bears an uncanny resemblance to Morticia from the Adam's Family.

'Excuse me, do you know what's happening?'

The woman cranes her neck and peers out of the window. 'Not sure. Oh, wait, I think I can see cattle on the track ahead.'

Pulling her phone out, she reads Zac's text message.

Plain clothes will be waiting for our man at York. Follow behind him as he gets off the train and raise your arm so our officers can identify Murphy. Arrest him and take him to Fulford Road station. I'm on my way there and will drive you home.

She replies with a thumbs up, as the train slows to walking pace. Her stomach grumbles with hunger and she could murder a coffee. A quick glance around at the pre-bought sandwiches, thermos flasks, and cold beers informs her there is no buffet car serving refreshments. Taking a deep breath, she relaxes back into the seat and casually gazes at the scenery outside. A sudden commotion of mild indignation and bemusements ripples through the carriage. Her eyes follow the gaze of the other passengers who are all gawping and pointing into the distance as a tall man, bedecked in an ill-fitting suit scampers across the fields, his cloak flowing behind him.

Jumping to her feet, she inspects the seat her suspect had occupied. She stares in dismay at a long black cane resting upright on the cushion, the pommel tucked neatly inside the top hat.

'Damn you!' she shouts, rushing to the carriage door as the conductor appears, looking duly concerned.

'Is that your man?' he says, pointing at the figure in the far-off distance already putting space between himself and the train, which is now creeping along like a lethargic, giant centipede.

'Yes! How did he escape? I thought the doors were centrally locked and couldn't be opened until the train came to a stop.'

He pulls an apologetic smile. 'It's a vintage carriage and all the doors are manual, I'm afraid.'

Prisha barely hears the reply as she drops from the coach, landing on squelchy ground which instantly soaks her feet.

She shouts up to the conductor as he begins to disappear. 'Where are we?'

'Pickering's a good three miles that-a-way!' he bellows, pointing south-westwards.

Two shrill blasts of the whistle and The Flying Scotsman picks up speed and accelerates away.

'Am I blessed?' she mumbles, staring at her trainers. 'I could weep.'

She pulls out her mobile and hits the call button.

'Prisha, what's happened?' Zac asks with urgency and prescience.

'The watery streak of piss has jumped from the train and is making a run for it.'

'Shite!'

'Don't worry. I still have him in my sights.'

'Don't tell me you jumped from the train as well?'

'Got it in one. He's heading towards Pickering, which is about three miles southwest of my current position.'

'I'm on the Whitby to Pickering Road now. Probably ten miles away. I'll call for back-up. Trail him but don't attempt to apprehend him.'

'Do you think I'm an idiot?'

'Good, lass. Keep in touch.'

She grins to herself. 'Christ, men are so gullible,' she murmurs, slipping her phone away and breaking into a steady jog. 'You said you couldn't wait to get out on the moors for a run. Now's your chance.'

He's already a good three hundred yards ahead, but Prisha knows button boots from the Victorian era are completely unsuited for long-distance running, especially on a badly maintained, gravel farm track. After five minutes she's closed the gap to less than fifty yards, as he slips and slides through potholes in the makeshift road. As she pulls her phone out to give Zac an update, she notices a boundary wall and a sign for a cattle grid. Stick Man looks fearfully over his shoulder at her as he tentatively picks his way over the horizontal iron rails. A muted yelp is followed by flailing arms and legs, a distinctive crack, then a howling scream.

'Aargh! My ankle, my fecking ankle!'

'Oh, dear,' Prisha purrs, as she slows to a walk and pulls her handcuffs from her belt.

'I've broken my fecking ankle,' he screams at her, writhing in agony, the bottom of his left leg at an unnatural angle 'Call an ambulance, for feck's sake!'

'Oh, stop your mewling, you great, big pussy! You should have used the gate.'

'Please!' he sobs.

Determined not to let him slip through on a technicality by claiming she didn't properly caution him, she perches her phone on top of the bypass gate and hits the record button.

'Peter Murphy, I am arresting you on suspicion of...'

53

The bulk of the major incident team can barely disguise their eagerness to retreat to their homes or reconvene at a nearby pub—a sanctuary for their fatigued bodies and unsightly bags accrued under sleep-starved eyes. Yet, in their way, stands Superintendent Banks, unspooling another meticulous oration in her hallmark style. Diligently, she offers gratitude to the team, and dissects the weekend's triumphs and failures with surgical precision.

It's gripping stuff.

'Team, this has been a wonderful result. A little girl successfully reunited with her family, and a suspected serial rapist securely in custody, with other serious charges pending. Now, I know how keen you all are to celebrate or, let's be honest, to get some well-deserved rest. But allow me a few moments to resonate on the sheer brilliance of this operation. Our consistently impressive adherence to police regulation benchmarks was, of course, at the heart of it. It's invigorating to see so many effective strategies in place, strategies we've emphasised repeatedly. Behind every positive resolution lies a fundamental bedrock: systems! Risk assessments, procedures, due diligence, media liaison, health, and safety, community consultation; the list is endless. These are the gears in the engine room, without which, the ship would be adrift in rough seas.'

Frank throws an embarrassed glance at Prisha, who, in turn smirks at Zac.

'Crock of shit,' he mouths silently.

'Remember, behind every successful conviction lies rigorous protocol. You all deserve a pat on the back.'

The team thinks she's finished and offers a ripple of applause. Unfortunately for everyone concerned... she's not finished.

'Before you leave, may I kindly ask everyone to complete your reports, timesheets, and expense forms. And let me emphasise to everyone - we will scrutinise your expense claims. Make sure every detail and receipt is beyond reproach. Once again, well done, team!'

'Sweet merciful shite,' Frank murmurs under his breath as Superintendent Banks turns on her heels and marches away not before barking her last order.

'Frank, Prisha, Zac, a moment if you please, in my office, now.'

Frank waggles his head. 'If I'd had my way, most of my crew would have been onto their third pint by now.'

Zac pats him on the shoulder. 'Home stretch, Frank, home stretch.'

Anne Banks slips into her fawn trench coat as the three officers line up in front of her desk, resembling wayward students awaiting instructions.

'I'd like to say privately, congratulations to all of you. You turned a weekend of hell into a very satisfactory Monday.'

'Thank you, ma'am,' Frank replies with minimal enthusiasm.

'You've pulled this one out of the fire, Frank. But let it be a lesson to one and all,' she adds, fastening the buttons on her coat, whilst throwing Prisha a barely hidden contemptuous glance.

'Ma'am?' Frank replies.

She gazes at him with her cobra eyes. 'Too many risks, Frank. Way too many risks. We are police detectives, not maverick hired guns. Rein it in otherwise there will be consequences.' She relents a little. 'Having said that, we'll take this one as a win.' Picking up her handbag, she turns to leave.

'Ahem... there is one small matter, Anne.'

She freezes and spins around. 'What?' she asks, fearing the worst.

'The death of Ginger Jack.'

'What about it? According to the pathologist's report, he died by hitting his head on the wood burner. An unfortunate accident.'

'Yes. So it appears. However, I was speaking with Charlene Marsden from forensics earlier and they've lifted some foreign fingerprints and DNA from inside his caravan.'

She scrunches her eyes up. 'Hardly surprising. And?'

'We are still investigating. Nothing to worry about at the moment, ma'am. I simply want to be one hundred per cent sure there is nothing untoward.'

'Then why mention it?'

'Ticking all the boxes, ma'am. Due diligence and all that.'

She scrutinises him with suspicion. 'Hmm... okay. Keep me posted. Now, I must dash as I have a media conference to prepare for and a debrief with the Chief Constable.'

In hushed silence, they listen as the click-clack of her heels recedes.

'Thank fuck for that,' Zac finally gasps.

'Aye, a walking, talking legalese pro forma.' Frank turns to Zac and pats him on the shoulder. 'Well done, lad.'

'Don't thank me, Frank.' He nods at Prisha. 'It's this one you should give the kudos to.'

'Yes, I know. But you make a good team.' He looks at Prisha, takes her hand, and pats the back of it. 'Excellent work, Prisha. I must admit, when you called me this morning and told me you'd found Rosie alive, well, I'm not ashamed to say I shed a tear or two.'

'Just doing my job, boss.'

Zack flicks a hand through his hair. 'How come you were coy with the Super about Ginger Jack's death?'

Frank's face hardens. 'The Millers have been through enough for the moment. I thought I'd give him one more night with his family. I'll call around there tomorrow about midday and make the arrest.'

'Do you want me to tag along?'

He gazes reflectively at a filing cabinet. 'No. I'll handle this one alone. He'll come quietly.'

Prisha attempts to break the impasse. 'Some of the team are heading to the Duke of York for a few drinks, Frank. See you down there?' she asks, expectantly.

Frank is dragged from his gloomy thoughts. 'What? Oh... no. Not this time. I think I'll head off home for a quiet night. Meera has some meals in the freezer.' He pulls his wallet from his back pocket and peels off two fifties. He hands them to Prisha. 'Stick this behind the bar for the gang, yeah?'

'Frank, you shouldn't.'

'Nonsense. Let your hair down. You're only young once. Not that a hundred quid goes far these days. Right, I'll see you two in a couple of days. Enjoy your time off.'

Prisha and Zac ponder thoughtfully as Frank shuffles from the office.

'Poor old bastard,' Zac mutters. 'First time ever he's not gone to the pub after a result.'

Prisha's face reflects her concern. 'Do you think he'll be okay?'

'Aye, he'll be right. I'll call around to his place tomorrow night with a takeaway and a six-pack of Guinness. That will cheer him up.'

'I'll join you.'

'That's the spirit!' he says with a chuckle. 'We need to stick together, you and me. No one else understands the shit we go through. Come on, let's head down to the battlecruiser and get smashed.'

Prisha grins. 'Yes! Sod it! Let's get hammered.' She pauses for a moment. 'I suppose we should invite Dinkel.'

'Aye, I guess so,' Zac replies, less than enthused by the idea.

Prisha laughs. 'Fair dues, Zac. He did some excellent police work on this case. I must confess, he is growing on me.'

'Aye, like a wart. Okay, Dinkel it is. For better or worse he's now part of the gang. But I'm telling you, if he starts off on one of his long-winded diatribes about something extremely boring that happened to him in his youth, then he's going to get a thump.'

54

Tuesday 3rd November – 11:20 am

With each step burdened by an unwelcome duty, Frank crosses the threshold as he's ushered into the living room by Jenny Miller. The rich aroma of ground coffee, a scent that once heralded shared confidences, now hangs heavy in the air—bitter and solemn. The familiar creak of wooden floorboards beneath the carpet groans at Frank's arrival.

'Keith, Frank's here to see you,' Jenny declares.

Keith tosses the newspaper onto the cushion of the couch at the side of him. 'Hi, Frank, how are you going old lad?'

'Would you like a cup of tea, Frank?' Jenny offers.

'Ahem, no thanks, Jenny. I don't intend on staying long,' he replies, embarrassed, as Keith rises from the settee.

'If you're here to check on Rosie, then you've just this minute missed her,' Keith chuckles. 'Scarlet's taken her shopping. They shouldn't be too far away. Ten, fifteen minutes and they'll be back. You've nothing to worry about, mind. She's as tough as nails is Rosie. Like nothing ever happened. It's amazing how kids bounce back, isn't it?'

Frank averts his gaze onto the threadbare carpet. 'Aye. Kids are resilient. Actually, I'm not here about Rosie.'

'Oh,' Keith says, pulling a frown.

'Is Riley home?'

'Riley?' His voice rises in pitch. 'No. He's out and about with some of his rugby mates.'

'I see.' Frank's gaze flicks from Keith to the pair of large Adidas trainers beside the TV, then to Jenny, who instantly looks away. Tension crackles. The subtle narrowing of his eyes speaks volumes, a silent broadcast of the grim purpose behind his visit.

Keith's voice breaks the charged silence. 'Oh, I get it. You're here to arrest me, right?' Resignation laces his words. Jenny collapses onto the settee, her sobs punctuating the still air. 'Jenny knows. I told her last night. I thought I had more time,' he mutters, accepting of his fate.

'I'm not here to arrest you, Keith. I'm here about your confession yesterday. There are a couple of irregularities.'

Keith frowns, then lightens a little. 'Such as?'

'You said Jack's caravan door was unlocked. I don't believe it was. He used a clothes peg, slipped through a hasp as a makeshift bolt. We found the broken peg on the floor. I think whoever entered gave the door a shoulder barge or a kick.'

Keith scratches his ear. 'Aye, maybe I gave it a shove?' he says, as if deep in thought. 'I had a lot going on and it's all a bit of a blur.'

'Then there's the poker,' Frank continues, hating every single word he utters. 'You said Jack picked it up off the top of the wood burner.'

'That's right.'

'The fire was still warm to the touch when I arrived at midday. If you broke into the caravan at two in the morning, the fire would have been roaring. If Jack had picked up the poker from the top of the fire, it would have left some sort of burn mark on his hand. I double checked with the pathologist; there were no marks consistent with a burn.'

A mock laugh, and an aching grin. 'It was dark. Maybe it was leaning up against the side of the bed. I'm not sure what the problem is, Frank. I may have scrambled a few details, but I have confessed to being inside Jack's caravan. What more do you want?'

Frank's chest heaves. 'We lifted fingerprints and a DNA sample from the caravan. One from the door and another from the sink. You said you were wearing gloves.'

'I think... oh, that's right. I had the lighter fuel in one hand, and I took one glove off to retrieve the lighter from my pocket. I must have touched something. That'll explain it.'

'The fingerprints and DNA don't match yours, Keith. The DNA is familial.'

Keith rubs a hand through his greying locks. 'Familial? I've told you before, I'm not the sharpest knife in the drawer, Frank. You may have to explain that one to me.'

'Familial is a technical term. It means the DNA contains markers which prove it came from a close family member... but not from you.'

Confused, Keith shakes his head. 'I'm not sure what you're driving at, Frank, but I've admitted what I did. The responsibility for that man's death is mine alone.'

Frank puffs his cheeks out. 'It's not your DNA, Keith. Nor is it your fingerprint. But you already know that, don't you?'

Anguish creeps across his face. 'Don't do this, Frank. It was me, okay. Take me in. What more do you want?' he pleads.

'I'm sorry, Keith. It's out of my hands. Once the wheels are in motion, well, there's no stopping them.'

Keith clamps onto Frank's arm. 'Please, Frank! I'm begging you. There must be something you can do? We can work this out. I can change my story to whatever works best.'

A creak from the stairs is followed by the young, imposing figure of rising rugby star... Riley Miller.

'Stop it, dad. It's over,' he says, his voice soft, gentle.

Keith spins around, anger overtaking desperation. 'Shut it, Riley! Don't say a word. For once in your life, keep your big bloody gob shut! We can figure this out together.' His grip on Frank's arm tightens as he glares into his eyes. 'The fingerprints, the DNA... you can make them go away, can't you, Frank? A mix up. Things get lost all the time. All you need is my confession. It's simple.'

Frank painstakingly peels Keith's fingers from his bicep, one by one.

'You know I can't do that, Keith. I'm sorry. I truly am.'

Realising the futility of the situation, Keith crumples onto the armchair, a broken man as Jenny sniffles into a tissue.

Riley steps forward. 'It's my DNA and fingerprints, Mr Finnegan. It was me who went to Ginger Jack's caravan early Sunday morning. The rest of what dad told you before is true, except for the fact it was me, not him. I wanted to frighten Ginger Jack, to get the truth. Find out where Rosie was. What had happened to her? I barged open the door, waking him. He sat on the edge of the bed and strapped his wooden leg on. I threatened him. I told him I'd lock the door and burn his caravan down if he didn't tell me what he'd done with Rosie. He stood up, grabbed the poker, raised it above his head, then his bloody wooden leg came off. He went down hard and cracked his head on the edge of the fire. I checked for a pulse, but there wasn't one. I knew he was dead as his eyes were wide open, staring at me. I panicked. I should have called an ambulance and fessed up. The shame I feel is overwhelming. I only meant to frighten the poor old bugger, Mr Finnegan. I never meant to hurt him... not an old man. Will I be charged with murder?'

Frank shakes his head. 'No. There was no intent to physically harm the old man. The charge will be involuntary manslaughter.'

Riley's eyes crease. 'What does that mean?'

'Manslaughter by an unlawful act. Breaking into his caravan. Verbal threats.'

Keith rocks back and forth in the chair, his chin resting on clasped hands. 'How long will he get, Frank?' he mutters, staring at the net curtains.

'Hard to say. Manslaughter can receive anywhere from a few months to life imprisonment.'

Keith grips his chest as Jenny's wailing intensifies.

'Life?' Riley whispers in a state of shock.

'Hold your horses,' Frank replies, raising his hand. 'In your case, it would likely be classed as lower culpability due to mitigating circumstances.'

'I don't understand,' Jenny cries, detecting a ray of hope in the ghastly drama.

Frank turns to her. 'Sorry, Jenny. What I'm trying to say is Riley had no intention of physically harming Jack. He went there out of desperation regarding his missing niece, meaning there were mitigating circumstances. It all depends on the crown prosecution service, and the judge. You have a clean record. If you plead guilty, give your full cooperation to the police, and produce some notable character references, then it's possible the judge may be lenient.'

'How lenient?' Riley mumbles.

'I'm not sure. Three, four years. Possibly less. With good behaviour, you could be out in eighteen months.'

'There goes his rugby career,' Keith groans.

'Not necessarily. You'd be surprised at the number of professional sports stars with police records. If the lad keeps himself fit, I'm sure he'll get other opportunities. He's only twenty-one.'

'What happens now?' Riley asks.

'I'll bring you in for questioning. Collect DNA, a blood sample, and a set of fingerprints. Then you'll be charged and remanded in custody.'

'You mean prison?'

'Aye.'

Keith gazes sorrowfully at Frank. 'Do me a favour, Frank, for me and Jenny. Don't put the cuffs on him. Spare the lad his dignity, please?'

Frank nods and musters a meagre smile. 'Aye, fair enough. I can serve the caution at the station,' he replies. His attention shifts to Riley. 'I'll give you some time with your mam and dad. I'll be in the car,' he adds, turning to leave.

'Frank!' Keith calls out.

'Yes?'

'If I hadn't come into the station yesterday, you'd have been none the wiser, would you?'

'Probably not. But what price a clean conscience, Keith? Especially for a young lad. No one should carry that burden for the rest of their life. Tell the truth, pay the price, then start afresh. Secrets are a cancer... believe me. Bye, Jenny.'

He ambles outside into the misty, damp air, the faint wails of Jenny's weeping trailing behind him like a funeral cortege. Under the grim, sombre sky, he exhales, his breath laced with regret.

'This job will be the death of me,' he whispers with a heavy heart. 'Christ, I'd kill for a cigarette right now.'

55

Saturday 7th November – 1:40 pm

Rosie's eyes widen in surprise as she stares at the car.

'What's this?' she asks, clearly bemused.

Frank chuckles. 'This is Beatrice, a 1968 Ford Anglia 105E Deluxe.'

'It's old,' she says with an element of uncertainty as Scarlet scurries down the garden path.

'Aye, she is. Nearly as old as me.'

Rosie looks up at Frank, then back at the car. 'It's not that old.'

'Oi! You cheeky monkey.' Foxtrot rises from the backseat and sticks his snout on the window, causing it to fog a little.

'A doggy! What's her name?' Rosie shouts with glee.

'It's a he, and his name is Foxtrot.'

A pout. 'Does he bite?'

'Old Foxtrot? Nah, he gets beaten up by the local cats. He's as soft as they come.'

Frank pulls open the car door and pats Rosie on the head as she clambers into the back seat and cuddles the dog. Scarlet climbs into the passenger side.

'Seatbelt, Rosie,' she says.

'Yes, mum,' she replies, rolling her eyes as Frank slams the door shut and jumps behind the wheel. He leans across to the passenger side and pops open the glove box.

'Now let me see what I've got in here,' he says. 'Ah, I wondered where they'd gone.' He pulls out a white paper bag of sweets and offers them to Rosie. 'Do you like Jelly Babies?'

'My favourites,' she says, beaming as she grabs the bag.

'That was a lucky guess of mine.'

'What do you say?' Scarlet prompts.

'Thank you, Mr Finnegan,' Rosie says, robot fashion.

'My pleasure, sweetheart.'

'Thanks for this, Frank,' Scarlet says, offering him a nervous smile.

'Least I could do. If something positive can come out of all this, that's all that matters. There's been enough doom and gloom. Time for a ray of sunshine.'

The car trundles along the road on the short drive to the top of West Cliff.

Scarlet turns to her daughter. 'Are you sure you want to do this, Rosie?'

'Yes.'

'Because, if at any point you want to pull out, then all you have to do is say the word.'

'No. I want to do it. It's better we all get along, isn't it?'

Scarlet smiles, masking her apprehension. 'Yes. Yes, it is.'

Frank parks the car and they all alight.

'Where is he? I can't see him?' Rosie says, perturbed, as Frank puts the lead on Foxtrot.

He spins around and spots the couple walking towards them. 'There he is,' Frank says, pointing.

'Who's that with him? Is that his girlfriend?' Rosie quizzes.

Frank chuckles. 'No, that's not his girlfriend. That's Prisha. Inspector Kumar, the lady who found you on the boat.'

'Oh. She looks different with her hair down.'

'You still want to do this?' Scarlet asks.

'Yes. Stop worrying, mum. He *is* my dad.'

'You've never seen him before, let alone met him.'

'I've met him hundreds of times in my head.' She thrusts the bag of Jelly Babies into Scarlet's hands and takes off like the wind, arms outstretched.

'She's like a lighthouse, that one,' Frank comments. 'Bad weather bounces off her.'

Blake Dufton stares in disbelief, drops to one knee and holds his arms out as Rosie flies into them. He hugs her tightly, sobbing into her neck. Prisha bypasses them and heads to Frank and Scarlet.

'What are you crying for, daddy?'

'They're tears of happiness, Rosie. I've never been this happy in all my life.' Rosie momentarily pulls away and offers him a severe frown. 'What's the matter, love?'

'If you want to keep seeing me, you must promise me one thing,' she states in a matronly manner, belying her tender years.

'Yes, anything. What is it?'

'You must promise not to get into trouble with the police ever again! Understand?' she declares, wagging her finger at him.

He clasps his hand over his mouth in a futile attempt to stifle the sobs. He crosses his heart.

'I swear. Cross my heart and hope to die. I will never break the law again. Promise!'

'Pinky promise?' Rosie says, still not entirely convinced.

They entwine little fingers. 'Pinky promise,' he replies as he shoots a generous smile at Scarlet, who is also wiping a tear from her eye. 'Now, we only have two hours, so what do you want to do? You choose. Anything at all?'

Rosie returns to being a little girl again and jigs excitedly from foot to foot. 'I want to get our picture taken under Whalebone Arch, along with mummy. Then I want to go to the Dracula Experience, and afterwards the amusement arcades. And some donuts and hot chocolate would be nice too,' she adds coyly. 'Although, I doubt you have much money as you've just got out of prison, but grandad gave me fifty pounds in case you were short.'

Frank and Prisha watch on in silence as the once broken family walk off heading towards Whalebone Arch.

'That was quite moving,' Prisha says, without too much emotion. 'Like I said to Zac, that little girl has been before.' She checks her watch. 'Ooh, I better dash.'

'Where are you going?'

'Meeting Adam at the brewery for a beer, then off for lunch somewhere swanky up on the moors.'

He stares at the amulet resting on her jumper. 'That's a nice charm. Did Adam buy you that?'

'What? Oh, yes, in a roundabout way,' she replies, fingering the claw, carved from Whitby jet. 'Enjoy the rest of your weekend,' she says, already on her way. 'See you Monday, Frank!' she calls back, waving.

'Aye, see you, Monday. Oh, to be young again,' he murmurs as his focus returns to the reunited family. He watches until they disappear from view. Glancing out to sea, he shivers as the mizzle returns.

'Hmm... the fog may have gone, but I don't like the look of those ominous black clouds rolling in. That doesn't bode well. Come along Foxtrot, old lad. Looks like it's just me and thee.'

Emitting a deep sigh, he sticks his hands into his overcoat pockets and heads to the car.

Thank you for reading. The dark underbelly of Whitby never sleeps. Pre-order the next gripping story today.

Book 7 – Happy Camp – Discipline, Godliness, Fun!

Keep In Touch

Your thoughts and feedback are incredibly important. If you enjoyed the book, please consider leaving a review on Amazon or Goodreads, or a review/recommendation on Facebook. Such reviews are not only deeply appreciated, but they also help fellow crime fiction enthusiasts discover and enjoy the DCI Finnegan series. Or even better, why not tell someone you know about the book? Word of mouth is still the best recommendation.

I thank you for giving me your time, a very precious and finite commodity.

In case you've missed any of the books, take a quick look at the **Also By Ely North** page.

All the best,

Ely North

Ely North Newsletter

Why not sign up to my entertaining newsletter where I write about all things crime—fact and fiction. It's packed with news, reviews, and my top ten Unsolved Mysteries, as well as new releases, and any discounts or promotions I'm running. I'll also send you a free copy of the prequel novella to Black Nab, **Aquaphobia – The Body In The River**

QR code below.

Also By Ely North - DCI Finnegan Series

Book 1: **Black Nab**
Book 2: **Jawbone Walk**
Book 3: **Vertigo Alley**
Book 4: **Whitby Toll**
Book 5: **House Arrest**
Book 6: **Gothic Fog**
Book 7: **Happy Camp**
Book 8: **Harbour Secrets**
Book 9: **Murder Mystery** – Pre-order (Dec 2024)
DCI Finnegan Series Boxset #1: **Books 1 – 3**
DCI Finnegan Series Boxset #2: **Books 4 – 6**

Prequel: **Aquaphobia** (Free ebook for newsletter subscribers)

*Note: All books are available from Amazon in ebook, paperback, and in **Kindle Unlimited** (excluding Aquaphobia). Paperbacks can be ordered from all good bookshops. **Boxset print editions are one book compiled from three books. They do not come in a box.** *** Pre-orders only apply to ebooks.

Contact

Contact: ely@elynorthcrimefiction.com

Website: https://elynorthcrimefiction.com

Follow me on Facebook for the latest https://facebook.com/elynorthcrimefictionUK

Sign up to my newsletter for all the latest news, releases, and discounts.

Newsletter Sign Up

Printed in Great Britain
by Amazon

49812574R00240